A JESSIE BLACK LEGAL THRILLER

by

Larry A. Winters

*For my parents,*
*thanks for everything!*

# 1.

Russell Lanford could hear the heavy thuds and clanks of the guns bumping together inside the nylon duffel bag, and he wondered if he should have wrapped the guns in paper towels or something. There was no real guide to this, unfortunately. He knew. He'd looked for one on-line. The problem was, most people who did what he was about to do didn't have time to speak their last words, much less pen a how-to manual. They made their final statements with hot lead. He slowed his gait and held his arm straighter in an attempt to minimize the swing of the bag. The last thing he needed was for one of the guns to discharge in the bag before he even arrived at the school. All of them were loaded—that had seemed prudent to him when he'd packed the bag in his bedroom, but now it made him nervous. As his online friend True_Man liked to say, he'd only have one chance at this.

He smiled grimly as he imagined the headline. *Teenager shoots himself in the leg en route to mass killing.*

He passed through the gate from the street to the grounds of the illustrious Stevens Academy. There were no metal detectors, no security officers. Stevens Academy wasn't that kind of school, after all. It was a private school for good kids. *Well-off* kids, which Russell understood to mean kids who's parents weren't rich, but had just enough money to get ripped off by sending their children to a fascist hellhole masquerading as an institution of learning.

Usually a guy named Cody Napier stood at the gate, but he was more of a crossing guard than anything else, and Russell knew that Mr. Napier liked to take a smoke break at 4pm every afternoon, and he had to do that in the loading dock on the other side of the school. It was 4:06 now, and Mr. Napier was nowhere to be seen. Passing the gate, he heard the sounds, carried by the breeze, of his fellow students. The school day—for which Russell had called in sick—was over. Now was the time that the campus buzzed with after-school activities—sports, newspaper, debate club, and a bunch of lame shit that kids did in an effort to beef up their college applications. *Because, you know, having straight A's ain't shit unless you also play on the varsity fencing team.*

Russell strayed from the cobblestone path leading to the school building. He inhaled the scent of recently cut grass as he crossed a vivid green lawn toward the athletic fields behind the school. It never ceased to impress him as an amazing contrast, emerging from the gritty, noisy city of Philadelphia and into this rarified, cloistered greenery. As a freshman, he'd felt lucky, privileged to be here. Fast-forward three years of living the life of a second-class citizen—a *loser*, a

2

*freak*—and all he wanted to do was tear it all apart. The duffel bag seemed to clank in agreement.

It was autumn, slightly chilly. The crisp breeze carried their voices to him as he neared the field where the cheerleaders practiced their routines. The bleachers were vacant, and he caught himself worrying that if he sat there, he'd stand out. Usually, he did everything possible to avoid notice. To blend in, disappear. But now? Why fucking bother? He marched straight to the bleachers, heaved the unwieldy duffel bag onto a bench, and sat beside it. His arm throbbed from the effort of carrying the duffel. He massaged the ropy muscles of his arm and let his labored breathing return to normal.

He was in position.

But he was not in a hurry. Not yet. As soon as he unzipped the gray Nike bag, then he would be in a hurry. Then every second would count as the police roared toward him, converging on this field at this school. He could imagine their confused radio communications now—"Steven Who's What? Where?"—as they used their GPS units to locate this shit-speck high school that otherwise didn't even exist in the consciousness of most Philadelphians. But the place would be world famous soon enough. Stevens Academy, grades 9-12, 994 students (minus the recently departed). Good old Stevens Academy, joining Columbine, Sandy Hook, and Umpqua Community College in the hall of fame.

He watched the girls. Long hair. Tight, perfect bodies. Their red and white cheerleader uniforms left little to the imagination. But more than their shapely thighs and perky breasts, Russell found his gaze drawn to their faces. There was something about their expressions—happy, smug, confident—that caused his chest to clench painfully. *He hated them.* They were so entitled, so proud of themselves, so sure that they deserved every happiness in life just because of the genetic accident of being born pretty. They didn't view their beauty as good fortune or luck. They viewed it as the natural order. Of course they were beautiful. Of course they were superior. Of course they would enjoy the privileges of popularity in high school (parties, boyfriends, the favoritism of teachers), followed by leisure and luxury later on (BMW SUVs, thousand-dollar watches, gleaming kitchens they didn't use), when they married men of means (like their fathers, like his). These cheerleaders would never know loneliness, or pain, or a hard day's work. They were above all that.

The world was a fucked up place, and it was all because of girls—of *women*—like these pretty little bitches.

His body vibrated with the energy of pent-up rage. He moved one shaking arm toward the zipper of the Nike duffel bag, and pulled. The metal teeth parted with a low zipping sound, revealing the shadowy space inside. Sunlight glinted off a black metal surface within. The Taurus 9mm? The Bushmaster .223 semi-auto? Where to begin, where to begin....

"Hey!"

His hand jumped away from the bag. Ms. Kerensa,

the cheerleading coach, had one hand up to her forehead to shade her eyes, and the other hand clamped angrily to her hip, as she stared up at him.

"What do you think you're doing?" she said.

The girls all turned to look at him. He saw expressions of annoyance, mostly, as if the intrusion of a lesser being (a loser, a geek, a beta male) into their exclusive and sacred space were an effrontery against nature.

"I'm talking to you," Ms. Kerensa said.

The woman's expression was severe, her features hatchet-like. Unlike her charges, Ms. Kerensa had not been blessed with a pretty face or a great body. Or maybe she had been. He supposed age robbed many women of their youthful beauty. Maybe he'd be doing some of these bitches a favor, sparing them from the eventual pain of realizing that what they'd assumed to be their God-given birthright was in fact fleeting and temporary, squandered in youth.

*Stay cool*, True_Man had said, *no matter what.*

Russell said, "I'm just sitting here."

"I see that. And you're making my team uncomfortable. You're making *me* uncomfortable. This isn't a show. Please leave."

Russell's hand dropped into the duffel bag. His heartbeat kicked up a notch as his fingers slid over the hard, cold steel shapes inside. His index finger eased inside the loop of a trigger guard and his hand curled around the textured stock of the grip—a motion that felt surprisingly natural, surprisingly *right*.

He didn't even know which weapon he'd grasped until his hand came out of the bag with the Beretta Neos rimfire pistol. Dad's favorite. The .22 caliber handgun's sleek, futuristic barrel caught briefly on the zipper. With a tug, Russell yanked it free. Like all of the guns in the bag, he'd loaded it with a full mag and chambered one round. This baby was ready to rock.

He barely noticed the look of horror that twisted Ms. Kerensa's face. He was already aiming down the sights at Maddy Nesbitt. Blonde hair, blue eyes, star of untold masturbatory fantasies. He aimed for center mass, admiring the swell of her chest even as his grip tightened on the gun and his finger pulled the trigger. His aim was slightly off—he'd never been the best marksman, despite many trips to the target range with his father—but no harm done. Blood burst from her throat and she flew backward as if flicked across the field by a giant. She landed in the dirt. Her cheerleader skirt flipped up to reveal her perfect thighs. The blast of the gunshot faded, and there was a moment when all was silent except for a little gurgle as Maddy choked to death on her own blood. Then her sounds were overwhelmed by the screaming of the others.

*Go time.*

At this point, it all came down to math. Stevens Academy's cheerleading squad boasted sixteen cheerleaders. He'd knocked one down, and a series of quick, well-placed shots would take down the other fifteen (and the coach, because *fuck that bitch, too*) before the cops arrived and ended him. The Beretta's magazine held ten rounds, plus the one in the chamber, which he'd just fired.

*Stay focused*, True_Man had said.

He fired shots in quick succession. The clap of each shot battered his eardrums, and he realized he should have brought his father's shooting earmuffs. He hadn't thought of that, and neither had True_Man. Too late now. *Crack! Crack! Crack!* The shots tore through the quiet of the peaceful afternoon, and he watched the screaming, panic-stricken girls fall one by one. Lissa Bernier. Peta Kent. Macey O'Reilly. Then the rest of the bitches scattered and his next shot missed. He lined up the sights on someone's back. It was Pam Speer. She went down like a ragdoll, blood erupting from a spot between her shoulderblades. Detta Sanborn. Brynne White. Coral Gaffney. Coral pinwheeled, blood spurting from her head, darkening her blonde hair. Then another miss.

He could hear police sirens in the distance. *Let them come. Let them come.*

One of the girls was sprinting for the school building. It was Sydney Devlin. How many times had he stared at her in American History, her cute, upturned nose, her long black curls, her even longer legs? She'd laughed at him once, he remembered, when Alex Tanner made fun of him for his stammering delivery of an oral report. Russell took careful aim, leading slightly in the direction of the building she was fleeing toward. *Crack!* Her head jerked and spewed blood. An amazing headshot, but he had no time to savor it. The Beretta clicked empty.

He tossed the gun (would Dad miss it?) and grabbed another one out of the bag. It was the Bushmaster. The .223 tactical rifle looked like a fully automatic death dealer straight out of *Call of Duty*, but sadly, it was only a semi-auto—one trigger pull, one round. It would have to be good enough.

Gina Franz. The rapport thundered under the open sky, much louder than the handgun had been. Mandi Fox. Jordan Dunn. Roni McClain. Skye Locke. It was so much easier to aim with the big rifle—why had he bothered with the handgun at all? Alene Rollins. Nola York. Nola was still alive, trying to crawl away, dragging her bleeding body. Her underwear bulged where she'd dropped a load in her cute little cheerleader panties. The smell of shit was faint but unmistakable. He put her down with a shot that entered the back of her head through her ponytail, and she stopped crawling.

The sound of sirens intensified. He heard tires squeal on pavement. Car doors opened and slammed. The cavalry had arrived, but too late. Too late.

The air was heavy with the stink of gunsmoke, blood, and shit. Dead and dying bodies littered the field, soaking the earth. Only Ms. Kerensa remained standing now. She was rooted to the spot where she'd stood when she told him to leave. The dumb bitch hadn't moved a step. She had no survival instinct whatsoever. None of these priveleged little princesses did, which was why they were all dead. He lined up a headshot and splashed the coach's brains onto the grass.

"Put down your weapon!"

Russell twisted around. Two figures approached from behind. He almost couldn't believe his eyes. The one in the lead was a woman! Tall, good-looking, with short blonde hair. Wearing a suit—no body armor or anything. Trailing behind her, seeming to huff and puff as he crossed the spongy terrain of the field, was a short, overweight man. He wore a shirt and tie, but no jacket, and his tie hung loose around his thick neck. Both of them held guns, extended out in front of them—just pistols, Glocks—aimed at him.

Was *this* the police response? *Seriously?* Two plainclothes cops with handguns? Where the fuck was the SWAT team?

It was the woman who'd shouted to him to put down his weapon. She raised her voice again. "Drop the rifle!"

The fact that she was pretty irritated him more than anything. He was supposed to be taken down by a man—by a team of men—in a blaze of glory. Not by one bitch and her fat-ass partner.

His hands tightened on the Bushmaster. This was it. The climax. The grand finale. All he had to do was raise the rifle and wait for their bullets to perforate him. *Suicide by cop*, the media liked to call it.

Only, now that the moment had arrived, he found that his body refused to carry out his brain's commands. The rifle barrel stayed where it was—aimed down, away from the cops.

And then, a thought sounded in his head.

Unwanted, un-asked for. *I don't want to die. I'm afraid to die.*

No. Hell no. That was not acceptable. He had to die here. That's how it worked. That's how it was done. The girls were dead. Bodies in the grass, vacant faces, tangled limbs, and blood-smeared cheerleader uniforms. He'd made his statement. Now he had to take his bow.

The woman cop must have sensed his reluctance. She held a hand, palm out, toward her partner, gesturing for him to hold off. Then she stepped closer to the bleachers. Moving cautiously. Her eyes flicked to the bodies, then back to Russell. He saw a muscle twitch in her throat.

"My name is Emily Graham," she said. "What's your name?"

Russell shook his head. *Don't talk to them. If you talk to them, there will be no turning back. Raise the rifle.*

"I'm here to help you," she said. "I'm a detective with the Philadelphia Police Department. How about you put down the gun and you tell me what's happening?"

*What's happening?* He almost laughed. Did this bitch think he was stupid? Where was the SWAT team? Where were the snipers? Why had his big moment been denied him?

Wasn't this just typical of his life? He never got what he deserved. And always—*always*—it was because of a woman. Even now, when he should be relishing his vengeance, all he felt was the impending horror of failure.

"Put down your gun," the woman said. "It's over."

And with an awful mixture of relief and dismay, he opened his hands and let the Bushmaster fall clanking to the metal bleachers.

# 2.

Jessie Black walked from the courthouse to the bar a block away. She paused at the door, tempted to keep on walking. Even though the trial was over, and her colleagues had summoned her here for an impromptu midday party to toast her victory, she was still in trial mode—on edge, full of adrenaline, thoughts running a mile a minute. Securing a guilty verdict always felt good, but she liked to be alone afterward, where she could think over what she'd done right and what she could have done better. Preferably with a cup of strong coffee. These days, she was more of a coffee drinker than a drink drinker, especially in the middle of the afternoon.

But she didn't want to disappoint her friends. She wouldn't be seeing them again for a week.

She walked inside and paused in the doorway for a moment as her eyes adjusted to the dim lighting. It was the right thing to do. The social thing. Besides, she deserved to celebrate now and then, didn't she? *Have a drink, accept a few congratulations, be a human being as well as an assistant district attorney.*

The murmur of conversation surrounded her, as did the smell of liquor. Celebrating courtroom victories at The Gavel had become a tradition. A lawyer hangout by virtue of its name and location—close to the Criminal Justice Center and City Hall—the ambiance was all glossy surfaces, chrome and glass, and well-dressed, well-spoken bartenders. Even at this early hour, men and women in suits crowded the bar and tables. Jessie spotted her crew at a round cocktail table near the middle of the room. She made her way through the crowd to reach them.

Warren Williams, head of the Homicide Unit in which she worked, jumped up from his stool. He gestured with one hand, offering her his seat, while lifting a wine glass from the table with his other hand and pushing it into her hand before she could decline. Judging by the half-empty bottle and the over-sized smiles of the other people at the table—Roland "Rolly" Westbrook, Dutch Shultz, and Marion Dallas, all homicide prosecutors like her—they'd already started the party. There was a plate of fried calamari on the table, mostly eaten. The marinara sauce explained a red splotch on Warren's shirt.

She took the wine but remained standing. "I should only have one glass. I can't stay long."

Warren's round face puckered in an exaggerated frown. "Jessie, this is a very fine vintage, courtesy of the DA's office expense account."

"Yeah," Rolly said. "Worth at least ten bucks." He flashed her a boyish smile that was known to work wonders on female jurors.

13

"That's how we roll," Dutch added as he refilled his own glass. "Like a boss." Dutch was a gray-haired lifer at the DA's office, pushing sixty. She had to admire his effort, even if less than successful, to keep up with the current street talk.

"Come on," Marion said. "It was a big case. You should celebrate a little. It's fun." Her heart-shaped face wrinkled as she gave Jessie a half-smile and beckoned her closer, as if she'd read Jessie's desire to brood over her victory in solitude. And she probably had. As one of the only other women in the Homicide Unit, she often seemed to watch Jessie with a knowing, been-there-done-that look.

Her companions watched her, waiting. All around them, conversations ebbed and flowed, glassware clinked.

"Ten-dollar wine, huh?" She examined her glass. The wine did smell good—almost like black cherries— and she supposed she could spare a little time. "Can't say no to that."

They smiled as she slid onto the stool and joined them. Warren lifted his glass in a toast. "To justice," he said, only half-ironically.

Rolly, Dutch, and Marion raised their glasses. So did Jessie. "To justice."

She took a sip. Cabernet, and a good one. More likely fifty dollars than ten. Apparently, putting a husband-murdering killer in prison for life warranted use of the DA's office AmEx card.

"Thanks," Jessie said. "Just as long as we're clear I

can't stay long."

Warren laughed. "Right. You need to pack for your big trip." He said it with mock-resentment—mostly mock-resentment, anyway, with a little real resentment thrown in, she was sure. Because she knew the DA's office was his life, and that he expected similar dedication from his prosecutors. He expected them to consider the DA's office as more than a job, more than something you would take a vacation from. Well, let him resent. Jessie hadn't taken a vacation in years. Not even a long weekend. If Warren didn't like the idea of losing her for a week, he would just have to deal with it.

Warren was right about one thing, though. She did need to pack. Her flight departed from Philly International tomorrow at 7:45 in the morning, and she hadn't even pulled her suitcase out of the closet. She'd ordered three new bikinis online, and they were still sealed in padded mailers (she could only hope she'd look good in them—if not, it was too late now to do anything about it). In about sixteen hours, she and Leary would board an American Airlines jet, nonstop to Punta Cana, where they would enjoy a week of beautiful beaches, great food, and a romantic suite. She'd be drinking piña coladas and strawberry daiquiris, and she intended to be very happy. The feeling hit her now just imagining it. Joy rose within her like the swell of a surf.

"Come on, Warren," Rolly chided. "Jessie earned some time at the beach with her boy toy."

Hearing Mark Leary described as a "boy toy" set

her teeth on edge. She wasn't one-hundred-percent what she should call him—boyfriend?—but "boy toy" definitely did not fit.

Thankfully Marion changed the subject before anyone could take it further. "Who cares about the beach? I want to hear about how Jessie put away Simone Rachelle, the great husband killer."

Warren shook his head. "Why can't these nut jobs just divorce each other like normal people?"

"I sat in the gallery on Wednesday," Dutch said, looking at her, "when you put the sister-in-law on the stand. Hell of a show."

"So glad I was able to entertain you," Jessie said. "That was my goal through the whole trial, obviously." She took another sip of wine.

"Obviously," Dutch agreed.

"What happened?" Marion said.

Dutch laughed. "So the victim's sister is up on the stand, and Jessie's asking her to describe the relationship between her brother and his wife, and the sister's pretty much laying the groundwork that the defendant, who we already know from the evidence was unfaithful, was also just a cold, nasty piece of work. And on cross, Rachelle's defense lawyer approaches the stand. Now, you gotta see it." He wobbled on his stool and almost fell off before grabbing the edge of the table and steadying himself. How much wine had the old guy had? "The defense lawyer—what's his name, Jessie?"

"Ned Perales," Jessie said.

"He any good?" Marion asked.

Jessie shrugged. "He's been around. Knows his stuff."

"Perales is this big fellow, okay?" Dutch said, resuming his story. "Tall, wide in the shoulders. Probably played football when he was in school. A giant. And the victim's sister is this tiny thing, maybe five feet tall, skinny as a flag pole. I could barely see her face over the top of the witness stand."

Rolly chuckled. "Leave it to Dutch to turn a routine courtroom exchange into a tale of David and Goliath."

Dutch shot him a watery stare. "Nothing routine about this exchange. Now, may I please proceed?"

Rolly waved his arm. "By all means."

"So the sister—this little thing, as I said—is sitting at the witness stand, and here comes Perales to conduct his cross-examination. Now, if I were him, I would have asked one, maybe two questions to throw some doubt on her impartiality, on her qualifications for evaluating another couple's marriage—whatever— and then get her off the stand as quickly as possible. Because juries love really small women. I don't know why, but they do. You ever notice that?"

They all shook their heads.

"They feel an instinct to protect them or something, I don't know," Dutch said. Jessie was trying to determine if he was slurring his words because he was really drunk, or if he was just having some fun with them. "What did I tell you, Jessie, my first piece of advice when you started in Homicide?"

The question snapped her back to the moment. "Don't buy the tuna salad from the deli down the street?"

"No. I mean, yes. That's true, too. But also, I said when it comes to really small women, children, and the elderly, go easy."

"I guess you're safe then, old man," Rolly said. Dutch frowned at him and refilled his glass.

"So Perales," he went on, "who never had the benefit of my wise counsel, starts really going to town on the woman. You know, dredging up petty grudges she might have had against her brother's wife—*Is it not true that Ms. Rachelle borrowed your crockpot, and did not return it?*—and poking around the sister's own lackluster marriage."

Jessie took another sip of her wine. As enjoyable as this was—and it *was* enjoyable, she had to admit—she needed to make a gracious exit quickly or she'd be packing all night. But interrupting Dutch mid-ramble didn't seem like the best idea.

"And then," Dutch said, "he goes that one step too far. He suggests, with his not-as-clever-as-he-thinks lawyer questions, that there might have been some kind of brother-sister incest thing going on."

Gasps all around the table, even from Warren.

"At which point I objected," Jessie said.

"But only half-heartedly," Dutch said with a smile, "since you knew as well as I did that Perales was digging his own grave."

18

Jessie shrugged noncommittally and drank more wine.

Dutch said, "At this point the sister flat out says to Perales, 'Are you implying that I was fucking my brother?' And Perales just stands there with his mouth hanging open. The judge tries to save him by reminding the sister that witnesses answer questions; they don't ask them. But she says, 'Your Honor, I'm just asking for Mr. Perales to clarify his question. Are you asking if I am a brother-fucker?'"

"She did not say that!" Marion said, looking astonished.

"She did," Dutch said. "And you could feel the mood of the jury turn against Perales. The judge looks at him, raises an eyebrow, and says, 'Would you care to clarify the question?' And Perales, who is now beet-red, says, 'I have nothing further for this witness.' I think that was the moment he lost the trial."

"Of course," Jessie said. "It had nothing to do with my presentation of the evidence, the direct testimony of key prosecution witnesses, or my closing argument. It's all because of one misstep by defense counsel."

Dutch grinned. "Yup."

Warren shrugged. "Hey, you know how I run the Homicide Unit. I don't care how you guys win, as long as you do."

Jessie hopped off her stool and smiled at her friends. "As flattered as I am by all the credit you're giving me for months of hard work, I really do need to leave now. But in a week, I'd be happy to hear all about how my whole career has been a series of happy accidents."

"I'll get started on a timeline right away," Rolly said.

She turned to leave, but paused when she heard the buzzing of a phone. She reached into her bag. At the same time, she saw Warren reach into his pocket. Then Rolly, Dutch, and Marion all found their phones, too. Jessie froze. A feeling of dread crawled across her skin.

"Uh-oh," Marion said, putting words to Jessie's thoughts. "This can't be good."

# 3.

Jesus Rivera, the District Attorney of Philadelphia, glared at himself in his bedroom's full-length mirror as he struggled to knot the bow tie under his collar. Usually the act was automatic—as an elected official in the country's fifth largest city, Rivera seemed to wear tuxedos more often than jeans, and say what you would about his leadership qualities (and his opponents certainly did), he was at least adept at dressing himself. But with the sound of his daughter weeping behind him while his wife struggled to console her, his fingers had become fumblingly useless. He also had to contend with the sounds of Cortney Abbott and Elijah Glynn, his political consultants, arguing at the other side of the bedroom as they debated the impact of this incident on his future in public office. Frankly, Rivera wasn't sure which was more disturbing.

A knock on his bedroom door preceded the entrance of Clara, his personal assistant, who quietly informed him that Warren Williams and Jessica Black had arrived. Then she ushered the prosecutors into the room.

Rivera tore his gaze from the mirror to offer his visitors a nod. It was the warmest greeting he could muster under the circumstances. Rivera knew they'd come straight from The Gavel, and he sincerely hoped that Warren's slightly flushed face didn't mean that the head of his Homicide Unit was drunk. Warren was sharp and politically astute—maybe more of a natural political animal than Rivera himself was, if he was being honest with himself—and Rivera needed his counsel today more than ever.

Jessica Black trailed behind her boss. As far as he knew, she had no political aspirations at all. Which was a shame. She had a look that would play well on TV. Tall and pretty, with lustrous black hair that fell just below her shoulders, but also professional-looking, with bright, green eyes full of both intelligence and compassion. Right now, those eyes were trying very hard (unsuccessfully) not to gape in awe at his palatial bedroom. Rivera would have smiled, if his heart were not being squeezed in a vise.

"A school shooting in Philly." The DA shook his head.

"It was bound to happen here eventually," Warren said.

"Yeah, but I was hoping it wouldn't be during my term in office."

Warren walked over to Rivera's wife and daughter, giving Ricki a hug, then hesitating in front of Nora, who was still crying. Warren looked like he might try to say something comforting to the fourteen-year-old girl. "You don't attend Stevens, do you, Nora? Did, uh, you know the victims?"

"She's just upset by the situation," Rivera said.

"The whole city's going to be upset by the situation," Cortney Abbott put in. "The country."

*No shit*, Rivera thought, but he stifled the angry reply. Cortney was old-school, a silver-haired, smooth-tongued adviser (or "political strategist" according to his LinkedIn profile), and although he had a penchant for stating the obvious, he was also a fount of good advice and had helped Rivera keep his office for several terms. Rivera wasn't so sure about his colleague, the much-younger Elijah. But Elijah was supposedly a social media whiz kid, and according to Cortney, they needed him. That's why he could bill four-hundred dollars an hour at the age of twenty-four. When Rivera had been twenty-four—which was longer ago than he cared to think about—he'd been making minimum wage at Macy's while attending law school at night.

"What's the plan?" Warren said.

"Right now, my experts here are trying to decide if I should keep to my schedule and attend a fundraiser for my church, or drop everything to show the city that this incident is my sole focus. Damn it!" His hands fumbled the bow tie for the hundredth time.

To everyone's surprise, Nora rose from her seat and came over to him. He looked at his daugter's red-rimmed eyes as she knotted his bow tie for him. "Here, Dad."

"Thanks, honey."

"What we want to avoid is a George W. Bush 9/11 embarrassment," Cortney said. "You know, reading *The Pet Goat* to a bunch of kindergartners while terrorists fly airplanes into the World Trade Center."

"This is hardly the same thing!" Rivera said. His daughter drew back, and he realized he'd failed to temper the anger, the harshness in his voice. More gently, he said, "The country's not in danger. The shooter is in police custody."

"Sixteen children dead," Cortney said, "along with a teacher. It's not 9/11 bad, but you better believe it's a crisis. For the city and for us."

"It's already trending on Twitter and Facebook," Elijah said. "You need to make a statement, get your voice out there."

Rivera wanted to groan, but he didn't. He stepped away from the mirror and paced. Jessica Black stepped out of his path, making room for him. He looked at her.

Why had Warren brought her along? But even as the question occurred to him, he thought he knew the answer. *Warren, you smart, sneaky bastard.*

"What do you think, Jessie?" he asked her.

She looked startled, but recovered quickly. "It's not really my expertise," she said.

Rivera shrugged. "I have enough experts. I want to know what you think, as one of my prosecutors."

He watched her lips press together as she gave the

question some thought. Again, he was struck by how photogenic she was. He'd been well-aware of how excellent a lawyer she was—she'd stood out as a courtroom all-star early on, and he'd followed her career with interest ever since—but he'd never really looked at her from this angle before. A political angle.

"Why not do both?" she said. "Make a quick statement to reporters on your way to the fundraiser? Send the message that the DA's office is taking this seriously, but that the city is safe and there's no need for panic."

"You just won the Rachelle case, right? The woman who killed her husband? That's what you were celebrating at The Gavel?"

"Yes." He saw her blush slightly. Then she smiled and nodded. "It seems wrong to celebrate anything now."

Rivera studied her for a moment, then did something every advisor he'd ever retained had told him never to do. He made a spur-of-the-moment decision, entirely on impulse. "I agree. It's time to put you back to work."

"I'm supposed to start a vaca—" She closed her mouth, shook her head. "Sorry. Of course. This takes precedence."

Ten minutes later, five of them were in a limo—Rivera, Ricki, and Nora dressed in their formal attire for the fundraiser dinner St. John the Evangelist Church was hosting at Reading Terminal Market, and Warren and Jessie dressed in their suits for the public statement the DA's office would be making just outside the event. The two political strategists followed in their own car.

Rivera caught Jessie's look of concern, and felt the first smile touch his lips since hearing the news of the shooting.

"I'm sure you were looking forward to your vacation," Rivera said, "but Warren was right to drag you into this. This shooter, what's his name—"

"Russell Lanford," Warren supplied.

"Usually, the shooters in these incidents kill themselves, and the public doesn't get the answers and the closure that come with a criminal prosecution. It's going to be different this time. Russell Lanford's trial is going to be under intense media scrutiny. I need to put someone in charge that I trust. Someone careful and meticulous, who I know will do a flawless job. And someone—" He hesitated, then shrugged. "Someone who will look good on TV. You're going to be representing the DA's office, Jessie. You're going to be representing me."

She looked at him, and those green eyes seemed to pierce him. "I understand. And I really appreciate your faith in me. I won't let you down."

Ricki placed a comforting hand on his knee and squeezed. It was his wife's signal that she was fully in his corner, that she approved of his decision to put this case in Jessie's hands. He appreciated her support, but didn't need it. He was already convinced he'd made the right call.

"Russell Lanford comes from money, apparently," Warren said. "Most kids at Stevens Academy do. So expect a good defense lawyer. I'm sure we'll face a motion to change venue away from Philadelphia, and a truckload of other pre-trial motions. They'll want the jury sequestered. You know the drill. It may be an open-and-shut case, but it's not going to be easy. We'll be busy for months."

Jessie nodded. "I know."

"If your travel plans included another person," Rivera said as delicately as he could, "you might want to give them a call now." He was aware, vaguely, that she was involved with a homicide detective on the Philly police force—or rather, a former homicide detective. The relationship had caused professional problems for both of them. It was the only blemish on her record, and one she'd survived. The detective, Rivera recalled, hadn't been so lucky. He'd been forced out of the police department.

"No," Jessie said. "I think that's a conversation I'm going to need to have in person."

They finished the ride in silence. Minutes later, they faced the cameras and the microphones, and Jesus Rivera told the people of his city that while Philadelphia would mourn this senseless tragedy, they could rest assured that the district attorney's office, in the person of its best homicide prosecutor, Jessica Black, would ensure justice for the dead.

# 4.

Leary was waiting for her in her apartment when Jessie finally made it home. She opened the door and found him sitting on the couch, watching TV. She wasn't surprised to hear the name "Russell Lanford" come out of the TV's speakers. She was sure every channel in Philadelphia had switched to nonstop coverage of the shooting.

"Hey," she said. Leary didn't rise from the couch to walk over and kiss her, which she tried not to take as a bad sign. She glanced at the TV screen, saw two talking heads babbling to each other about gun control. Had he seen the statement Rivera had made to the press? He must have. "Sorry I'm late."

"You looked good. On TV, I mean, when Rivera introduced you as the avenging angel of justice."

*Yup, he'd seen it alright.* "I'm going to go out on a limb and guess you're not happy with me right now," she said.

"Good deduction. Maybe *you* should have been the detective instead of me."

Leary had been a homicide detective with the

Philly PD—that's how they'd met—but after some departmental politics had flat-lined his career, he'd resigned and entered the private sector. Now he worked for Acacia, a large corporation that owned and operated several retail companies in the northeast. She didn't know much about the day-to-day details of his new job, but her sense was that he missed his days with the PPD. He was a loss prevention specialist now, consulting with management about potential areas of risk, like vandalism, embezzlement, shoplifting, safety, and security, and although he still conducted investigations, they were a far cry from the murder cases he used to work. Looking at him now, she wondered what pained him more—that she had been pulled into the Russell Lanford case, or that he had not.

"There was nothing I could do," she said.

He arched an eyebrow at that. "You could have called me before you agreed to cancel our vacation and head up the prosecution."

Had she owed him that? Their relationship was still a relatively new thing, and they were still feeling out the rules. Jessie was thirty-three, and she'd been on her own for a long time. An independent, professional woman. She didn't think she needed to ask anyone's permission before making a decision at work. On the other hand, they had planned the Punta Cana trip together. Leary had taken a week of vacation days. He'd paid for half of the airfare and resort fees.

"If there are cancellation charges, I'll pay for those," she said. Anger flared visibly in his eyes, and she immediately regretted her words.

"I looked for your suitcase," he said. "I found it at the back of your coat closet, empty. You didn't even start packing. Did you ever plan to go on this trip?"

"Of course I did! I've been looking forward to it for weeks. I was busy with the Simone Rachelle trial."

"You're always busy with a trial."

Jessie dropped onto the couch beside him. She touched his arm, and he did not pull away. That, at least, was a good sign. "Look, the District Attorney himself asked me to handle this case. What was I supposed to say?"

Leary sighed, and the anger seemed to fade from his face. "I know. I'm just disappointed."

"Me too."

She leaned forward and kissed him. He kissed her back, finding her tongue with his. A very good sign. His arms wrapped around her and pulled her close. Her body pressed against his.

"You know," she said, "I ordered three new bikinis, and I haven't had a chance to try them on yet."

He grinned, and his blue eyes lit up. "No time like the present."

"Who says we have to go all the way to the Dominican Republic to have a good time?" She ran a hand down his arm, massaging his bicep, and then clasped his hand in hers. Their fingers intertwined.

"Not me."

Later, after she'd confirmed that the bikinis did, in

fact, look good on her, and both she and Leary had energetically explored the possibilities for having a good time right here in her apartment, she forced herself to sit down at the little desk in the corner of her bedroom and boot up her laptop.

"Back to work already?" Leary said. "Are you sure you're done with me?" He was stretched out on her bed, his lean, muscular limbs twisted in the sheets. His hair stood out in sandy blond spikes where her fingers had made a mess of it, and a sheen of perspiration shined in the patch of hair between his pecs. He propped himself up on one elbow, the tattoo of a hawk visible on his bare arm. Even as sated as she felt right now, she was pretty damn tempted to climb back into bed.

"I need to check if the police report has been emailed to me," she said.

He yawned. "Who's the lead detective?"

"Emily Graham. She and her partner were a block from the scene when the first 911 calls came in. They were the first to arrive."

"Graham?" Leary made a face.

"Not a fan?" Graham was a recent addition to the Homicide Division, and Jessie had not worked with her yet.

"Just watch your back," Leary said.

She took her hands from her keyboard and turned to face him. "What do you mean by that?"

"Probably nothing. But she has a reputation for, I don't know. Not working well with others."

"Didn't *you* have a reputation like that, too? And we both know you didn't deserve it."

"Good point."

"I'll give her the benefit of the doubt. But I'll also keep your words in mind." She turned back to the laptop, and started opening emails.

She spent most of the next few hours reading the police report. Like most cops, Detective Graham had composed her narrative in stilted sentences, as if every word had been pulled forcibly from her brain. As a general rule, cops hated to write, and their reports showed it. But the facts shined through the prose, each one more vivid than the one before, and they were horribly compelling in spite of the flat delivery. Dead girls. Dead *children*, even if teenagers rarely thought of themselves that way. Lives cut tragically short.

There were photographs, too, of course. A shockingly young face with a hole through the right cheek, bits of bone exposed, shattered teeth. A chest with a hole over the left breast, the material of the brightly colored cheerleader uniform singed. Bullet casings in the grass underneath the bleachers. She clicked through photo after photo and forced herself to study each one closely, even as her stomach started to knot up in protest. There was something about crime scene photos, something sickeningly voyeuristic, that always made her feel queasy—as if by looking at them, she was perpetrating a second violation of the victims. But she knew the guilty feeling was irrational. Looking was necessary. It wasn't a violation of the dead; it was the first step toward avenging them. She needed to absorb the crime into herself, in all its gory detail, needed to know it as intimately as the killer, in order to be as effective as possible at trial.

"You coming to bed?" She heard Leary yawn, but didn't turn away from the laptop.

"Soon."

"Okay. But I'm beat. I'm going to turn off the light."

The room darkened, and she blinked against the sudden glare of the monitor. Part of her wished Leary would just go back to his own apartment instead of spending the night. She immediately chastised herself for the thought. *That's me, Jessie Black, lovey-dovey girlfriend.* Once a case got its teeth into her, she had a tendency to block the world out, and that unfortunately also included loved ones. That's why she kept photographs near her workspaces, both at home and at the office—one of her father and her (both of them about a decade younger than they were now, holding each other awkwardly as they posed for a picture at her law school) and the other (more recent) of her brother Alex, his wife Carol, and their two kids. Glancing guiltily at the man sleeping in her bed, she supposed she'd need to add a third photo soon, to remind herself of what was really important in life. She returned her attention to the murders. It was a long time before she went to bed.

When she woke up the next morning, the view

beyond her window was still black and Leary was sleeping deeply. She dressed as quietly as she could and slipped out, wanting to arrive early at the DA's office and organize her file on Russell Lanford. When she got there, her first call of the day was to Detective Emily Graham, to arrange a meeting at the crime scene. Even more so than photos, crime scenes were gut-wrenching. But like photos, indispensable.

"There's not much to see," Graham said. She sounded distracted, and Jessie could hear noise behind her—people, phones, the din of Police Headquarters. "Everything's in the report."

"I want to tour the scene anyway," Jessie said. "It's just something I need to do. Part of my process."

She heard Graham sigh through the phone. The put-upon reaction didn't surprise her. When cops needed something, the prosecutors were their best friends, but when the prosecutors needed something, they were pain-in-the-ass lawyers. And Leary had warned her about Graham's reputation for not working well with others. The line was quiet for a moment. Then, with clear reluctance in her voice, Graham said, "I can meet you at Stevens Academy in fifteen minutes."

Jessie wouldn't have minded a ride. Although she owned a car, she kept it in a garage and only used it for excursions outside Philly. Police Headquarters was close enough that Graham could have picked Jessie up on the way, saving her the trouble of hailing a taxi. But she didn't need to be a mind reader to know that asking for a lift would be pushing her luck. So she forced a cheery voice, said, "That's perfect," and ended the call.

Outside, the autumn breeze swept her hair back. She breathed the cool air, enjoying the aroma of dry leaves and crisp air beneath the usual city-smells of asphalt and car exhaust. The sun peeked between the buildings of the Philly skyline, warming her face.

"Excuse me, Ms. Black, but do you have a moment to speak?"

She turned to find a man standing beside her. Her first impression was *wealthy executive*. He wore an expensive-looking business suit, the jacket buttoned. It looked good on his tall, narrow frame. His shoes gleamed. His head, almost as shiny as his shoes, was smoothly bald. His cheeks were clean-shaven. He was holding two cups of coffee, one in each hand. He extended one of them toward her. "Coffee?"

A thin ribbon of steam wafted from a hole in the plastic lid of the travel cup. She looked at it for a second, tempted, before shaking her head. "Thanks, but I'm not really in the habit of accepting coffee from strangers."

He nodded, frowning, and turned to look for a place to set down the cup. After a few seconds, he gave up and continued to hold both cups. "I'm Wesley Lanford," he said. "I believe you're prosecuting my son."

She took a step back, almost involuntarily. "We shouldn't be talking, Mr. Lanford."

"There's something I need to tell you."

"Were you waiting for me out here?" The thought that this man, no matter how respectable-looking, had been watching the entrance to the DA's office so that he could intercept her made her feel suddenly vulnerable even in broad daylight.

"I wanted to speak with you in person. I didn't think you'd agree to meet, so I came here."

"You should talk to the police, not to me," she said. "I'm sure Detective Graham will contact you to arrange an interview soon, if she hasn't already."

"I know what Russell did was horrible," he said. "And I'm not here to defend him, or make excuses for him. He deserves most of the blame. But—"

"*Most* of the blame?" She knew she should just walk away, catch her taxi before she was late to her meeting with Graham, but the man's words irked her.

"That's what I want to speak with you about." He sighed, looked around again for a place to unload the second coffee cup, and finally just bent down and placed it on the pavement next to his fancy shoes. "Have you heard of Vaughn Truman? Manpower?"

She had no idea what he was talking about, and this whole conversation was inappropriate. She was the attorney prosecuting his son. He was a potential witness. Even a potential co-defendant, if the police found evidence of culpability. By talking to him now, outside of proper channels, she could be jeopardizing her case. "Mr. Lanford, I really need to go. Whatever you need to say, the police—"

"They call themselves men's rights activists.

Ridiculous, right? There's a website—Russell called it a *forum*. People post messages there. Anonymously, using fake names. Someone on that website manipulated Russell. I'm not saying Russell wasn't already thinking ... terrible things. But this person on the website gave him ... I don't know ... the final push. Do you understand what I'm telling you?"

"Not really." She took another step away from him, craning her neck and hoping to spot an approaching taxi.

"I'm saying there's another bad actor here. Russell's just a troubled kid—more troubled, obviously, than I ever realized. But this other person is ... is *worse*. Hiding behind a fake identity and manipulating a susceptible teenager—"

"Worse than murdering seventeen people?" The words came out before she could stop them, cold and angry. He gaped at her and the blood seemed to drain from his face. This time he was the one who took a step back. The side of his shoe hit the coffee cup and knocked it over. The plastic lid dislodged and coffee pooled on the sidewalk.

"I'm just trying to explain," he stammered. "There's another bad actor here—"

Jessie felt another rush of fury. She hadn't realized how angry the senseless shooting had made her until now, face to face with the shooter's father. "If there is, I doubt it's some guy on the internet. More likely, it's someone closer to home. Someone who provided an unstable fifteen-year-old with access to handguns and rifles and ammunition."

Lanford blanched even paler. "I'm a firearms enthusiast. A collector. There's nothing wrong with that. I have the appropriate licenses. I keep everything in a top-of-the-line gun safe." For the first time, his cool expression broke and she saw uncertainty, maybe even regret. She felt a pang of sympathy for this man. "I don't know how he got the code."

"Did you have it written down somewhere?" she said. Her voice had softened.

"No. I was careful. Extremely careful."

Jessie shook her head. "I need to go," she said again. "I'm sure you're going through hell right now. I understand the instinct to look for someone else to share the blame with your son." *And with you,* she thought, but didn't say. "But I'm not the right person to talk to. Maybe a loved one, or a therapist."

She raised her hand and a taxi pulled to the curb. Before Lanford could say more, she slid into the backseat and closed the door. She watched him through the window as the car pulled into traffic. He looked forlorn, lost. And maybe, she thought as the taxi turned a corner and he passed out of sight, angry, too.

The vibration of her phone pulled her from her thoughts. It was Graham. "Are you still coming?" The detective sounded annoyed.

Jessie glanced at her watch. She was late. "I got held up. It's related to the case. I'll be at the school in five minutes and I'll fill you in then."

She heard the detective huff a frustrated breath into the phone. "I don't have a lot of time."

"I'll be there in five minutes."

Jessie hung up. As a general rule, she liked to give people the benefit of the doubt, but Detective Emily Graham was not making a good first impression. She wished Leary was still working Homicide. But that part of his life was over, and she supposed they would both have to adjust to that. Right now, she had a job to do. She took a deep breath and prepared herself for the crime scene.

# 5.

Jessie felt a familiar jolt of adrenaline as the taxi turned a corner and the grounds of Stevens Academy came into view. A low, square building, constructed of dark red brick, sat a good distance back from the street. Grass surrounded the building, still mostly green, despite the chilly autumn breeze that ruffled it. A fence surrounded the property, looking more decorative than functional. Beyond the fence, a wall of double-parked cars and vans, many bearing the insignia of the Philadelphia Police Department, and just as many emblazoned with logos like NBC and FOX NEWS. Busy-looking men and women dotted this landscape, but no kids. She knew the school had closed today—presumably out of respect for the dead, concern for the psychological welfare of its surviving students and faculty, and to clear the way for law enforcement to work—and there was something decidedly ominous about a school without kids.

"Jeez," the driver said. He rolled the steering wheel, pulling over. "Can't get you any closer than this, looks like."

"This is fine. Thanks." She paid him and prepared

herself to run the media gauntlet. She'd done it before, many times. Another one of those skills they don't teach you in law school.

The barrage of questions began the moment the first reporter recognized her face, and then the reporters all converged on her like hungry animals. She had to walk past what felt like a hundred video cameras. She held her head up and kept her gaze straight ahead, walking silently and trying to project a *determined prosecutor* image. She knew one of the reasons Rivera had chosen her for this case was that he'd thought she'd "play well" on TV, but she still cringed inwardly at the thought of seeing herself on the news later. Some prosecutors reveled in the quasi-celebrity that seemed to come with their office, but it had never held any appeal for her. She'd entered the profession to help people, not to worry about whether her makeup would hold up in full HD.

Her media escort fell back as she crossed the police line at the gate and entered the school property. Even then, she didn't drop her guard. She knew from bitter experience that the news outfits' cameras had longer range than high-powered rifles. Helicopters wheeled overhead. There was no privacy at a crime scene, especially an outdoor crime scene.

She showed her ID and told one of the uniforms at the gate why she was here. He extended an arm, pointing grimly toward a field to the left and behind the brick building.

Her heels made a crunching sound in the grass as she reached the athletic field. The two detectives came into view—Emily Graham and her partner, a veteran homicide detective named Tobias Novak who had to be pretty close to retirement by now. They met her at the yellow tape barricading the area where the murders had occurred the day before. Novak handed her latex gloves and paper shoe covers and she quickly pulled them on before stepping over the police perimeter. She felt a flutter in her chest and her heartbeat kicked up a notch.

"Good morning, counselor," Graham said.

"Detective," Jessie returned. She'd thought she'd heard a note of sarcasm in the woman's voice, but had decided to ignore it. She shook Graham's hand. Their latex gloves squeaked together. "Good to meet you, even if the circumstances are...." She left the rest unsaid, and Graham nodded curtly.

There was a moment in which Jessie could almost feel Graham sizing her up, and she supposed she was doing the same. The detective was about five-seven, athletic body, good taste in suits. Mid-twenties, maybe early thirties. Short blonde hair. A direct, intelligent stare. She made a solid, professional impression. *A solid prosecution witness*, she thought. Be an assistant DA long enough, and you start to assess everyone you meet based on how well they'd do on the witness stand.

But there was something about Graham that made Jessie uncomfortable, too. A confrontational posture, a look in her eyes that was angry, maybe even disdainful.

"What's the good word?" Novak said. His big smile instantly diffused the tension, and she saw Graham visibly relax. Like most young homicide detectives, Graham had been paired with an old-timer. In this case, a *real* old-timer—Toby Novak had seemed ancient to Jessie the first time she'd met him when she'd started at the DA's office years ago. Now he had to be sixty-five at least, and he looked it.

"Hi, Toby." Jessie looked around, taking in the field, with its ominous crime scene markers and tape. "So, Detectives, you want to walk me through it?"

Graham waved a hand toward a cluster of yellow plastic signs extending from the grass, each about the size of an index card and bearing a number in bold, black print. Markers placed by the crime scene techs to mark the locations of bodies and bullets. "The girls were practicing over there," Graham said, "and the perpetrator did his shooting from the bleachers over there." She pointed to the bleachers, where more crime scene markers indicated the locations of casings and other evidence. "I mean, you looked at the photos, right? What else can I add? You've seen the evidence log."

In other words, *Why are you wasting my time?*

"I just want to get a feel for the crime. On a gut level."

"Is that a new addition to the prosecutor playbook?" A challenge flashed in the young detective's gaze.

"No. Just my personal style."

Graham shrugged. "When Toby and I arrived, the girls and the coach were sprawled on the grass where you see those markers. Blood everywhere."

Jessie stared hard at the grass and thought she could see a slight reddish stain, but that could just as easily be her imagination. Outdoor crime scenes were always the most difficult to preserve because of the elements. Rain, wind, animals. And what nature hadn't removed, the crime scene techs had, after carefully photographing, bagging, and logging all of the forensic evidence, and transporting the bodies of the victims to the Medical Examiner's Office.

Still, the scene retained an eerie echo of the violence that had occurred here. And even though this echo was unpleasant to experience, it was the reason Jessie made a habit of visiting crime scenes. She suppressed a shiver as she approached the patch of grass where seventeen women had died.

"Watch where you step," Graham said.

"She knows," Novak said. "This is far from Jessie's first rodeo."

"Then she should know there's no point in dragging us out here."

Jessie took a breath. She had been hoping to avoid a direct confrontation with the detective, but she saw now that it was inevitable. Better to clear the air now. "Do you have a problem working with me?"

Graham watched her evenly. "I have a problem working with anyone who interrupts my work."

"Assisting the DA's office *is* your work."

"Oh, so you're my boss now? My lieutenant should find that pretty interesting."

"I'm not your boss. The police department and the DA's office work together."

"This isn't my first rodeo either, Ms. Black. But you're the first prosecutor to order me around like her personal butler."

"I'm helping you. You want your arrest to end in a conviction, don't you?"

"Lanford? It's a foregone conclusion."

"No conviction is a foregone conclusion. Anything can happen in the courtroom."

Graham snorted. "*That* I believe. Fucking lawyers."

Novak cleared his throat loudly. "Emily, that's enough."

The detective shot her partner an annoyed look, but her expression softened as Novak's unspoken thoughts seemed to get through to her. She turned to Jessie with a look that was almost apologetic. "Sorry, I.... I'm just having a bad morning."

Jessie returned her attention to the crime scene, careful to watch where she stepped. Even though most of the evidence was gone, you never knew for sure, which was why preservation of the scene was so important. She'd come here to get a feel for this hideous crime at a gut level so that she could do a better job prosecuting Russell Lanford; the last thing she wanted to do was contaminate evidence. "Walk me through it, please."

Graham seemed to hesitate for a second. Then she said, "We found Lanford standing on the bleachers there. He had a rifle in his hands. There was a duffel bag on the bench. To his right. The bag was full of guns and ammo."

"Full?" Jessie said. "This was a normal-size duffel bag?"

"Yeah," Graham said. "I'm not exaggerating. We found a ton of hardware. More than he'd ever need for one cheerleading squad, even if his aim had been bad. Which it wasn't, by the way. Kid knew how to shoot."

This time, Jessie did shiver. "The firearms were registered to his father?" she said.

Graham nodded. "Apparently the guy is a collector. Properly licensed, kept them in a safe, all the right things. Or so he claims." Her voice shifted subtly. Jessie might have missed it once, but she'd been working with cops long enough to pick up on it now.

"The father interests you?" she said.

Graham's gaze came up, and for the first time, Jessie thought she saw a hint of respect. "Yeah. I mean, nothing at the level where I'd include it in an official report, but.... There's something."

Before Jessie could press her for more details, Novak chuckled. The sound was so intensely inappropriate for the situation that both Jessie and Graham swung their heads to look at him. He was holding an iPhone about an inch from his face, smiling hugely.

"Jesus Christ, Toby," Graham said. "You're

criticizing *my* behavior? Put that thing away."

"Joey's dancing," the older detective said. "You gotta see this."

Graham exchanged a glance with Jessie and said, "His grandson."

"Hold on a sec," Novak said. "I need to *Like* this."

Graham let out a weary sigh. "Novak can barely operate a police car laptop, but put his grandkid on the screen and suddenly he's Mark Zuckerberg. He spends more time liking, favoriting, and tweeting than he does solving crimes. Why don't you just retire already?"

He put his phone away. "Because you still need me."

Graham shook her head with a mixture of amusement and annoyance.

Jessie said, "I ran into him earlier today. The father, Wesley Lanford. He tried to tell me something about an internet message board that might have influenced Russell. Something about men's rights?"

"Yeah, he tried to sell that line to us, too," Graham said. "Asking us to look into this website as if his son had been brainwashed or something. We shut him down pretty quickly."

"You weren't interested in what he had to say?" Jessie said.

"No," Graham said. She started walking away from the crime scene markers, apparently satisfied that she'd done all she needed to do here and that it was time to leave. "You know the drill. We're trying to build an airtight murder case here. The last thing we want is the police file filled with theories about unknown third persons that the defense can use against us at trial."

"You agree with that?" Jessie said to Novak. But he was already looking at his phone again, another big smile on his face.

"What?" he said, looking up quickly. "Sorry, I missed the question. I was multitasking."

"Jesus," Graham said under her breath.

*These two were definitely going to be a challenge to work with.*

"Never mind," Jessie said. Then, to Graham, "In my experience, that kind of strategy doesn't work. If it's out there, the defense will find it, so the more information we have, the more effectively we'll be able to counter their arguments."

"I'll keep that in mind," Graham said.

"It probably doesn't matter much in this case," she said, ignoring the detective's sarcastic tone. "Whether Russell Lanford was influenced by someone he met online, or just by his own damaged psyche, we have him at the scene, with the murder weapons and the victims. It's a strong case."

"Exactly," Graham said.

Novak burst out laughing. He held up his phone. "You gotta see this video of Joey at the playground!"

Before either of them could respond, the sound of a cough drew their attention to a man approaching them from the direction of the school building. Jessie didn't recognize him, and she was pretty sure he wasn't a cop. He was average height, with a slim build. He wore khaki pants and a sport jacket that fluttered behind him in the breeze.

Graham threw her partner a look. "Not this guy again."

"He's just trying to be helpful," Novak said. "School's closed. What else is he gonna do?"

"He's not trying to be helpful," Graham said. "He's trying to cover his own ass."

"Who is he?" Jessie said.

"School principal," Graham said. "Pretending to help us, but every chance he gets he reminds us that neither he nor the school could have prevented the shooting. No one was blaming the school, anyway. He's wasting his breath and getting in our way."

Novak shook his head. "You're too young to be this cynical, Emily. Some civilians actually want to help the police."

Graham shot Jessie a knowing look. "You'll see."

The man waved awkwardly as he drew closer. He had brown eyes that looked tired, dark brown hair, and a brown goatee with a few strands of gray. His face was long and narrow, attractive in a hangdog kind of way. If she had to guess, Jessie would say he was in his mid-forties, but he wore the weary expression of an older man.

"Jessie Black, meet Clark Harrison," Graham said. "Ms. Black is the prosecutor who will be handling

Russell Lanford's case for the district attorney's office."

Harrison seemed to study her for a second before extending his hand. "Nice to meet you." He had a firm, dry grip. "I saw you on TV. Like I told the detectives, if there's anything I can do to help, please let me know."

"And like I told you," Graham said, "we don't need anything more at this time." There was an edge in her voice, but if Harrison noticed it, he didn't let on.

"Anything you need. Stevens Academy takes student safety very seriously. I do, too. This is our first serious incident that anyone can recall—"

"As you've told us several times," Graham said. She gave Jessie a sidelong glance.

"Do you have kids of your own?" Jessie asked the principal.

The question seemed to catch him off guard. "No, but we plan to. My wife and I. When we're less busy with our careers, you know."

She did know, all too well. She thought of Leary and wondered if they'd ever find the time to take their vacation together, much less anything that required serious commitment.

"Don't wait too long," Novak said. "I did, and now every day I worry whether I'll live to see my grandson graduate high school, or get married, or—" A notification appeared on his iPhone screen and he looked at it, grinning widely. Jessie caught a glimpse of a child's smiling face.

"I just want to help," Harrison said again.

The man looked sincere, and Jessie could see the frustration in his eyes. Novak had been right—some civilians did want to help the police. But Graham had also been right, in that those civilians often got in the way.

"The best thing you can do to help is let the police and the DA's office follow their process," Jessie said. "I know it's difficult, feeling like there's nothing you can do, but sometimes you just need to trust the system."

*Trust the system.* She'd spoken those words, or words like them, too many times to count. To grieving families, traumatized witnesses. And she never felt wholly convinced herself. When something bad happened, there was a human instinct to *do something.* Trusting a faceless system to handle it—especially one as flawed as the criminal justice system—was tough for most people. As terrible as crime was, sometimes it seemed that the feelings of helplessness and impotence that followed were worse. But Graham was right—being a principal did not equip a person to assist the police, and Harrison would best serve them by staying put.

Novak's phone lit up again, and Jessie began to feel the same irritation that Graham had shown. But the display did not show a child's face this time. Only text. Graham pulled out her own phone, which was also vibrating.

"Excuse us for a moment, please, Mr. Harrison," Graham said.

The detective took Jessie's arm and tugged her

away from the principal. They walked together to the bleachers, where they would be out of earshot of the civilian if they spoke in whispers.

"What's wrong?" Jessie said.

"We just received a message from the jail. Russell Lanford killed himself."

Jessie felt the blood drain from her face. "What? How?"

Graham shook her head. "I'll get the details, but apparently he hanged himself."

"How could this happen?" Jessie said. "He should have been closely watched. He—"

"There's no sense arguing about it here," Graham said. The detective's gaze turned to Harrison, Novak, and the crime scene.

"You're right." Jessie said. She needed to head back to the DA's office immediately, where she was sure Warren was impatiently awaiting her.

## 6.

Warren was waiting for her in his office in the Homicide Unit. "Well," he said, "I guess you can go on your vacation now."

Jessie thought of the cancelled plane tickets and hotel reservations, but bit her lip. Outside Warren's office window, the sky had turned overcast, and she could practically feel the chilly air. The balmy weather of the Caribbean seemed a million miles away.

"What?" Warren said. "You don't look happy."

"Why would I be happy?"

"I thought you wanted to go on vacation. Check Expedia—you can probably book something last-minute on the cheap."

"And you know this from experience?" As far as she could remember, Warren had never taken a day off, not even a sick day. She'd even caught him working on Christmas and New Year's.

He blew out a sigh. "Now you don't want to go on vacation anymore." It was a statement, not a question, and as soon as she heard the words, she knew they were true. The Lanford case had sucked her in and wound her up—and now, just like that, it was over, leaving her with a feeling of unfinished business.

She tried to express this. "I just feel...."

He waved away her words. "I know how you feel. Rivera's not happy either, believe me. He made a promise to the city. A promise to deliver justice. Closure. Russell Lanford's suicide makes that promise impossible to keep."

Jessie paced in front of her boss's desk. In the past, he probably would have asked her to sit down, but he'd apparently learned that pacing was part of how she worked. Moving. Thinking on her feet. He turned to his computer, checking email and letting her do her thing. She was grateful.

"Maybe there's still a chance to fulfill Rivera's promise," she said, stopping.

He looked up at her. "What do you propose? Sit Russell Lanford's corpse at a defense table and pretend he's alive, *Weekend At Bernie's* style?"

She could always count on Warren for some tasteless gallows humor. Seventeen dead—eighteen counting the teenage killer hanged in his jail cell? Perfect time to roll out the 80's movie references.

"This morning, I ran into Russell Lanford's father. I mean, I didn't run into him. He found me. He wanted to tell me about a website that Russell had been frequenting."

Warren made a face. "Why would he want to tell you that?"

"He thinks someone on this website influenced

his son. He wanted us to look into whether, I don't know, there might be another person to blame for what happened at the school."

Warren barked out a laugh. "Come on, Jessie. We're not that desperate."

She tried to laugh with him, but it felt forced. He looked at her and his eyes narrowed.

"You're not serious?" he said.

"What's the harm in talking to him, finding out more? There's no trial to jeopardize now—Russell Lanford is dead. Worst case scenario, we learn nothing useful, offer our condolences, and walk away. No downside."

"It's a waste of time," Warren said. "That's the downside. Look, if you don't want to take your vacation, I'm certainly not going to try to change your mind. I've got six new cases I can assign you. If that's what you really want."

"Let me think about it."

"Please do," he said as she turned toward the door. "Maybe even ask that boyfriend of yours for his opinion."

Jessie nodded—feeling more than a little chastised that she hadn't even considered asking Leary—and left the room. She walked down the hallway to her own office. She sat at her desk, opened the web browser on her PC, and navigated to Philly.com. The Stevens Academy incident continued to dominate the news, with Russell's suicide now taking center stage.

She forced herself to leave the news sites and go

to Expedia. A search for Punta Cana filled her screen with colorful photographs of vacation resorts, which should have been a welcome change from the stark, painful pictures she'd just been looking at. But her mind refused to focus on palm trees and tropical beaches.

Like the rest of Philadelphia, she wasn't ready to let go of her case yet. And she wasn't convinced that talking to Wesley Lanford would be a waste of time.

# 7.

An hour after Warren told her to put the Lanford case behind her and head for the tropics, Jessie found herself visiting Police Headquarters instead. The so-called Roundhouse (a name derived from the shape of the building, which resembled twin circles) was about as far from an island resort as you could get. No ocean breezes or Mai Tais here—just stale coffee, stale air, and the smell of tired, overworked city cops.

But there was something comforting about the familiar sights and sounds of the Homicide Division's open floor plan. She passed the desk where Leary used to sit before he left the PPD, and a pang of nostalgia burned in her chest. She pushed the feeling aside. She hadn't come here looking for memories.

She saw Novak first. The detective sat tilted back on the rear wheels of his swivel chair, his smiling face buried in his iPhone. She located Emily Graham at a similar desk a few feet from Novak, curled over a keyboard and staring into her monitor.

Jessie peered past the woman's blonde hair and saw Russell Lanford's name on the screen.

"Paperwork?" she said.

Graham jumped, then threw Jessie an irritated look. "Ninety-nine percent of this job," she said with a frown. "At least it feels like that sometimes."

"Maybe you'd like to go somewhere with me for a few hours, do something a little more exciting?"

A creased line appeared between Graham's eyes as she regarded Jessie with obvious skepticism. "Depends what you have in mind. In my experience, 'exciting' usually means something different to a cop than it does to a lawyer." She said the word *lawyer* as if speaking of a rare and unpleasant zoo attraction.

"I'd like to interview Wesley Lanford. Learn more about the website that supposedly played a part in the Stevens Academy shootings. Just to tie up loose ends."

Graham pushed away from her desk and turned to face Jessie. "First of all, investigating crimes is a job for a detective, not a lawyer." Jessie caught an angry emphasis on the word *lawyer* again. "Second, there are no loose ends." Graham returned her attention to her computer. "The investigation's over. I'm closing out the file now. Why don't you go back to the DA's office and focus on a live case? Preferably one with a different lead detective?"

Jessie put a hand on Graham's wrist to stop her from moving the mouse. "Can you wait a day before you do that?"

"I could, but I don't see why I should."

"Do you have a problem working with me, Emily?"

Graham froze. The direct question, and use of her first name, seemed to have caught her off guard. "No."

"You sure seem to."

Novak's shadow fell over them. The older detective had stowed his phone in the sagging pocket of his suit pants. He looked first at Jessie, then Graham. "What's up, partner?"

"We're fine," Graham said. "Go get a cup of coffee."

Novak seemed to study them. "You don't look fine."

"Get me a cup, too," Graham said.

Novak's eyes narrowed. "You don't like coffee."

"Or lawyers, apparently," Jessie said.

Novak sighed. "That was this is about? Christ sakes, Emily, we talked about this."

The detective avoided his gaze. "I said we're fine."

"Then why can I feel the tension from across the room?" Novak said.

"Our illustrious legal counsel doesn't think we should close out Lanford. She thinks there are loose ends. I disagree. There's nothing more to it." Jessie could see anger and embarrassment in the woman's eyes. "Certainly nothing personal."

"Loose ends?" Novak said. "Everyone's dead."

"Maybe not," Jessie said. She still believed that whatever Graham's problem with her was, it was personal. But she could sense the time was not right to force the issue, especially with Novak present. She allowed the conversation to shift back to Lanford. Part of her felt silly in persisting when everyone else seemed ready to throw in the towel, but she had a gut feeling that there was more to this case than they realized, that not *everyone* involved was dead.

"What are you saying?" Novak leaned his hip against the side of Graham's desk. The flimsy furniture rocked and a pen rolled off the surface. Graham caught it before it reached the floor.

"She wants to visit the shooter's father," Graham said.

"The guy you said you had a hinky feeling about," Novak said. "Sounds kind of like you're in alignment on this." There was a subtext Jessie sensed but couldn't quite decipher. Novak had a determined glint in his eyes.

"Humor me," Jessie said. "One conversation. We hear the man out, look at the website, see if there's anything to his claims. If it comes to nothing, you can drive straight back here to finish your paperwork." But if there *is* something there, she thought, maybe we're back in business.

"You don't give up," Graham said. She pushed back from her desk. "I'm guessing you were a precocious child? Always challenging things, arguing, asking questions? Did your mommy and daddy tell you you'd make a great lawyer one day?"

"My mother died when I was four. I don't remember what she might have said about my future career. And as for my dad, I think he assumed I'd be president of the United States."

Graham and Novak both looked taken aback. Jessie forced her lips into a casual smile—*no big deal*—and looked at her hands. Why had she brought up her personal history? It was none of Graham's business, and besides, she didn't want to get her way by playing the dead-mother card.

"Sorry," Graham said. She seemed to look at Jessie a little differently. *Seeing me as a person, maybe?* At least the woman wasn't totally devoid of empathy.

Jessie waved away the condolences. "It happened a long time ago."

"I mean about not being president," Graham said. She smiled tentatively. "Must have been tough for your dad to see his daughter throw away all that presidential potential by embarking on a dead-end career in the prosecutor's office."

Jessie smiled back. She felt herself relax. They'd transitioned to the safe territory of cop banter. "He's working through the disappointment."

"So," Novak said. "We going to Chestnut Hill or what? I'll drive."

The Lanford house was a sleek, modern mini-mansion in Chestnut Hill, one of the most expensive neighborhoods in Philly. Novak parked the unmarked sedan in the driveway, and he, Graham, and Jessie stepped out of the car and took in the view. The two-story house presided over an immaculate lawn—there was not a single fallen leaf within its bounds, even though the neighbors' yards were strewn with them. Tall, majestic trees rose like columns near the house. The air felt cool on Jessie's face, and she thought she smelled pumpkins, apples. Behind them, two kids wheeled past on bicycles, fearlessly riding in the middle of the quiet residential street. The word that came to mind was *idyllic*. And yet, this place had spawned a monster.

The front door opened and Wesley Lanford looked out at them. The expression on his face was mostly sadness. But also, Jessie thought, hopeful. He hadn't thought they'd come.

Jessie and the detectives climbed the path to the front door. Lanford shook their hands and guided them into his house. The entryway was brightly lit, clean and inviting. They passed through it to a kitchen, where Lanford gestured to a large oak table and said, "Make yourselves comfortable. I can brew coffee."

"Coffee would be great," Jessie said. She pulled a chair out from the table and sat down.

"I'll try not to spill this one on my shoe," he said. It was meant as a joke—a callback to their first meeting outside the DA's office—but he didn't seem capable of a smile.

Novak lowered himself into one of the kitchen chairs with a heavy grunt. Then he pulled out his phone. He hadn't checked for grandson updates during the whole car ride over here—Jessie thought it was a wonder he wasn't trembling from withdrawal.

Graham didn't sit. She prowled around the

kitchen, staring at the top-of-the-line fixtures. "Nice house." Graham managed to make it sound like an insult.

"Yes, I'm going to miss it."

"You're planning to move?" Graham said.

He nodded. His expression seemed to say, *What else can I do?* Jessie supposed it wouldn't be easy to stay here after what had happened. Even if the constant reminders of his son didn't destroy him, the resentment of his neighbors probably would. Being the parent of a mass murderer tended to decrease a person's popularity.

Graham made her way to the granite countertop. She lifted a photograph from a pile of papers and held it up. "Your wife?"

In the photo, Lanford stood with his arm around the waist of an elegant-looking blonde woman. He wore a tux and the woman was in a black gown. Tables in the background—a formal event of some kind.

Lanford finished spooning coffee grounds into a stainless steel Cuisinart coffee maker before turning to look. "That's Tanya. We're not married."

He flipped on the coffee maker. A gurgling sound filled the kitchen, along with the rich aroma of coffee.

"Is Tanya Russell's mother?" Jessie said.

"No." Lanford looked uncomfortable now. Clearly he hadn't been expecting to talk to them about this subject. "His mother—Caroline—left about ten years ago."

"She left?" Graham said. "Or you left her? Tanya's what? Ten years younger than you?"

"No," Lanford said. "I mean she left. Just walked out one day, while I was at work and Russell was at school. She called us that night, from a motel in Ohio. Said she was sorry but she didn't like her life with us anymore and wanted a new one. I filed for divorce later, when it became clear she wasn't coming back."

"That must have been hard for Russell," Jessie said.

Lanford nodded. "Hard for both of us. But we got through it. Or—I guess I thought we did." He carried two mugs to the table and put one in front of her, the other in front of Novak. "Cream or sugar?"

Jessie added half-and-half to her coffee. Novak drank his black. Graham declined and continued to move around the kitchen even after Lanford joined Jessie and Novak at the table.

"Russell used your guns when he shot those people," Graham said.

Lanford looked at her with an expression of defeat. "Yes. I kept them in a safe. I don't know how he got the code."

"You have a lot of guns."

"I'm a collector."

"Nice hobby. Did Russell take all of them, or do you have even more?"

"Is that relevant?" Lanford said.

"Maybe," Graham said evenly.

"He left one. Maybe he couldn't fit in his bag. A Browning X-Bolt SSA Predator, bolt action. Good for hunting."

"Good for hunting," Graham repeated flatly.

Lanford's eyes flashed. "I own my guns legally. I've fully complied with the law."

Jessie sipped her coffee. She waited to see if Graham would pursue the topic, but the detective seemed satisfied for the moment.

"Why don't you tell us about the message board?" Jessie said.

Lanford rubbed the bridge of his nose. "I think I better just show you."

He stood up and led them through the house. Carrying her coffee, Jessie followed him up a wide, spiral stairway to the second floor. Passing open doorways offering glimpses of large, well-appointed rooms, Jessie couldn't help comparing Russell Lanford's home to the two-bedroom ranch in south Jersey where her father had struggled to raise her brother and her with as many creature comforts as his factory job afforded. She and Alex had cheered when their dad brought home their first VCR—an unimaginable luxury. By comparison, Russell had grown up in a palace. How could a kid with so much to be thankful for turn into a twisted killer?

"This is—I mean *was*—Russell's bedroom," Lanford said. Jessie braced herself—she'd visited killers' lairs before, and had the nightmares to prove it—but when she entered the room, all she felt was deeper confusion about Russell. Other than exhibiting the same luxury as the rest of the house, his room was utterly normal. A double bed (unmade), a small desk with a MacBook on it and an open math textbook, a pair of jeans tossed over the back of a chair, movie posters on the walls (one corner of an *Avengers* poster coming loose where the tape had unstuck from the wall). Somehow, the ordinariness of the room was more chilling than pentagrams or animal bones or a bag full of hair and nail clippings—all of which she had seen, and found plenty disturbing at the time.

Lanford stepped past her and opened the MacBook. The screen lit up and he touched the trackpad, opening the Safari web browser.

"Do you use adult filters to keep him off the porn sites?" Novak asked. It seemed like an odd question, and Jessie wondered if he was looking for facts about Russell or advice for his own grandkid.

"We used to." Lanford leaned over the desk and typed a web address into the address bar. "Russell always found ways around them. I don't think the filters would have blocked this website, anyway. It's just a message board, a forum where people post messages and respond to each other. Here." He drew the chair out from the desk. "Why don't you sit down?"

Jessie sat. Lanford had navigated the web browser to a website called Manpower. The layout was minimalist. A banner at the top read "MANPOWER: Men's Rights." Below the header was a list of forum threads, organized in order of the date of the most recent response. She knew from her own experience on other message boards that clicking on a thread would lead her to a page displaying the messages posted by the users—basically a public conversation. She didn't see any real names—the users all used handles like Redpill2 and FightTheFemale.

Her eyes scanned down the list of thread topics: *Bitch cop sues police department after failing physical fitness test. Blatant man-shaming by radical feminist whore group at University of Michigan. Another false rape allegation—let's dox this cunt.* It went on and on, the anger and vitriol practically pulsating from the screen.

"Detective, you want to take a look at this?" she said.

Graham had been surveying the room, an expression of impatient boredom on her face. At Jessie's question, she sighed and came over to the desk. With Graham hovering at her shoulder, Jessie scrolled down to show more threads. "What am I looking at here?" Graham said.

"Anger," Jessie said.

One thread caught her eye: *Coverage of Stevens Academy shooting shows typical anti-male bias.* She clicked on it and found huge blocks of text, diatribes against the media's supposedly unbalanced coverage of the shooting. *Why no mention of the poisonous cheerleader culture? Because the feminist agenda seeks to maintain its sexual leverage that begins in our schools!*

Graham shook her head dismissively. "Anger on

the internet?" she said dryly. "We must re-open the case immediately."

"I think you should take this more seriously," Jessie said, trying to hide her annoyance.

"Thanks for the tip."

Jessie's stomach felt nauseated. The coffee she'd enjoyed moments before now felt heavy, and a sour taste filled her mouth. Still, she couldn't fully dismiss Graham's sarcasm. The Manpower message board was certainly disturbing, but exposure to fringe people usually was. If Russell had been a frequent participant on this board, then Jessie could believe he'd been influenced by its nasty propaganda. But that didn't rise to a level impacting the case. It didn't justify further investigation, especially when their shooter was already deceased. She sighed. Time to extricate herself from this situation, get out of here, and flush this toxic language from her memory.

*And then what? Book a flight somewhere sunny and lose herself with a Michael Connelly novel in one hand and a mojito in the other?*

"Mr. Lanford, we appreciate your bringing this to our attention." She started to get up from the chair. "If we have any follow-up questions, we'll call you—"

"Wait," he said. "There's more I need to show you." He leaned over, put his finger on the trackpad, and navigated to a bookmarked page.

It was another page from the Manpower boards. The dates on the messages indicated that they had been posted the previous week. The thread topic was

*So Disgusted.* The user who'd started the thread went by the name Betaloser. "Betaloser is—*was*—Russell," Lanford said.

"He told you his user name?" Jessie said.

"I wish he had. I wish he'd talked to me about any of this stuff. I would have set him straight. But no, he kept all of this a secret from me. I only learned about the website and his user name when someone sent me an anonymous tip."

"A tip?" Graham gave Jessie a pointed look. Her voice sounded dubious, and Jessie knew why. A witness or suspect claiming knowledge from an anonymous source was the police investigation equivalent of a person asking for sex advice on behalf of a "friend."

"I received an e-mail about an hour after Russell was arrested. At first I thought it was some kind of cruel prank. But then I read the posts on the website. I know my son's writing, his voice. These posts—it's him. It's Russell."

"Who sent you the email?" Jessie said.

"It came from a Yahoo Mail account. Whoever sent it didn't sign their name. It just said 'Tipster.'"

"Betaloser," Jessie said, looking at the laptop screen.

"Beta is one of the terms these people use," Lanford said, "You know the old chestnut that women are only attracted to jerks? People were saying that back when *I* was a teenager—it's nothing new. Now apparently they call those jerks 'alphas.' According to this Manpower nonsense, women are only attracted to alpha men. And betas are the opposite, the nice guys who get walked all over. Russell apparently felt that he was a beta and a loser. I wish I'd known before it was too late to help him, to show him how great he was and how much he had to look forward to in life." Lanford's voice cracked on the last word.

Jessie read the first post by Betaloser: "I've been a lurker on the forum for a few weeks, and I've learned so much from you guys. All this time I've been lonely and unhappy and frustrated, and I didn't know why. But now I do. Thanks to all of you, I finally see through the illusion. I see what women have done to us. What they continue to do to us. And I'm mad. Fuck that. I'm disgusted."

There were a handful of sympathetic responses: "Welcome to the club, Beta!" and "We're all furious. How else can we feel?" and "Lots of good reading on the site. Check out the FAQ if you haven't already. Written by VT himself."

"VT?" Jessie said.

"Vaughn Truman," Lanford explained. "I looked him up. He's the founder of Manpower. He got rich off this website, believe it or not. You see all these Google ads around the side? This site generates a ton of ad revenue."

The next response in the thread was posted by a user calling himself True_Man. She pointed at the screen. "True_Man, with an underscore," she said. "Do you think that's him?"

"I did at first," Lanford said. "But not once I read True_Man's posts. The real Truman is too smart to post crap like that. I think True_Man with an underscore is just a disciple. A *dangerous* one. Look at his post."

Jessie read True_Man's response to Betaloser: "If you're so disgusted, why don't you stop being a pussy and do something about it?"

Jessie leaned forward. From this point on, although other users added their comments from time to time, the rest of the page was a conversation between Betaloser and True_Man.

Betaloser: "Do something like what?"

True_Man: "Send a message."

Betaloser: "That's what I'm doing right now."

True_Man: "Not to us. To them. To the bitches at your school. Do you have access to guns?"

Betaloser: "You're joking, right?"

True_Man: "Think how good it would feel. How right. To get some revenge on those bitches. You could do it, Beta. You could knock them off their pedestals. Put them in their place, finally. You'd be a hero to us."

Betaloser: "I think you're joking."

True_Man: "PM me."

That's where the conversation ended. Jessie stared at the screen for a moment. "That's it?"

"PM means private message," Graham said. She was staring at the screen over Jessie's shoulder. The boredom seemed to have left her voice.

"You'd need to sign in as Russell to access his private messages," Lanford said, "and I don't have his password. But now you see why I needed to show you this, right? This guy, True_Man or whatever his real name is, he must have convinced my son to kill those girls. I know my son was the shooter. I know that. But this ... creature ... *pushed* him."

Jessie glanced at Graham. There was a crease of frustration above the bridge of her nose. Jessie thought she knew what the detective was thinking. That all of this was awful, a hideous example of the worst impulses of human beings, but there wasn't enough here for them to act on. There was no case.

"We need to see the rest of the conversation," Jessie said. "The private messages."

Lanford grimaced. "I must have tried a hundred words trying to guess his password."

"You looked for a piece of paper he might have written it down on?" Graham said. "Or a document file on his computer or phone where he might have recorded it?"

"I looked everywhere," Lanford said.

Jessie stood from the chair. She said, "Maybe there's another way."

# 8.

Warren looked up from his desk as Jessie entered his office. The room seemed even more crowded than usual. In addition to the stacks of documents that always made a labyrinth of the floor, there was also a large box to step around.

He watched her maneuver around it. "Jessie, this isn't really a good time. I have a meeting in five minutes—"

"I need to talk to you about the Lanford case."

"You mean the one I told you was closed?"

"I spoke with the father again, Wesley Lanford, and he showed Detectives Graham and Novak and I Russell's computer—" Her voice cut off as Warren's body bobbed up and down. "Did you just bounce?"

He looked at her sheepishly. His body rose and fell again. She heard a quiet, rubbery *squeak*.

"It's just something new I'm trying."

She came around his desk. His office chair was gone. In its place was a giant blue exercise ball.

"You're sitting on an exercise ball," she said.

"It's a *stability* ball. That's what it says on the box." He pointed to the box she'd had to walk around to get into his office.

"Is there a difference?"

"I'm not sure." There was another squeak. His thighs seemed to flex in their suit pants, and his body rose and fell.

"Is that comfortable?" she said.

"Not really. Listen, like I said, I have a meeting in five minutes—"

"I'm sorry, it's just...." Jessie couldn't suppress a smile. In her years as a homicide prosecutor, she'd seen Warren pursue various initiatives to get into better shape. Generally these initiatives didn't last long. "You'd have to see yourself to understand."

"You're saying I look ridiculous." It was a statement, not a question.

Jessie shrugged. "Kinda."

Warren's face reddened. "Laugh all you want, but this is the best idea I've had yet. I'm improving my health by doing something I'm already good at— sitting. I'm going to build my core strength, exercise my abdominal muscles, and burn calories, all just by sitting on this ball all day instead of a chair."

"Sounds like you've done some research on this."

Warren's gaze shifted, a tell-tale sign that he had not. "I read a few Amazon reviews." He looked at his watch. "I told you—"

"I know. Meeting in five minutes. I'll make it

quick, okay?"

He sighed and gestured for her to continue.

"I want to stick with Lanford. There's more to the shooting than we originally thought. There were other people involved, and especially one of those people, who goes by the online handle True_Man, appears to have pushed Russell Lanford to commit the crime. But most of their communication was in the form of private messages, and we don't have the password to access them."

"I really hope this is not going where I think it's going."

"I want to seek a warrant requiring the company that owns the website to hand over the private messages and the real identity of True_Man."

Warren sighed. "That's where I thought it was going."

"There could be something more here, Warren. More than a typical school shooting. We may only be seeing the tip of a big, deep iceberg."

"Jessie." Warren raised a hand to stop her. The movement unbalanced him and his torso dipped to the right. His hand shot out and clutched the side of his desk just in time to avoid a fall.

"You still have your real chair, right? You didn't throw it away?"

"You realize you're talking about compelling a tech company to undermine the privacy of its users. When the government does that, tech companies tend to resist. Do I need to point you to recent cases involving Facebook, Google, Apple—"

"Manpower isn't Facebook," Jessie said. "And besides, Facebook lost that case."

"Until their next appeal. Do you really want to tie up our office in endless appeals just because the shooter's father showed you some disturbing posts on an internet message board?"

"Our warrant will be narrowly tailored, directed at specific posts and a specific user's ID. I'll cross every T and dot every I to make sure it holds up on appeal."

Warren rolled his eyes. "You don't hear what I'm saying."

"It's a little hard to hear anything over all that squeaking."

He bounced. He looked at his watch.

"Russell Lanford is dead. The city is hosting a memorial service for the victims, and then the public will move on. I don't see an upside to keeping this case open."

"The upside? We have sixteen murdered teenage girls, and one murdered coach. A memorial service is not going to address that in the same way that a criminal prosecution would. The city is aching for justice."

The word *ache* seemed to strike a chord with Warren, and she wondered how his "core" was feeling right about now.

"Justice. You love that word, don't you? You and Rivera both."

"It's more than a word."

"That it is." She followed his gaze to his watch. Her five minutes were up. Warren rose from his spherical chair and sidled past her toward the door of his office. "I'm sorry. I need to run."

"At least tell me if I can send Graham and Novak back to Stevens Academy for some further investigation into what was going on in Russell Lanford's life just prior to the killings. They might find more probable cause to support a warrant."

"I understand how frustrating it is to have to let this go. Whatever Wesley Lanford showed you on his son's computer, I'm sure it was disgusting, or heartbreaking, or both. And you want to do something about it. But there are limits to the power of the district attorney's office. We don't police the internet."

"I agree that there are a lot of uncertainties. But isn't it better to look for answers than to just assume there aren't any?"

"Not always."

"You know I'm experienced enough to distinguish a good murder case from a lost cause. Give me one week. Let me see what I can learn. If the detectives and I can't turn up a solid reason to continue with the case, I'll let it go. But if we find something—if there's a real case here—you'll be glad you gave me some leeway. And so will Rivera."

Warren stepped across the threshold of his office doorway. Half in, half out. "I'm late for my meeting.

Believe it or not, you're not the only prosecutor working cases here."

"Please, Warren. I have a feeling about this one."

His eyes closed and he let out a sigh. A long moment seemed to pass. "Christ, you're tenacious."

"Please."

"Okay," he said at last. "One more week. See what you can find."

# 9.

The next morning, Jessie met Detectives Graham and Novak outside Stevens Academy. The school had reopened, but Jessie wondered how many parents had chosen to keep their kids home today. The students who had come in walked the halls with blank, faraway expressions that reminded Jessie of photos she'd seen of shellshocked soldiers. No one talked. Aside from the sound of footsteps on linoleum, the hallways were silent—which felt chillingly out-of-the-ordinary for a high school. The somber atmosphere that pervaded the air seemed to extend to Jessie and the detectives. They did not speak to each other as they made their way to the principal's office for their interview with Clark Harrison. Novak didn't even check his phone for grandchild updates.

They needed more information about Russell Lanford's relationship with the Manpower website. The principal had voiced his desire to help their investigation. Talking to him about the troubled student seemed as good a place to start as any.

A receptionist greeted them in the outer vestibule of the office. She was a gray-haired matron with reading glasses hanging from a chain around her neck. Across from her desk was a row of three small chairs aligned against the wall, all of them vacant at the moment. For a second, Jessie was sixteen again, and a pang of fear shot through her at the sight of those chairs. She'd sat in a similar waiting area when she'd been caught trying a cigarette with two of her friends in her junior year of high school. She knew before even being ushered inside that Harrison's inner office would feel familiar, too. Private school or public school, Pennsylvania or New Jersey, city or suburb— somehow every principal's office was the same.

Jessie glanced at Emily Graham. The expression on the detective's face implied that she was having similar thoughts. Jessie grinned at her. "Bring back memories?"

Graham quirked an eyebrow. "I was a model student."

"Right on time," Harrison said. "I'm glad you reconsidered my offer. It's a relief to finally be able to assist the police. Come on in."

Jessie, Graham, and Novak squeezed into Harrison's office. An old desk dominated the windowless room. There was a bookshelf on one wall and his diplomas on the other. Two small, uncomfortable-looking chairs faced the desk. Jessie didn't sit down, and her thoughts must have been obvious from her expression.

"Don't worry," Harrison said, "I won't give you detention."

"Thanks for agreeing to see us on short notice," Graham said. Jessie noticed that the detective didn't sit down either. "We just have some follow-up questions about Russell Lanford."

"Okay," Harrison said. He looked at his own chair and hesitated, as if unsure of the etiquette of sitting while his guests stood. "It's a little cramped in here, isn't it?" he said. "Why don't we take a walk?"

"Great idea," Jessie said.

They followed him through mostly-empty hallways. As they passed lockers, trophy displays, and bulletin boards, Jessie felt more high school memories boil to the surface. Names and faces she hadn't thought about in ten years or more came to mind as clearly as if she'd just graduated. Maybe she should take a cue from Novak and get on Facebook, try to reconnect with some of her old friends.

"In here," Harrison said. He unlocked an unmarked door between two classrooms, reached inside, and touched a switch. Banks of fluorescent lights pulsed to life inside. "This is the teachers' lounge."

The room was sparsely furnished with three battered Formica tables, an ancient-looking refrigerator, and a kitchen counter. There was a microwave on the counter that looked crusted with grime and emanated a stale popcorn smell. A coffeemaker beside it looked dirty enough to make even a caffeine junkie like Jessie turn away. Above their heads, the drop ceiling was stained with cigarette smoke.

"Nice," Novak said.

Harrison let out a laugh. "No, it's not. But no one has much time to use it anyway, so what does it matter?"

"What do you mean?" Graham said. She walked closer to the counter and wrinkled her nose at the microwave.

"Apparently, in the old days, the faculty used to hang out in here, gossip about the students, play cards. But that was a different era. Now, with longer classes and shorter lunch periods, there's no time for socializing. When I was teaching, I would sometimes eat my lunch in here. I had 28 minutes for lunch." He shook his head, smiling ruefully. "It's so much better to be in the administration. I eat in my office now. I take as long as I want."

"It's good to be the king," Novak said. When no one responded, he said, "Mel Brooks? *History of the World Part I?*"

Harrison smiled politely and shrugged.

"When did you stop teaching?" Jessie said. "Do you miss it?"

"A little over a year ago. I do miss it, a little bit. The kids, mostly. But getting the principal gig was a huge step up for me. I don't think I could ever go back. If I ever lose this job...." He shook his head, as if the thought were too painful to think about. "So you said you have more questions about Russell?" He pulled a chair out from one of the tables—its metal legs squealed against the linoleum—and sat down. "I'm kind of surprised. I mean, doesn't his suicide end the investigation? You're not, you know, looking to place blame on Stevens Academy for his suicide—"

"No, nothing like that," Graham said.

"I guess the Philly PD is just really thorough," Harrison said.

Graham shot Jessie a look and said, "Something like that."

"We're interested in talking to people who might have known Russell on a personal level," Jessie said. "Friends. Teachers he was close to. Anyone he might have confided in."

"Confided about what?" Harrison said.

"Extracurricular activities," Graham said.

"Hobbies, interests outside of school, that sort of thing," Jessie said.

"Why do you want to know about his hobbies?"

"Just being thorough, like you said," Graham said.

Jessie sensed Harrison didn't like their vague answer, but when no additional information was forthcoming, he said, "Personally, I don't know about his hobbies."

"Friends?" Jessie said.

Harrison looked uncomfortable. "I don't think Russell had any friends."

"He didn't have *any* friends?" Jessie said.

"Not that I can think of. That's not, you know, all that unusual for some high school kids. It's not something a school would generally be expected to take action about."

"Mr. Harrison," Graham said with a trace of exasperation, "I give you my word that we are not here to place blame on the school."

Harrison nodded, but didn't look convinced. Definitely a tightly strung guy. "Maybe if you told me a little more about what you're looking for. When you say hobbies, or extracurricular activities, or whatever, what do you mean?"

Jessie did not want to specifically mention the website. The evidence would be stronger if it was offered without prompting. "What about teachers?" she said. "Was Russell close with any of his teachers?"

"Teachers he confided in? No, I don't know of any. Russell Lanford was a quiet kid. He kept to himself. Obviously if we'd only known what was going on in his head, we would have tried to help him, but"— Harrison spread his hands—"there was no way for the school to know."

Graham was pacing the length of the teachers' lounge now, clearly finished with the interview. Novak, sitting at another table, was looking at his phone.

"Okay, Mr. Harrison," Jessie said. "Thank you for your time. If you think of anything else, anyone who Russell Lanford spent time with, please let us know, okay?"

"I will. Of course." Harrison rose from his chair. "Let me show you out."

# 10.

As they walked down the hallway with Clark Harrison, Jessie kept her eyes open—for what, she wasn't sure. All she saw was the sad spectacle of students and teachers trying to go back to their ordinary routines as if a horrific mass murder had not just rocked their school to its foundations. They passed classrooms only half-filled, a few quiet kids in the hallway, and administrative offices that seemed to exude solemnity. At the school's entrance, when Harrison opened the door for them, the anticipation of getting out of the place brought her a sense of relief. The weight of the grief at Stevens Academy was oppressive.

"Thanks for everything you're doing for the school," Harrison said. It seemed like a weird comment—they hadn't done much of anything—but the principal seemed sincere enough. They said goodbye.

As soon as Jessie and the two detectives stepped outside, the media crews at the edge of the school grounds came alive. The news vans, camera people, and reporters were no longer here in full force, but the media outlets had been savvy enough to keep some on hand, just in case. Now someone pointed a video camera in their direction. *They'll take anything at this point before the story fades completely*, Jessie thought.

"Jackals," Graham muttered.

Jessie did not respond. Her gaze had drifted from the reporters to the school's faculty parking lot, where something caught her eye amidst the cars.

"More like vampires," she heard Novak say to his partner. "Feeding off the blood of a tragedy."

"And you say *I'm* the dark one?" Graham said.

Jessie said, "Who is that woman over there, wearing the purple sweater?" She pointed into the lot where two women, one in a sweater and pants and the other in a form-fitting skirt-suit, were talking next to a late-model Toyota Camry. She knew the woman in the suit. *All too well.*

Graham's gaze followed her pointing finger to the woman in the sweater. "Christiana Weaver. One of Russell Lanford's teachers. We interviewed her as part of the initial investigation. I don't know who she's talking to, though."

"I do." Jessie headed for the parking lot, anger already rising in her chest. She sensed Graham and Novak coming after her, and she was glad. A show of force would be useful.

"Excuse me," she said when she reached the two women. "The media has not been granted permission to enter school property, as I'm sure you are well aware, Ms. LaVine."

Shira LaVine turned, then beamed at her as if they were the best of friends. "Jessica Black! So great to see you again. How are you?"

"Is there a problem here?" Graham said as she reached them. Her eyes narrowed as she focused on LaVine.

"No problem," Jessie said. "Ms. LaVine was just leaving. Right?"

The woman in the purple sweater, Chistiana Weaver, looked from the reporter to the police and seemed to shrink into herself.

LaVine's friendly smile slipped, but only for a fraction of a second. Then it returned, brighter than ever. "Detective Graham. Let me introduce myself." She extended a well-manicured hand to the detective. "Shira LaVine. I write for the *Philadelphia Inquirer*."

Her hand hung in the air. After a moment, she lowered it, somehow managing to make the gesture seem graceful rather than awkward. The reporter was smooth, Jessie would always give her credit for that. But maybe the better word was *slippery*.

Graham looked at her partner, and spoke to him without taking her stare off of LaVine. "Detective Novak, it seems Ms. LaVine has accidentally wandered away from the designated press area. Would you please escort her back to her friends at the gate?"

Novak looked up from his iPhone. "What? Oh, sure. Come with me, ma'am."

The teacher, Christiana Weaver, had watched the confrontation in silence. Now, as Novak led LaVine away and Jessie and Graham turned their attention on her, the teacher took a step back. She was chewing her lip hard enough to draw blood. Jessie noticed for the first time that she was holding a thin, manila folder in her hands. "I should really, um, get back to my classroom now."

She tried to step around them. Graham blocked her path.

"Just stay here another moment, if you don't mind," Jessie said. "Your name is Christiana?"

"Christy. I teach English. My AP class is actually starting in a few minutes, so...."

She spoke in a quiet voice and seemed to be avoiding eye contact. Jessie wasn't sure if she should interpret these signals as signs of a guilty conscience, or if the woman was just shy. Weaver was young and pretty, but seemed to be trying to hide both under shapeless, conservative pants and a bland sweater. Jessie thought of the claims of "sexual leverage" that users of the Manpower forum charged women with using to get ahead in the workplace, and she almost laughed. In Jessie's experience, most women erred on the side of downplaying their gender, like Weaver, whose blonde hair was held back in a knot and who wore little in the way of jewelry. Jessie remembered dressing similarly during her first few years at the DA's office, when she'd feared sending the wrong signals or not being taken seriously.

Jessie decided to give her the benefit of the doubt and be direct. "What were you talking about with Ms.

LaVine?"

"I ... do I have to answer that?"

"Is there a reason you don't want to?" Jessie said.

"Well, I...." Weaver's voice trailed off.

"Let me be clear," Graham said. "If you are withholding information from an active investigation—"

"But I didn't know it was active," Weaver blurted. "I mean, when Russell killed himself, I just assumed it was over, and there'd be no harm in, you know...."

"No harm in what?" Jessie said.

"It'll be better for you if you just tell us everything now," Graham said. "Trust me."

Weaver sighed, and her posture seemed to slump with defeat. "It's embarrassing. I mean, this is going to make me look like a bad person or something, but I'm not. I'm a good person. It's just ... a teacher's salary...."

"Go on," Graham said.

"Russell's a student—I mean, he *was* a student—in my writing class. I always assign the kids personal essays. It's a good way for them to focus on the writing itself, instead of research and that sort of thing. I ask them to write about themselves."

"And you were, what?" Graham said. "Trying to sell a few of Russell's essays to the *Inquirer*?"

"Just one essay," Weaver said. She cringed. "I told you this would make me look like a bad person."

"What's the essay about?" Graham said. "*How I Spent My Summer Vacation?*"

"No," Weaver said. "It was about women. Russell's views on women. Here." She pulled a sheet of paper from the manila folder and handed it to Graham.

Jessie watched from beside her as Graham unfolded the sheet. There was a typed, single-spaced report: *Discrimination Against Men, and How It Has Affected Me, by Russell Lanford.* Scanning the paragraphs that followed, Jessie saw the now-familiar rhetoric of the Manpower website. There was no date on the essay.

"When did Russell write this?" Jessie said.

"Two weeks ago."

"You didn't think to bring this to anyone's attention in the administration?"

"I did! I walked it over to Clark Harrison's office and showed it to him. I even made a copy for him."

Jessie and Graham exchanged a look. Interesting that the super-helpful principal of Stevens Academy hadn't mentioned it.

"What did Harrison do after you showed him the essay?" Jessie said.

Weaver shrugged. "As far as I know, nothing."

They would have to ask Harrison about that.

"Did Russell turn in any other assignments like this?" Graham said.

"No, nothing like that one."

"Did you assign him other personal essays?"

"Yes, one other one, but—" She bit her lip.

"You didn't think it would sell as well to the

media?" Graham said. Her tone dripped disdain.

Weaver nodded. Her gaze was locked on her shoes. "It was about how he didn't want to move to Delaware. It wasn't very interesting."

Jessie saw Graham's brow furrow, and sensed that they were thinking the same thing. When Russell Lanford's father had told them he was moving, they had both assumed that the decision to move had come *after* the shooting, as a response to the anger directed at him from his former friends and neighbors. Now it appeared that the decision to move predated the shooting. Was that relevant? Did it mean something?

"Am I in trouble?" Weaver said.

"Don't talk to the media again," Graham said. "Don't give them anything. Definitely don't *sell* them anything. We'll forget this happened, this time."

Weaver looked massively relieved. "I won't. I swear to God. Thank you!"

Graham nodded. "We'll call you if we have further questions."

Weaver hurried back to the building and her waiting English class. They watched her go.

"What do you think?" Jessie said.

"I think she's an asshole."

"Yeah, but aside from that. Harrison saw that essay, knew about it, but didn't do anything."

Graham seemed to consider. "The paper is stupid—hateful even—but it's not explicitly threatening. What was Harrison going to do? Put a red flag in the kid's file, potentially ruin the kid's future over a one-page essay? Kids say stupid things all the time. It's part of being a teenager. I cringe when I remember some of the stuff I wrote and said when I was younger."

Jessie couldn't deny the logic. "Okay, but why didn't he tell us about the essay? It's clearly relevant now."

Graham shrugged. "Because he's in cover-up mode, trying to protect the school and save his job at all costs. If he told us about the essay, he'd have to admit not acting on it when Weaver first brought it to his attention, and that would put everything he cares about at risk."

"So you don't want to confront him about it?"

Graham grinned. "I didn't say that."

Novak rejoined them as they started to walk back toward the school's entrance. "We're going back?" he said. "I missed something, didn't I?"

Jessie sighed. "Nothing particularly useful."

"Don't be so sure," Graham said, walking at her side. "We learned that Wesley Lanford was planning to move his family out of state, and that Russell was unhappy about it."

"That information is even less useful than the essay."

"Is it?" Graham said.

"It means something important to you?" Jessie said.

"You know I don't have a good feeling about Wesley Lanford. The guy just, I don't know, sets off my asshole detector."

"Being an asshole isn't a crime," Jessie said. "The guy did bring Manpower and True_Man to our attention. He's trying to do the right thing."

"Look at it from another angle," Graham said. "Dad wants to take his hot young girlfriend to a new state for a new life. But his pain-in-the-ass, weirdo kid doesn't want to go along. So, what's a way to get rid of the kid? Give him some guns. Put some crazy ideas in his head about dying in a blaze of glory. Think about it. What if Wesley Lanford *is* True_Man?"

"That's a little far-fetched, don't you think? For one thing, Lanford claims he didn't learn about the website until *after* the shooting."

"Yeah," Graham said with a sneer. "From an anonymous email. How convenient. It's just as likely—*more likely*—that he already knew about the site. That he found it on Russell's computer or Russell told him about it."

Jessie still wasn't convinced. "Then why would he tell *us* about it? Why would he want us to look for True_Man if he's True_Man?"

"Who knows? He's a rich guy who probably arrogantly believes himself smarter than and superior to everyone else. Maybe he's playing with us. Laughing at us."

Jessie let out a breath. "I guess it's a theory." Not a theory she was inclined to believe, but if her experience digging into the actions and motivations of criminals had taught her anything, it was to be receptive to the seemingly unbelievable. "It still brings us back to needing a warrant for the identification of True_Man."

Graham held up the essay. "Maybe our helpful principal will be more forthcoming when he sees this."

# 11.

This time, Principal Clark Harrison dispensed with the niceties—no praises for the thoroughness of the Philadelphia PD, no leisurely walk to the teachers' lounge. He barricaded himself behind his desk and sat rigidly and with his eyes narrowed.

"What are you trying to imply?" he said. His gaze shifted between Graham and Jessie, as if unsure of the greater threat—Novak, with his ever-present smartphone, apparently posed none. "Is this about liability? It is, isn't it? I knew I shouldn't have believed a word you said. The school has insurance, but...." His voice trailed off. "Look," he said. "I didn't do anything wrong. Does it help anyone if I lose my job? Does that bring anyone back to life? What is the point of this ... this *persecution*?" He glared at them.

"Are you finished, Mr. Harrison?" Graham said.

He frowned and wrung his hands. "What do you want from me?"

"You could start by explaining why you didn't tell us about the personal essay the first few times we spoke," Graham said. "And then, after you've explained that, you can tell us all of the other things you've been holding back."

Harrison licked his lips. The anger in his gaze was giving way to panic. "Other things? There aren't any other things. You make it sound like this is some kind of cover up."

Graham shrugged, as if to say, *if the shoe fits....*

Jessie suppressed a laugh. Graham's abrasive demeanor could be pretty entertaining when it wasn't aimed at her.

"How is the essay even important at this point?" Harrison said. "The students are dead. Ms. Kerensa is dead. Russell Lanford is dead. Does that sound cold? Maybe. But it's true. What's the point in looking back now—with perfect hindsight—and second-guessing what I should have made of a stupid essay written by an angry, angsty teen? Neither of you are in education. Who are you to judge me?"

Graham leaned toward him. Jessie could tell by the glint in her eyes that she wasn't ready to let Harrison off the hook so easily. He cringed back from her. "Ms. Weaver made something of it, didn't she?" Graham said. "And without the benefit of perfect hindsight. She found the essay disturbing enough to bring to your attention."

"What did you do when she showed it to you?" Jessie said.

Harrison's mouth opened and closed. Clearly, he did not want to answer. Jessie wondered if they should *Mirandize* him, but decided that would only cause him to clam up further. The *Miranda* warnings were only required when a suspect was interrogated while in police custody. Here, Harrison was in his own office and not even really a suspect. Although she could imagine Graham arresting him for obstruction of justice, just out of spite.

"You did nothing, isn't that right?" Graham said.

Harrison swallowed hard. "Please, you need to look at this from my perspective. Disciplinary action is part of my job. I deal with the school's 'bad kids' on a daily basis. Russell Lanford wasn't one of the bad kids. At least, he wasn't at the time. He was quiet, brooding, obviously unhappy—but so was I when I was fifteen. Why taint the kid's file by flagging his essay as potentially threatening? Why make a big production out of a paper he probably dashed off between episodes of South Park? That was my thinking. I was cutting the kid a break because I felt bad for him."

Graham nodded. "Would you have cut him a break if his paper had been about hating blacks instead of hating women?"

Harrison let out a strangled laugh. "That's hardly the same thing."

"What about Jews?" Graham pressed. "Is Jew bashing okay at Stevens Academy? Or what if he wrote a diatribe against gays? You would have let those essays slide, too?"

"Of course not. Stevens Academy has a zero tolerance policy for any kind of bigotry."

"But this essay was only about hating women, so it

was tolerated."

Harrison sighed. He looked deflated and defeated. At this point, Jessie felt bad for the guy, but she wasn't going to come to his rescue. If there was a chance that Graham's questions might shake some important piece of information loose, she wanted to be here to hear it.

"Like I said, in hindsight, I maybe should have been more concerned about his essay. Bad judgment. But I didn't do anything wrong."

"Is there anything else you haven't told us?" Graham said, changing tack. "Any other secrets? Because it would be much better to get them out now. As you just learned, these things have a way of bubbling up to the surface."

"No." Harrison shook his head vigorously. "No other secrets."

Graham arched an eyebrow. "You told us that Russell Lanford didn't have any friends, that he wasn't close with any students or teachers. Was that the truth, or were you just trying to steer us away from learning about the essay?"

"It was the truth. Russell was a loner."

"Ms. Weaver said he was upset about having to move to Delaware. If he was so friendless and alone, why would he care?"

Harrison looked pained. Jessie could only imagine what he was thinking right now about Weaver and her big mouth. "I have no idea. There are lots of reasons a kid wouldn't want to move. Maybe he liked his house. Who knows?"

"Okay," Graham said. "I guess we're done for now."

Harrison nodded but apparently couldn't quite bring himself to speak.

"Hold on," Novak said from the back of the principal's office. "I have a question."

Jessie had almost forgotten the older detective was in the room. Now, she turned to see him approaching Harrison's desk with an intent look on his face.

"After you read the kid's essay," Novak said, "did you check out the website?"

"The ... website?" Harrison said.

"The Manpower website. The forum he talked about in his essay." Novak held out the essay, then looked meaningfully at the computer on Harrison's desk.

Harrison wet his lips again. "I don't think so."

"Really?" Novak said. "So if we look, we won't find it in your browser history? If we send your PC to the police lab, they won't uncover it?"

"Uh, well, I...." Harrison stammered. "I might have looked at it once, the day I first saw the essay. You know, real quickly, out of curiosity. I don't really remember."

Jessie stared at the man, incredulous. How could anyone read that venomous message board and not immediately seek help for the impressionable kid who'd been taken in by it? Harrison was right to worry about his job. He didn't deserve to keep it.

"There seem to be a lot of things you don't remember," Graham said. "A lot of things you didn't do wrong."

Harrison just nodded, speechless.

Graham rose from her chair. Jessie took her cue and did the same. With Novak, they headed for the door.

"Are you going to go after my job for this?" Harrison said. "Or the school? Are you going to claim we're responsible for what happened?"

Graham said, "We'll be in touch." Then they left.

Outside in the fresh air, Graham turned to Jessie and said, "How'd I do?"

The question took Jessie off-guard. She peered at the blonde detective, looking for signs of sarcasm. "Are you asking me?"

"I'm sure not asking *him*," she said with a dismissive shrug in Novak's direction.

"I didn't think you cared what I thought."

Graham frowned. She looked hurt. "Look, if you don't want to answer the question—"

"I thought you did great. You backed him into one corner after another. He gave up everything he knows, and he's scared enough to tell us more if he remembers anything else. I was very impressed, and I've worked with a lot of detectives."

"Thanks."

Jessie glimpsed a vulnerability in Graham's

expression that the woman had never let show before. Acting on intuition, she said, "Listen, Emily, maybe we got off on the wrong foot. Do you, uh, have plans for dinner tonight?"

Graham seemed to study her for a moment. "I don't think—"

Jessie felt her face redden. "No, I mean, if you're busy, don't worry about it. I was just thinking—"

"The truth is I'm supposed to go on a date. A guy my mother met at her doctor's office." Graham groaned.

"You don't sound too excited about it."

"Believe me, I'd skip it if I could."

Jessie thought for a second. "Can you change it to a double date? You and him, with me and Leary?"

Graham nodded slowly. "That would be less excruciating."

The woman was full of compliments, Jessie thought, already regretting this. "Great," she said.

Graham turned to Novak and said, "What the hell are you smiling about?"

# 12.

"Hold on," Leary said. "Let me get this straight. You invited Emily Graham—who's been nothing but standoffish toward you—along her date—whom apparently not even *she* likes—to join us for dinner on one of the exceedingly rare occasions when we're able to get a romantic night to ourselves?"

"Well, of course it sounds bad when you put it that way." Jessie wrung her hands.

"And you're telling me now, half an hour before our reservation?"

Le Virtù was a fine Italian restaurant in East Passyunk Crossing. Jessie had been wanting to try it for months, ever since reading a bunch of enticing reviews online. So, while she still wasn't sure if asking the confrontational detective to dinner would turn out to be one of her best ideas or one of her worst, she figured even in a worst case scenario, she'd still get to enjoy a great meal.

Leary was less enthused.

"Look," she said, "it was a last minute decision. And it wasn't easy to get the restaurant to change our reservation from two to four. I had to name drop the DA's office before they agreed."

"Lucky us," Leary said.

"You're really upset?"

His look of incredulity might have been humorous under other circumstances. "What were you thinking?"

"If I don't forge a bond with this woman, my ability to win this case is going to be impaired. And who knows how many cases down the line? There's nothing worse than a detective and a prosecutor not getting along—I've heard horror stories, and I'm sure you have, too. There was a moment today when she seemed to warm up to me. I decided to take advantage of it."

"Exactly. *You* decided."

"I have a feeling Emily's not so bad once you get to know her," she said.

"Oh, so now she's *Emily* instead of Graham? For God sakes, Jessie, you're barely on a first name basis with me!"

"Leary—" He glared triumphantly at her. She started over. "*Mark*, it's just one dinner. Please just do this for me as a favor. I'll make it up to you."

"Well," he said with a hesitant smile, "now we're getting somewhere."


Le Virtù was located at the end of East Passyunk Avenue, off Broad Street. There was a pleasant-looking patio, but the night was too chilly for outdoor dining, so most of the patrons were inside. Jessie and Leary waited at the curb, where a valet was parking cars.

When Graham and her date arrived, Jessie almost did a double-take. Graham looked surprisingly elegant in a dress. It was hard to believe this woman was the same hard-edged cop she'd gotten to know since the shooting.

"You look great," Jessie said as they walked inside. Jessie gave the hostess her name, and they waited by a bar. Quiet sounds, like the clink of silverware and the low babble of voices, created a soothing atmosphere.

"You clean up pretty well yourself," Graham said. "You must be Leary. I don't think we've actually met."

"No, you must have joined the Homicide Division just after I left," Leary said.

"This is Troy Eckert," Graham said, introducing her date.

He turned out to be unexpectedly normal-looking, considering that Graham's mother had apparently met him randomly in a doctor's waiting room. He had a firm handshake and wore a conservative suit. When Leary asked him what he did for a living, he said he was a commodities trader downtown. "How about you? Emily said you used to be a detective?"

Jessie sensed Leary's discomfort with the subject, but he did a good job hiding it behind a friendly smile. "Yeah, I had a few years of adventure," he said in a light tone, "but that's behind me. Now I work in the private sector. Loss prevention."

"Oh, that's interesting," Eckert said. "What made you decide to leave the police department?"

Leary was spared from having to answer this question when the hostess, holding four menus to her chest, politely interrupted them. "Your table is ready. Would you like to follow me, please?"

"Thanks," Leary said, and Jessie heard the relief in his voice.

The hostess guided them behind the bar to a small dining room. Most of the tables were filled and the noise level was loud, but not unpleasantly so.

They ordered a bottle of wine and settled into the obligatory small talk while looking at their menus. The wine loosened them up a little bit—as did the pasta course, which was homemade and amazing—but Jessie noticed that Graham wasn't saying much. Her date, on the other hand, seemed to have an endless supply of long stories to recount in minute detail. Several times, she had to brush Leary's hand away as he tried to pinch her leg.

When the waiter arrived with their entrees, Jessie's nostrils filled with the aromas of garlic, pasta, meat, and other savory smells. Her mouth watered. She smiled at Leary through the steam rising from their plates. He smiled back.

She had ordered brodetto, a seafood stew. She paused a moment just to smell it—hints of saffron and wine and red pepper—then turned her spoon through shrimp, calamari, and big chunks of monkfish and sole. She tasted the stew. "Oh, this is good."

Leary lifted his knife and fork. He'd ordered the porchetta, which the menu described as roasted pork belly served with cicerchie and broccoli rabe. It looked delicious, and judging by the expression on his face as he chewed his first bite, it tasted as good as it looked. "Damn," he said with approval.

Graham brought a forkful of her dinner—a beef dish—to her mouth. She frowned.

"Something wrong?" Eckert said, pausing with his knife and fork.

"It's just not as well done as I'd like," Graham said. "I'll say something."

Eckert shook his head. "Let me." He raised a hand into the air. When the waiter didn't respond immediately, he loudly cleared his throat and said, "Excuse me! Waiter!"

The dining room went silent. Jessie felt the gazes of the other people focus on their table. She gritted her teeth and tried to ignore the stares.

"Yes, sir?" The waiter said. "Is there a problem?"

Graham said, "It's no big deal. If you could just take my plate back and make it slightly more well done—"

"Actually, it is a big deal," Eckert said. He grabbed Graham's plate off the table and thrust it into the waiter's hands.

"I'm very sorry to hear that. I'll run it back to the kitchen."

"You better," Eckert said. "This isn't how she

ordered it. And we expect you to take it off the bill, too."

The waiter looked abashed. "Certainly, sir."

"Now she has to sit here while we all have our dinners. Ridiculous!"

"My apologies, sir." The waiter took Graham's plate and hurried away.

Every other person in the room had watched this exchange, and now Jessie heard the murmur of conversation as the silence broke and people started to talk again—probably about them.

"Excuse me," Graham said. She stood from her chair. "I need to use the ladies' room."

Jessie stood, too. "I'll go with you."

She felt bad leaving Leary at the table with Eckert, but she supposed it was just another thing she'd have to make up to him.

In the restroom, Graham stood in front of the sink, staring at her reflection. Her gaze ticked to Jessie as she entered the room and came up beside her. "This is why I don't do blind dates," Graham said. "I knew I shouldn't have let my mother talk me into this."

"His heart is probably in the right place."

Graham stared at her. "Seriously?"

And they both burst out laughing. "Okay, I agree. It's a turnoff."

"It's a warning sign," Graham said. "You can tell a lot about a person from the way they talk to waiters. The guy is clearly a dick."

"So it seems."

"Boring, too," Graham said. "I think I listened to about ten seconds of his ten minute story about leasing his car. I was thinking about our case the whole time. Thank God I had that on my mind, or I'd have died of boredom."

"Me, too," Jessie said.

Their eyes met in the mirror.

"What were you thinking?" Graham said.

Jessie shrugged. "Mostly about getting a warrant to compel Manpower to give us the identity of True_Man and access to the private messages. The more I think about it, the more I think this is a criminal conspiracy case."

"Conspiracy?" Graham seemed to mull it over. "I hadn't thought of it that way, but I guess that fits. Aiding another person in the planning or commission of a crime, or soliciting someone to commit a crime. And there has to be an overt act, right?"

Jessie saw her own surprised expression in the mirror. "You know the Pennsylvania Criminal Code."

Graham shrugged. "I've picked up bits and pieces."

"If we can get the warrant," Jessie said, "I think the private messages will give us evidence that True_Man solicited Russell Lanford to commit the crime, and maybe even aided him, too."

"And there's no question regarding the presence of an overt act," Graham said. "Seventeen people were killed."

"Right. We'll have all we need to charge him."

"Assuming we can also find out who *he* is—and assuming he's not sitting in an internet cafe in China or somewhere equally beyond our reach."

"Right." Jessie took a deep breath. "I think we should draft the warrant application first thing in the morning. Do you want to meet at my office?"

Graham nodded. "Okay."

When they returned to the table, Leary looked like he wanted to kill himself. But a moment later, the waiter returned with Graham's dish—now cooked perfectly to order—and they quickly absorbed themselves in the delicious meal.

On the way home, Leary said, "Was our double date everything you hoped it would be?"

"Actually, yes."

"You and Emily seem pretty chummy now."

"Nothing brings two women together like disliking the same man."

"So, mission accomplished, I guess."

"And as a bonus, we did some good brainstorming on our case."

"Really? When did that happen?"

"In the bathroom."

Leary nodded. "Of course."

"Sorry you had to endure Eckert."

Leary shrugged. "At least the food was good.

And"—he shot her a mischievous grin—"I believe I've earned some special attention tonight?"

She grinned back. "Tonight, you'll have all my attention."

## 13.

Six AM the next morning, the DA's office was a ghost town. Jessie had to flip wall switches to illuminate their path step by step as she led Emily Graham to a conference room on the floor of the Homicide Unit. The detective was silent, and Jessie could practically feel the waves of anxiety pulsing from her body as she tailed her down the hallway. Despite her enthusiasm the previous night, Graham didn't want to be here. Jessie remembered the labored sentences in her police report. Apparently, writing was not Graham's activity of choice.

As a lawyer, writing was second nature to Jessie. In some ways it was her preferred method of communication. In briefs and other court documents, she could organize her thoughts in coherent, persuasive arguments that she could never seem to match while speaking on her feet. Sometimes she forgot that most people didn't share this view, and many went through life limiting their written output to texts and Facebook updates. Cops didn't have that luxury, though, and she didn't need to remind Graham of that.

"You always start work this early?" Graham said.

"I like the quiet. You?"

"I usually run in the morning," Graham said. "Clears my head. Helps me prepare for the day."

"Sorry. I guess we could have done this later."

"No, let's get it over with."

In Pennsylvania, a search warrant application consisted of two parts: the legal application, presented by the DA's office, which laid out the request and argued that probable cause existed to justify a Constitutionally-valid search and seizure, and the factual affidavit, a sworn statement by an officer or detective describing the facts that supported the argument.

Typically, the detective would draft the warrant application, an assistant DA would review it, and then it would be filed. But sometimes, Jessie preferred to work directly with the detective. The process helped to make sure she and the detective were on the same page—critical if and when the warrant was challenged by defense counsel in a pre-trial motion to suppress evidence—and it made Jessie an active player rather than a rubber stamp on the detective's words. Today was one of those times that she believed working on the warrant application together would benefit the case, especially since Graham had helped Jessie solidify their argument the night before.

Jessie opened the conference room door and walked inside. She took a seat and opened her laptop on the long, oval table. Graham opened an identical laptop, one of the loaners the DA's office kept for guests.

"Okay," Jessie said. She smiled. "Let's knock this out."

"I feel like I'm in college again. But not the fun part."

Jessie thought about that. "How about if we order breakfast?"

Graham arched an eyebrow. "Are you serious?"

"Sure. The diner around the corner doesn't mind delivering here. They make incredible bacon, egg, and cheese sandwiches. What do you say?"

"I say I don't know how you maintain your figure."

Jessie shrugged. "I'm blessed with an amazing metabolism. They have salads, too, if you want—"

"Screw that. I'll get mine with a side of hashbrowns."

Jessie laughed. She pulled out her phone. The diner's phone number was already in her contacts list, and she had their order placed within a minute. "Done," she said, putting down her phone. "Feeling more like the fun part of college yet?"

"A little," Graham conceded with a half-smile. "Food has definitely improved our working relationship."

"Yes. Maybe we should just eat constantly when working together."

"I'm good with that," Graham said. She looked at

her laptop and her frown returned.

"Just write down what happened when we interviewed Wesley Lanford," Jessie said, "what he said and showed us. I'll help you through it."

They worked together on the affidavit for fifteen minutes. Then Jessie's phone vibrated, interrupting them. Their food was here.

An hour later, the conference room reeked of greasy food, Jessie's stomach felt full-to-bursting, Graham looked dazed, and they had a completed application for a search warrant.

Their request to the court was straightforward. They were asking the court to issue a search warrant requiring Manpower to locate and produce information—specifically, the identity and all user information and content (including private messages) of True_Man.

"What do you think we'll find?" Graham said.

"A monster," she said, and they sat in silence for a moment contemplating that.

# 14.

Later that day, Jessie's phone vibrated. She looked at the screen and saw that the identity of the caller was blocked. She answered anyway. "Jessica Black."

"Hi. This is Brenda Townsend." When Jessie didn't respond, the caller added, "Judge Katz's clerk?"

"Oh, right. Hi, Brenda." Jessie remembered her now—a young woman who'd just graduated from law school and was clerking for Judge Clifford Katz. Katz was the judge reviewing her application for a search warrant of Manpower's records on True_Man. "Is this about the warrant?"

"Uh, well, yes." Brenda sounded uncomfortable, and that made Jessie uncomfortable.

"Is there a problem?"

"The judge would like to speak with you in person, if that's okay. He has an opening at 2. If you could meet him in his chambers...."

"I'll be there," Jessie said.

"Great." Brenda sounded relieved. "I'll let him know."

\* \* \*

Jessie entered Judge Katz's chambers. She found him hunched over his desk, one hand gripping his mouse, playing what looked like an intense game of solitaire on his PC.

"You wanted to see me, Your Honor?"

His bright blue eyes zeroed in on her from beneath bushy gray brows. "Jessie, come on in. Have a seat. Relax."

She did as the judge commanded, taking a seat in one of the chairs facing his desk. "It's kind of hard to relax when I don't know why you called me here. Is there a problem with the warrant application?"

He gave up on his solitaire game and leaned back in his chair. "Maybe. I'm not sure."

She wanted to ask him what that meant, but she kept her mouth closed. Katz was an old-timer. He'd been on the bench since before Jessie went to law school. Hell, probably before she'd gone to high school. Whatever he had to say, he'd get to it in his own way.

"This school shooting," he said. His voice was low, rumbling. "Terrible thing."

"Yes."

"I love kids. I'm not sure if you knew that about me, but it's true. They're our future. I truly believe that. And they're delicate. So delicate. They don't realize it, don't believe it. So it falls on us to protect them."

She nodded. In fact, she did know that Katz loved kids. She knew that he donated generously—in the form both of money and time—to children's charities and organizations. She knew that he dressed as Santa (even though he was Jewish) every Christmas at a homeless shelter so that kids who had nothing could make their heartbreakingly simple wishes—and, whenever it was within his power to do so, he made those wishes come true. What she didn't know was why he seemed to want to talk about this now.

"You mind if I take off my shoes?" he said. "My wife bought me new shoes and they're killing my feet."

"Don't worry about me," she said. Hell, he could take off his shirt, too. Just as long as he gave her her search warrant.

Katz yanked off his shoes and let out a sigh. "Much better." Then, with barely a pause, he said, "This warrant application. I don't know. I think it's a stretch."

"Your Honor, the application meets all of the requirements under the Pennsylvania Rules of Criminal Procedure."

He waved a hand. "I'm not talking about formalities."

"Then what?"

"Where's the probable cause? Do you really expect to find evidence that a crime was committed on this ... what did you call it ... message board?"

"Yes."

"Which crime?"

"Conspiracy."

He grunted. "Conspiracy to commit murder, Jessie? Really?"

She leaned forward. "All of the elements are there, Your Honor." She counted them off on her fingers, thankful her earlier brainstorming sessions with Graham had prepared her. "Intent. Agreement to aid in the planning or commission of a crime. Overt act."

"I know the statutory elements. And I'm sympathetic to the district attorney's office's desire to seek justice here. But come on. Russell Lanford killed those kids. No one helped him—certainly not by talking to him on some internet page."

"I think I can prove that's exactly what happened. But only if you grant my application for a search warrant."

The judge sat back in his chair, thinking. Rather than stare at him, she looked around his chambers. He'd turned a utilitarian office into a warm space, practically a den. All it needed was a fireplace and more comfortable chairs. But Jessie knew better than to allow the ambiance to lull her. Katz had a warm side, no doubt—call it his Santa side—but he was also a shrewd judge, battle-hardened by years on the bench and even more years prior to that as a trial lawyer. And no judge liked to be reversed on appeal.

The judge said, "I won't pretend that what I read in Detective Graham's affidavit didn't disturb me. It's terrifying, what the internet makes possible, the dangers it poses to kids. I mean, don't get me wrong. I'm not naïve enough to believe it was ever truly possible to protect kids during their teenage years. You know, the years when they're at their most stupid and most susceptible to bad influences. Before the internet, in my day, parents worried about their kids being corrupted by the bad seed who hung out on the street corner, the greaser wearing a leather jacket and showing off his switchblade. But now ... now that bad seed is everywhere. He's in your phone." Katz shook his head ruefully. "But conspiracy? The Pennsylvania Criminal Code just wasn't drafted with the internet in mind."

"The laws were drafted to be flexible," Jessie said. "To accommodate a changing world. If True_Man conspired to commit murder, the technology he used is irrelevant."

Katz sighed and tilted his chair forward, pinning her with his stare. "You're a good prosecutor, Jessie. One of the best, to be truthful. So I'm going to give you some leeway this time. I'm going to issue the search warrant."

"Thank you, Your Honor—"

Judge Katz raised a knobby finger, signaling that he was not done. She closed her mouth. "But," he said, "I want you to understand the risks. For both of us. The risk for me is a spanking from the appellate court. I can handle that. At this point in my career, I don't need to worry about my record, only my retirement fund. But the risk to you is potentially more dire."

"I know, Your Honor. The inadmissibility of evidence."

He nodded. "If an appellate court rules my search warrant unconstitutional, then everything the warrant leads you to—up to and including True_Man's identity—will be off limits. Fruit of the poisonous tree. Your whole case will vanish in a puff of judicial smoke and True_Man will walk."

"The search warrant will stand," she said. "Even if I have to defend it before the Supreme Court."

Katz smiled, and a raspy laugh escaped his throat. "Now that would be a show."

Jessie nodded. "Let's hope it doesn't go that far."

The judge's face grew serious again. "Okay, Ms. Black. You have your search warrant. Let's see what you find."

## 15.

The city held a memorial service for the victims of the Stevens Academy shooting at Fairmount Park, a large municipal park along the waterfront that served as a frequent venue for public concerts and other, happier events. Walking through the crowd of mourners with Leary, Jessie saw a lot of teenagers with their parents. She tried to imagine what it would be like to struggle with the reality of a school shooting at that age. It was hard enough for a thirty-three year old. Her heel came down on something and she almost tripped. Leary caught her. She looked down. There were candles scattered on the ground.

"Careful," Leary said. "There was a candlelight vigil here last night. The grass is littered with candles, flowers, condolence cards."

A dais had been set up near the river, with a podium and several folding chairs. The mayor was standing at the podium and seemed to be studying his notes as tech people set up equipment in front of him. Jessie recognized a few of the people sitting in the chairs—community and religious leaders. No sign of Jesus Rivera. As far as he was concerned, Jessie knew, the Russell Lanford incident was no longer a matter for the DA's office.

Jessie hoped to change that soon.

She and Leary found a pocket of space in the crowd just big enough to accommodate them if they stood hip-to-hip. As always, an almost electric current raced through her when their bodies touched. She didn't know whether to be happy or irritated about this—it seemed even the tragedy of seventeen murdered people couldn't damp her attraction to Leary, and she wasn't sure how she should feel about that.

"Hello," the mayor said. His voice boomed across the park. "I want to welcome you all, and thank you for coming together to honor our lost friends and loved ones on this very somber occasion."

The mayor spoke for fifteen minutes. Most of his talking points were predictable. He expressed solidarity with the families and friends of the victims. He called for an end to hatred and violence. He cited a desperate need for nationwide action to address the senseless tragedy of school shootings. He sounded sincere—even wounded—and Jessie thought in this case he might be. He had two children of his own. He was affecting.

She wiped her eyes. As a new speaker took the mayor's place at the podium, she observed the crowd. The mayor's speech had struck a chord, and many faces were shining with tears. Teenagers were crying into their parents' shoulders. Bodies were hitching with ragged sobs. She saw one man—a six-foot giant with a full beard and trucker hat—who was openly weeping. She looked up at Leary. His cheeks might be dry, but his eyes were red and shined more than usual. She took his hand in hers and squeezed.

She was mildly surprised when he skirted the subjects of gun control and violent media, but then realized he'd only delegated them to the people sitting behind him. A plea for stronger gun control in Pennsylvania would be coming in a subsequent speech, as well as some finger-pointing at the graphic violence that TV, movies, and video games exposed to the country's impressionable youth.

Jessie would have preferred her leaders to keep politics out of this memorial service, but she'd been working for the government long enough to know there was zero chance of respect for the dead outweighing an opportunity to advance an agenda. This fact didn't disgust or upset her as it might have ten years ago. It was simply the way things were.

Sometimes, she knew, killers liked to haunt the funerals of their victims. Was True_Man here now, in Fairmount Park, among the hundreds of people who'd come to grieve and pay their respects? *That* thought *did* disgust her.

*I will find you.*

Her phone vibrated. Looking at the screen, she saw Warren Williams's name. "I need to take this," she said to Leary.

"Here?"

She nodded.

"Work?" he said.

"Yeah. Maybe Manpower complied with the warrant." It seemed too quick for that, but she felt a surge of hope anyway. If she could just put a real name to the person she knew as True_Man, her conspiracy case would begin to come together.

She scanned the park for a space where she could step outside the crowd. There was none. The memorial service had drawn a huge number of mourners. They stood practically shoulder-to-shoulder now, waiting for the next speaker.

With no other option, Jessie put her phone to her ear, plugged her other ear with her finger, and ducked down. "Warren? I'm at the memorial service. Can't really talk." Someone shot her a dirty look, and her face flushed hotly. "Is this about the warrant?"

"You could say that."

"Good news?"

"A lawyer representing Manpower, LLC reached out to the district attorney's office today." His voice was hard to hear over the sound of the crowded park.

"Warren? Tell them to contact me or Emily Graham to coordinate handing over the data."

"That's not why they called me." The people around her faded as she strained to hear. "It was to request that this office voluntarily withdraw the warrant."

"What?" Anger spiked through her. "What did

you tell them?"

"I declined. Obviously."

"Good."

"Not good. My take on this lawyer? He's not finished. Manpower isn't going to willingly comply with the warrant. And worse, they're going to refuse publicly. They're going to try to make a media event out of this."

"All publicity is good publicity," she said.

"What? I'm having trouble hearing you," Warren said.

"I said all publicity is good publicity."

"Maybe for sleazy websites. Not for elected officials. This is going to get messy. There's going to be a fight."

"The law's on our side."

"Are you even listening to me?" She could hear his exasperation even over the background noise. "This isn't just about the law. This isn't your everyday, ordinary murder. This is a school shooting in Philadelphia. It's news. And you need to control the news. If there's blowback, if Rivera is made to look bad, you will be looking for a new job. A new career. Do you understand what I'm saying?"

She didn't, really. As far as she understood, the only thing that mattered was that she do everything in her power to bring an evil man—a man she now believed to be a killer by proxy— to justice. But Warren was a political creature, and he wouldn't want to hear that. So she said, "I understand."

"Good," he said. The call ended.

"Everything okay?" Leary said as she straightened up and put away her phone.

"No," she said. At the podium, a middle-aged man was talking about young lives cut short, bullet casings on a football field, cheerleader uniforms riddled with blood and bullet holes. He was talking about a community in pain, a city in need of action. "Nothing is okay," she said.

They stood together, silent, listening.

When the service ended, they walked out of the park together. She leaned into him as they walked. His body was reassuringly sturdy, strong, exactly what she needed.

# 16.

Graham and Novak did not attend the memorial service. Novak seemed to think this was because Graham couldn't face the immensity of the sadness that the event represented, but that wasn't it. She wanted another crack at Wesley Lanford, and she thought showing up at the man's house during the memorial service of his son's seventeen victims would be excellent timing to put him off his game—whatever game he was playing. She still wasn't sure what game that was, but she knew something was *wrong* about the guy, and she intended to flush it out, using every strategy at her disposal.

She stood with Novak at the front door of the Lanford house in Chestnut Hill. When he answered the door, she started with, "Is your girlfriend here today, Mr. Lanford?"

"Detective Graham," he said, obviously surprised by their visit. "Detective Novak. Come in, I guess. Tanya's here. Why?"

"We'd like to go over some questions with you, and with Tanya as well, since we missed her last time."

"Right now?"

"That isn't a problem, is it?"

"No." He walked them into the house, where they were met by a blonde woman who looked even more striking in person than she had in the photographs Graham had seen during their previous visit. *A trophy wife, no doubt.* "This is Tanya. Tanya, these are the detectives investigating the ... you know...."

Tanya nodded gravely. "I'm so sorry to meet you under these conditions," she said. She shook their hands. Graham met her gaze and tried to gauge her sincerity. The woman looked away. Her hand trembled when she shook Graham's. She was nervous, and probably hiding something.

"So, how can we help you?" Lanford said when they reached the kitchen. "Is it about the Manpower website? Have you looked into that?"

"We're in the process of looking into it," she said, "but that's not why I'm here. I wanted to ask you a few more questions about your upcoming move to Delaware."

"Okay," Lanford said. "What do you want to know?"

"Why don't you start by telling me why you lied before."

Lanford and Tanya exchanged a glance. Graham caught it and knew she was on the right track. These wealthy fathers were all the same—no sense of familial responsibility, always looking to move on to the next best thing. "I didn't lie—"

"The last time we were here, Jessica Black asked you about the move. You implied that you were moving to get away from the notoriety caused by Russell's actions."

"Well, that's partially true."

"Partially true? I'm not familiar with that concept. Are you, Novak?"

Novak looked at her blankly. She doubted he'd been paying attention, but he was quick enough on his feet to turn to Lanford and say, "Why don't you help us understand?"

Lanford's gaze shifted around the room. He looked trapped. "We'd already started planning the move before the incident," he said. "But the incident, well, it *accelerated* things, I guess. Originally, we planned to sell this house first. Now, given everything that's happened, we're going to move to Delaware now and live there while we try to sell the house. Is that important for some reason? I don't understand."

"I'm just wondering why you didn't explain it that way the other day? Why did you lie to two homicide detectives and an assistant district attorney?"

Tanya let out a little gasp. Lanford's face flushed. "No, no, I never lied. Maybe I got distracted and didn't correct what Ms. Black said, but I never lied—"

"Tell me about Russell's mother," Graham said.

If her previous questions had discomfited him, this one really threw him for a loop. He practically reeled back in his chair, almost knocking it over. Beside him, Tanya looked stricken, as if this were the last subject on Earth she wanted to hear about. *Hit a nerve?*

Lanford cleared his throat and sat up straighter, regaining his composure. "What does Russell's mother have to do with any of this?"

"The last time we spoke, you indicated that she left when Russell was young."

"That's right. It was about ten years ago."

"Where did she go?"

"I have no idea. She called that night from a motel in Ohio, but I don't know if she stayed there or moved on. We didn't keep in touch. When she left, she left our lives completely—"

"She didn't stay in contact with Russell? Check in on him?" Graham said. She loaded the questions with an incredulous tone. "Novak, you're a parent and a grandparent. Does that sound right to you?"

Novak glanced up. "No it does not."

"I never said it was *right*," Lanford said, seeming to bite out each word. He looked pissed off now. That was good. When a suspect was pissed off was when the good stuff had a tendency to slip out—which was fortunate for Graham, since she seemed to have an innate talent for making people angry. "It's what happened."

"I'm trying to understand how and why," Graham said. She made her voice extra calm and patient, knowing that tone would aggravate him even more.

It worked. He looked like he was about to

explode. Before he could, Tanya put a hand on his hand and massaged it in a comforting gesture.

"Maybe some things just can't be understood," Tanya said. She looked sadly at Lanford, then at Graham. "Caroline made a selfish decision. Terribly selfish. It's hard to comprehend how any mother could leave her little boy behind and never look back, but that's what happened. It is what it is."

A tear welled in Lanford's left eye and then rolled down his cheek. *Nice touch*, Graham thought, *but I'm onto you.*

"How do you know what happened?" Graham said to Tanya. "Did you know Wesley at the time?"

"What are you implying?" Lanford said.

"I'm asking if you and Tanya knew each other at the time your wife disappeared."

Lanford bared his teeth. "She didn't *disappear*. She left. And yes, Tanya and I knew each other. *Platonically*. There was nothing going on. We weren't having an affair. She worked as a secretary at my company."

"I see." Graham shot her partner a look. Novak didn't return it. He was checking his phone.

"You must have a hell of a data plan," she said to him.

"Huh?" he said, looking up. "What?"

"Never mind." Turning back to Lanford, she said, "Did you call the police when your wife left? File a missing persons report?"

"You're a cop. You would have access to those records. You already know I didn't."

Graham shrugged. "Sometimes records get lost. I like to be thorough."

"You like to badger and intimidate people," he snapped. "And I don't appreciate it. Where is Ms. Black? She's a lot more professional than you are."

"She's at the memorial service for the women your son gunned down."

Lanford exhaled as if gut-punched. "Listen, I'm the one who reached out to the police. To the DA's office. *Me.* I've been cooperating one-hundred percent, despite my deep, personal loss. I think that entitles me to the benefit of the doubt. Or, at the very least, some respect and sensitivity."

Graham let him reprimand her. When he ran out of steam, she said, "The police department greatly appreciates your cooperation in this matter, Mr. Lanford. As I said, we're only being thorough."

"Are we done?"

"Almost. Just a few more questions."

"Fine. Ask."

"How did you know your wife left of her own free will and wasn't kidnapped or injured or killed?"

"I told you. She called us."

"And that was that? You made no attempt to get her to come back?"

"It didn't seem worth the fight—"

"The mother of your only child? You didn't care

132

enough to at least try?"

Lanford stood up. "I think I need to get a lawyer before I speak to you any more."

Graham cursed silently. She'd built up a nice momentum with Lanford, and now he'd slammed on the brakes. But she forced herself to smile knowingly at him as if this were a victory and not a setback. Let him think he'd just tipped his hand, confessed.

"I think that's a good idea," she said, giving the words a suitable tone of menace. She rose from her own chair, and touched Novak's arm to signal him to rise as well. "Let us know when you and your lawyer are ready to help us get to the truth."

Lanford stormed away, leaving Tanya to walk them out. The blonde looked at Graham with uncertainty as she opened the front door. Graham had seen the look before, on the faces of people who wanted to tell her something but weren't quite ready.

Graham looked in the woman's eyes. "Despite what you may think, I am here to help."

Tanya nodded. "I know."

Graham handed her a business card. "My cell phone number's on there. If you ever need me, call."

Tanya nodded again.

"I mean it."

"Okay."

Then Graham stepped outside, into the daylight. Novak followed.

# 17.

The next morning, Jessie arrived at work to see a man she recognized as a local process server standing at the security desk, chatting with the guard about college football. There was nothing out of the ordinary about this. The DA's office was served every day with various motions and court filings. But the way the guard's gaze swung toward her while the process server droned on about a Penn State quarterback told her that the document in his hand was for her. A pit opened in her gut. This was about the search warrant Judge Katz had issued. She knew it before even taking the document from the security desk.

She skimmed the title: MOTION TO QUASH SEARCH WARRANT.

*You gotta be kidding me.*

She looked up from the document and glared at the process server. He took a step back and raised his hands. "Hey, come on. I'm just the messenger."

"I know." She forced a smile. "Don't worry about it." It was a stupid thing to say—why would he worry; he'd done his job, and it was her problem now—but the words succeeded in dissipating the tension. The men went back to their conversation about football. And she headed upstairs to face Warren.

She found her boss still trying to run a Homicide Unit while balanced on a giant rubber ball. She wondered how long he'd stick it out before this exercise scheme went the way of all the others he'd tried.

"Manpower filed a motion to quash the search warrant." She handed him the papers, then watched him scan through them while bouncing gently. "You don't look surprised."

"Well, when they called me yesterday to request that the DA's office voluntarily withdraw the warrant, I didn't think that was a coded love message."

"This is annoying, but I'll take care of it."

The bouncing stopped, and he looked sharply up at her. "Annoying? Is that the word you're planning to use when the press asks why the DA's office has been accused of trampling the Fourth Amendment? You know, the one about unreasonable searches and seizures?"

Jessie made a face. "Maybe 'meritless' would sound better."

His hard stare continued to drill into her. "Remember what we talked about. Jesus Rivera put you on the Russell Lanford case to make him look good—not to make him look like Big Brother." The ball squeaked, which only seemed to increase his agitation.

"I said I'll handle it, Warren."

"I know you will. Privately, if possible." He skimmed through the motion again, then pointed to the phone number of Manpower, LLC's legal counsel. "They're represented by a law firm in Ohio, but they're using Noah Snyder as local counsel. Reach out to Snyder and see if you can set up a meeting. Out of the public eye. Make a deal, something both sides can live with."

Jessie highly doubted such a deal existed. She wanted their data, and they didn't want to give it to her, despite a search warrant. But she nodded. Warren was in charge. If he wanted her to try to reach a mutually acceptable compromise, she would try.

"I'll call Noah and try to set something up."

"Good." He turned to his computer screen, apparently ready to move on to other matters, put out other fires.

"In the meantime, I'll start working on my opposition brief," she added as she turned to leave. "Just in case."

Warren gave her another sharp look, but didn't comment.

# 18.

Jessie made the call to Noah Snyder as Warren requested, and proposed a private meeting to try to work out a compromise around her warrant and Manpower's reluctance to comply with it. Snyder was a Philly criminal defense attorney who ran a small firm that mostly defended drunk driver and domestic violence disputes. She wouldn't necessarily describe him as a bottom feeder, although many in the DA's office did. She knew he was a skilled lawyer in his own way. She wasn't surprised when he agreed to meet. She couldn't remember ever trying a case against him, as he always convinced his clients to take a plea agreement rather than go to trial. But she was surprised when he called her back five minutes later with a location. The Sofitel Philadelphia, one of the city's most upscale hotels, located in the heart of downtown Center City. Pretty far from Snyder's usual low-rent haunting grounds.

As if sensing her thoughts through the phone, Snyder said, "Vaughn Truman is staying there."

"The owner of the company is here in Philly?"

"I guess he considers this pretty important," Snyder said. "Or maybe he just wanted to try a good cheesesteak. His reasons aren't really my concern, but he's here, and he wants to hear your proposal personally."

*My proposal?* The only thing Jessie wanted to propose was that he comply with her valid and legally binding warrant. "I'll be there," she said.

Now, as she entered the gleaming lobby of the hotel, she wondered just what she was going to be up against. A high-speed elevator shot her fourteen stories up to Truman's floor.

The door to his room was open, but two blank-faced men in dark suits blocked Jessie from entering. She noted the bump at the hip under each man's suit jacket—sidearms—and the buds in their ears. Security, and seemingly high-end security at that.

"Raise your arms, please, ma'am," one of them said.

"You're going to frisk me?" She looked past the men, through the open doorway, and saw three more men inside. One of them sat in a leather armchair. She recognized him from his photographs. Vaughn Truman, the primary owner of Manpower, LLC. "Seriously?" she said, loud enough for Truman to hear her.

"It's okay," Truman said. "Let her in, please."

The security men stepped aside and Jessie walked into the room. Only the word "room" didn't really do the place justice. Truman wasn't just staying in a room, or even a suite. He'd taken occupancy of two suites of the top floor. If it was meant to intimidate Jessie, it didn't. She'd faced adversaries with deep pockets before, with similarly expensive war rooms, and beaten them.

"Sorry about that," Truman said. He rose from his chair and crossed the room to shake her hand. "I've learned the hard way to be careful."

"I guess you make a lot of enemies when you're in the hate business."

Truman took the insult with a wry smile. He was handsome—better looking in person than his photos suggested. That surprised her, and she wasn't sure why. Maybe part of her had believed on a subconscious level that hate would corrode a person from the inside out and render them ugly. That was naïve, obviously. History showed how frequently the most hateful people were also the most charming and charismatic—and, yes, good-looking—which only increased their dangerousness. As Vaughn Truman took her hand in a firm handshake, she sensed that he was no exception. "Pleasure to meet you in person, Ms. Black. And thank you for proposing this meeting. I'm hoping we can work something out that will make everyone happy, without the need for a lot of courtroom shenanigans. May I call you Jessie?"

She glanced at the roomful of men. "Why do I feel outnumbered here?"

Truman smiled. His expression radiated friendliness and calm warmth. *Yes, very dangerous, indeed.* "Well, you're a lawyer and I'm not. As confident as I am that we can come to a meeting of the minds, I'd be pretty foolish if I didn't bring along some legal minds of my own, right? The tall guy by the window is Adrian Rohr. He's Manpower's lawyer, does all of our legal work." In other words, Jessie thought, a corporate lawyer with no experience in criminal law, much less Philadelphia criminal law. "The other guy," Truman continued, "I believe you already know."

Noah Snyder lifted a hand in greeting. He was holding a glass of Scotch. A bottle of Glenlivet stood on the table behind him. Living it up on his client's dime. *Real professional.* He grinned smugly at her.

"Noah," she said by way of greeting.

"Always fun, Jessie. I assume it goes without saying that this meeting is for settlement purposes only. Under Section 408(a) of the Pennsylvania Rules of Evidence, nothing said in this room is admissible in court by either party."

"Noted," she said through gritted teeth. Snyder might not be the city's brightest legal mind, but he knew the laws that counted.

"Good." Snyder returned to his drink.

Truman waved a hand toward the other side of the room, where two leather couches faced each other across a glass coffee table, at the corner where floor-to-ceiling windows offered a breathtaking view of Center City.

She walked to one of the couches and took a seat. She placed her attache case on the table, but didn't open it. She leaned back and crossed her legs.

Truman said, "Can I get you a drink? Water? Something stronger?"

"I'm good, thanks."

Truman sat across from her. His lawyers and bodyguards remained standing. "I never mix alcohol with business, either," Truman said. "Not to say I judge anyone who does, as long as it doesn't impair their work." He cast a glance at Snyder, who suddenly looked less smug, "but personally that's not how I roll." And then that smile again, bright as a camera flash, warm as a best friend's embrace. "So, let's get to it. Why is the Philadelphia District Attorney's Office so keen on violating the trust and privacy of my website's users?"

He was trying to frame the issue in his favor, albeit with a winking tone. Jessie didn't take the bait. "Why is Manpower unwilling to comply with a court-ordered warrant?"

The corporate lawyer, Rohr, cleared his throat. "That warrant was granted based on an *ex parte* communication with a judge. Manpower wasn't afforded an opportunity to present the judge with an opposing viewpoint."

"That's how warrants work," Jessie said. "The judge found probable cause. Maybe you need a refresher course on criminal procedure."

Truman stuck out a hand toward his lawyers, palm out. "Let's not turn this into a legal pissing contest." He turned back to Jessie, and with a knowing grin, added, "Not yet anyway. I want you to know that I appreciate that you reached out to us to try to work this out in a non-adversarial mode."

"Jessie doesn't have a non-adversarial mode," Snyder said. He emptied the remainder of his Scotch down his throat. "Just FYI."

"Well," Truman said, spreading his hands, "even adversaries can make treaties, right?"

"The Commonwealth needs access to the identity and private messages of the Manpower user called True_Man," Jessie said. "By the way, that's not *you*, I assume. Truman, True_Man.... Just a coincidence?"

Truman laughed. "You're joking, right?"

"You're avoiding the question, as well as resisting the warrant—"

"My name lends itself to an obvious pun. I never claimed my users were brilliantly creative. I'm not True_Man."

"So it's like an homage," Jessie said. "You're something of a celebrity in MRM circles, right?"

He elevated an eyebrow at that, and an indulgent smile lit his face. "The men's rights movement? I'm not invited to their parties anymore. They call Manpower a splinter group and they call me a...." He turned to his lawyer, Rohr. "What did they call me in that interview last month, Adrian?"

"A self-aggrandizing extremist," the lawyer said.

"Right." Truman smiled at Jessie and winked. "But really I'm just misunderstood."

"Is True_Man with an underscore also misunderstood?"

"I wouldn't know."

"If you read Judge Katz's warrant," Jessie said, "you know we have probable cause indicating his involvement in criminal activities."

"Judge Katz issued that warrant," Rohr said, "before hearing our counter-arguments. We're confident we can persuade him—"

Truman's hand came up again, silencing him. Then the leader of Manpower stood from the couch and walked over to the floor-to-ceiling windows. He gazed out at the city. "Did you know there's a demonstration happening right now, in Rittenhouse Square? Gun control." He smiled sadly and shook his head, as if the demonstrators—and people in general— were hopelessly misguided. "Gun control. A stale debate, Republicans versus Democrats, the same arguments over and over. Meanwhile, a much bigger issue goes unnoticed." He turned from the windows to stare directly into her eyes. "Privacy. Our loss of privacy in the face of relentless government intrusion."

"So privacy is your cause of the day? I thought you were fighting for men's rights."

She watched for a flinch, or any telltale sign that she'd stung him, but Vaughn Truman's expression remained placid.

"I'm fighting for equality," he said. "That's my cause."

She wanted to laugh, thinking about her own male-dominated field, but didn't think doing so would help her obtain this man's cooperation. She settled for a skeptical-bordering-on-sarcastic tone. "You believe men are being denied opportunities?"

"I know they are."

Again, the urge to laugh, which she repressed. She also repressed the urge to debate him—even though she longed to question how he could possibly square this view with studies about salary disparity, workforce imbalance, and a hundred other examples of men enjoying a privileged status in almost all societies worldwide.

"You think I'm full of shit," he said. He smiled thoughtfully at her.

"What I think about your politics isn't the point, Mr. Truman—"

"Vaughn."

"I'm here because of a criminal matter. I'm asking you to turn over information that could be critical in bringing a murderer to justice."

"Or just censoring political speech," he said, "in violation of both the First and Fourth Amendments."

"This type of speech isn't protected."

"Because it's, in your words, 'hateful'?"

"No, because it constituted the planning of a criminal act."

"You can't prove that."

"I'm pretty sure I will be able to once you give me

copies of True_Man's private messages."

His smiled widened, still as warm and familiar as that of a close friend. "I hear you demanding the same data listed in the warrant. True_Man's identity and the private messages. I thought you were here to discuss a compromise."

"I'm here to try to persuade you to do the right thing and comply with the warrant."

"Then you're wasting your time."

Well, at least she could tell Warren she tried. She sighed and began to gather her things.

Truman said, "Gender roles in this country—in most countries—require men to take on the financial burden of supporting their wives, their families, while women are not even expected to work. A man is denigrated if he fails to pick up the tab at a coffee shop so that his date can sip her latte for free. Does that sound like equality to you?"

"You don't need to justify your politics to me."

"The world is rife with this type of gender discrimination," he continued. "Western society relies on male sacrifice—forcing men to work so that women don't have to, ranking men based on their earning potential, shaming men if they show emotion, discounting the role of fathers as opposed to mothers. I could go on."

She didn't doubt that. Beneath his calm and reasonable façade, she sensed he was a zealot. And there was no negotiating with a zealot. Truman was right about one thing. This meeting was a waste of time. "None of this is relevant to the matter of your website user's culpability in the murders of seventeen people."

"Our government goes out of its way to protect women at the expense of men. How many divorced men are cut off from their children?"

Jessie shook her head. "Mr. Truman—"

He let out a breath. "Sorry. This is a cause I feel passionate about."

She decided to try one more time, for Warren's sake, before giving up this meeting as a total lost cause. "You said the men's rights movement disowned you. Isn't that a bad thing for your cause? You can't really believe the way to achieve equality for men is to protect a member of your group who perpetrated a violent crime."

Truman settled back against the leather couch cushion. "I respect the men's rights movement, even if the feeling isn't mutual. But they don't understand that there are extreme factions in every movement, and that they are necessary. Exaggerated rhetoric is needed in order to overcome public indifference. To draw attention. That's Manpower's role, and we'll continue in that role with or without the approval of the core movement."

"Is that why you've personally come to Philly? To use Russell Lanford's heinous actions as a means of gaining publicity and drawing attention?"

Truman shrugged. "The news stories about the murders will reference my website and people will check it out. Most people will be deaf to our arguments, but some won't be. So yes, that's one of the reasons I'm here."

She shook her head as realization dawned on her. "*You're* the one who sent Wesley Lanford the anonymous email about his son's participation on the website. To ensure that Manpower became part of the story."

Truman glanced at his lawyers. "Is that a crime?"

"Not the last time I checked," Snyder said.

"In that case, yes," Truman said, returning his attention to Jessie. "I sent the email."

"Then finish what you started," Jessie said. "Turn over the identity of True_Man and the content of his private messages. Show you're one of the good guys."

"The good guys don't aid the government in tearing down the privacy rights of its citizens," Truman said. "Today you want True_Man's messages. Next week, who knows? Maybe you want us to hand over the rest of our users."

"That's your gameplan?" Jessie said. "A slippery slope argument? Might work on a jury, but I doubt you're going to convince Judge Katz that a warrant for the records of a hateful criminal conspirator will inevitably lead to the destruction of all privacy on the internet. I guess I'll see you in court." She started to stand up.

"Sit down," Truman said. His tone was authoritarian, the voice of someone used to giving orders and being obeyed. "I'm not done."

"I am." Jessie took her attache case from the table. "And you'll be done, soon enough. Count on it."

Truman leaned forward. The leather couch cushion creaked. He wasn't smiling anymore. All the warmth was gone from his face, leaving hard lines and a cold stare. "Vindictive," he said. "A womanly trait."

"What's your problem with women, anyway? Did the mean girls reject you in high school?"

He let out a bitter-sounding laugh. "Look at me, Jessie, and imagine me twenty years younger. Does this look like a face a high school girl would reject? I drove a Mitsubishi 3000GT. Remember those? Looked like a Ferrari. I played varsity football. The sluts practically assaulted me in the hallways. I think I spent more time in the janitor's closet than his mop and bucket. Getting my dick sucked by stupid sluts hardwired to prostrate themselves to the strongest alpha male."

They glared at each other until the silence was broken by a sloshing sound. Snyder refilling his glass of Scotch. The lawyer looked embarrassed. But the other lawyer, Rohr, did not. He looked half-angry, half-reverent. Jessie thought of those old Hair Club For Men ads that used to run on late night cable. Rohr wasn't just corporate counsel for Manpower. He was also a client. No, a *believer.*

"Then why?" she said. "Why does the men's rights movement call to you? Instead of, say, saving the whales?"

A cloud seemed to move across the man's face,

darkening it. "I married young, stupidly, to one of those high school sluts I was just talking about. Her name was Angela. The marriage fell apart almost instantly. Snyder, bring me one of those Scotches, please. Neat."

The lawyer poured his client a drink and brought it over with a nervous glance at Jessie. Truman slammed back the drink with such ferocity that she heard the rim of the glass click against his teeth.

"I thought you didn't drink while conducting business," she said.

"Exceptions to every rule." He made a face as the burn of the whiskey reached his stomach. "Anyway, Angela didn't realize that out of high school, her new hubby would be an average Joe instead of an all-star jock. I was bringing home a starting salary for a high school graduate, respectable but nothing to get excited about. I had no standing in society, no power. Angela thought she'd hitched herself to an alpha male, but in the real world, I was just a guy. I didn't live up to her expectations. She thought she was entitled to more." He put his empty glass on the table. "You ever been married, Jessie?"

"No."

"We divorced, and it was ugly. Angela wanted huge amounts of alimony. She really believed she was entitled to it. That I *owed* her. But if I'd agreed to pay even half of what she was asking for, I would have been signing up for the life of a slave. When I refused, she lied to the police and had me arrested on charges of domestic violence. Probably her lawyer's idea. It's a disgustingly common tactic, I've learned."

He glared at her, whether to indicate his resentment of women or lawyers or both, she couldn't know, but the anger in his gaze was so intense she had to break eye contact and look out the window.

"The charges were false," he said, "complete lies, but because she was a woman and I was a man, they were simply accepted as true with no evidence. I was perp-walked out of my own apartment in handcuffs, in front of the neighbors, everyone. Angela told me she'd drop the charges—all I needed to do was agree to the divorce settlement she'd proposed, with all the alimony. Spend the rest of my life slaving away so she would never have to work. I refused. We went to trial. I won. And that felt good. But before I won, I spent six months in jail while the trial dragged on, and during that stint in jail, I lost my job, most of my friends, and what little money I had left, which went to my defense lawyer."

It was a chilling story, and it struck Jessie temporarily speechless. She had to remind herself that all of this was beside the point. She needed Manpower's data about True_Man because that user had conspired to commit murder. The political ideas of the website through which he'd chosen to communicate were not the issue.

"What I gained in jail was a cause. A calling. I know that's a long answer to your question, but there it is."

Jessie took a deep breath. "That's a terrible story. No one should have to go through an ordeal like that. I'm sorry for what happened to you."

"Thank you."

"But," she added, "I am also sorry for the sixteen teenage girls and one woman who were gunned down at Stevens Academy. And it's my job to ensure that they receive justice, just like you eventually did. To do that job, I need your company to give me the identity of True_Man and a copy of the private messages exchanged between True_Man and Russell Lanford. Can we come to an arrangement now, or do we need to battle it out in open court before Judge Katz?"

"Another thing I learned in jail," Truman said. "Never back down from a fight."

# 19.

After their encounter at the Sofitel, Jessie would have been happy never to see Vaughn Truman again. But one day later she shared a courtroom with him. Jessie sat at one counsel table, while Truman sat with his lawyers at the other. Judge Katz presided.

In the gallery behind them, a smattering of spectators and press filled about a third of the seats. Even Truman's publicity efforts had failed to generate more than minimal interest in what would surely be a dull recitation of legal arguments. Jessie sensed that the low turnout displeased Truman.

The judge looked more distinguished in his judicial robes than he had with his shoes off in chambers. He stared thoughtfully from beneath his bushy gray eyebrows at his courtroom. Since there was no jury—or defendant, for that matter—no one bothered with the pomp and ceremony. The judge dove right in. "First of all, Mr. Snyder, I'm a little perplexed by the timing of this motion."

Snyder said, "How so, Your Honor?" though Jessie was certain he knew exactly what the judge was getting at.

"As you know," Katz said, his voice becoming stern, "the proper time to contest the validity of a search warrant is during the criminal proceedings, when the person who is the subject of the warrant—assuming that person is even charged—will have ample opportunity to file a motion to preclude."

"But that's just the point, Your Honor," Snyder said calmly. "It's like you just said. This person might not even be charged. But his or her privacy is at risk *now*. His or her constitutionally protected right to be free of unreasonable searches and seizures is being threatened *now*. And my client, Manpower, an organization in which this person placed his or her trust, isn't prepared to aid the state in violating those rights in the hopes that one day in the future the wrongs will be redressed."

"That's very poetic," Katz said. He was smirking, and his voice couldn't sound less impressed. "But it's not how the law works, is it?"

"Your Honor," Jessie said, sensing a chance to press her advantage, "the Commonwealth takes issue with Mr. Snyder's insinuation that the search warrant was obtained by unconstitutional means. That's not the case. This Court reviewed a lengthy affidavit by Homicide Detective Emily Graham and found sufficient probable cause to believe that the warrant will reveal evidence of criminal activity. The person who is the subject of the warrant therefore enjoyed every protection of the Constitution and corresponding Pennsylvania statutes."

153

"Oh, come on," Snyder said, scoffing. "Probable cause? You're looking for messages from a guy who may or may not have encouraged Russell Lanford to kill a bunch of people. Even if you find such messages—and there's no particular reason to believe you will, by the way, since True_Man and Betaloser could have been corresponding about hemorrhoid cream for all anyone knows—even if you find messages from some sicko about how great it would be to kill people, that's a far cry from committing criminal activity, in my opinion."

"Maybe," Jessie said, annoyed, "but nobody here particularly cares about your opinion."

"Let's keep it civil," Katz cautioned.

"Your Honor," Snyder said, "the Fourth Amendment stands as the last shield against unlawful police activity, protecting privacy, and freedom, which cannot exist without privacy. Do you really want to toss that aside, so that an assistant DA and a homicide cop, thirsty for blood after a school shooting, can find a scapegoat?"

Katz leaned back in his chair, seeming to think this over. "Is there any truth to what Mr. Snyder is saying?" he said, looking at her. "Is this really just a witch hunt, Ms. Black?"

"It is not, Your Honor. The warrant is narrowly targeted. We know that a specific user of the Manpower message board discussed the shootings with Russell Lanford prior to the crime. We know that the two also exchanged private messages. We have sufficient probable cause to believe that the private messages will demonstrate that these two individuals jointly planned the shooting. This planning rises to the level of conspiracy to commit murder, which certainly qualifies as criminal activity, despite Mr. Snyder's personal opinion to the contrary."

Katz raised his hands for silence before Snyder could burst forward with a retort. "Okay, counselors. I've heard enough. I'm denying the motion to quash. The search warrant stands."

"Thank you, Your Honor," Jessie said.

Snyder mumbled a barely audible thank-you of his own and began to gather his things. Jessie watched him and his client and was not surprised to see that Vaughn Truman did not look particularly disappointed with the ruling. Now he'd have a chance to deliver a stirring speech to the public about how the state was trodding over the rights of Manpower's users—further evidence, no doubt, of the terrible inequality suffered by males.

"One more thing, Your Honor," Jessie said. Snyder froze.

"Yes, Ms. Black?" Katz said. She could tell his patience was wearing thin.

"The Commonwealth is concerned that Manpower will stall or outright defy this Court's ruling. We therefore request that Manpower be ordered to comply with the warrant within twenty-four hours, and that this Court place Manpower, LLC, and its owner, Vaughn Truman, in contempt of court if they do not comply."

This was a stretch, she knew. It would mean a visit to a jail cell for Vaughn Truman if he continued to play games with her. But as soon as she saw the color drain from Truman's face, she knew she'd made the right call. He'd been to jail, and he apparently had no desire to make a return trip.

"Granted," the judge said.

As expected, a press conference was assembled on the courthouse steps, and Vaughn Truman stood before the cameras talking about a "travesty of justice" and a "gender biased judiciary" and the "relentless erosion of the rights of ordinary people to come together to discuss ideas." He said, "All ideas—even unpopular ones—need to be protected. This setback will not stop Manpower or the broader men's rights movement. It will only stir us to fight harder."

Jessie had managed to escape from the courthouse unseen, and watched this circus act from the shadows of a doorway across the street. She wanted to avoid giving the cameras any "reaction shots" to run with. Unfortunately, at least one person spotted her. Noah Snyder.

He sidled next to her in the cozy archway of the building. "You really kicked my ass in there." He was smiling, though. It was all fun and games to him.

"You had no case."

He shrugged. "I know. But it's always fun putting the DA's office through its paces."

"And wasting taxpayers' money."

"They won't miss it."

"When can I expect to receive my data?"

Snyder watched Truman, who was still holding forth about grave injustice. "Pretty damn soon. You heard Vaughn's story back at the hotel. Believe me, that man has no interested in going back to a jail cell. That was a slick move, getting Katz to threaten contempt of court." He looked at her appreciatively. "Rivera should count his lucky stars he has you working for him."

"And all this speech-making for the media? What's the point if Truman's done fighting?"

Snyder laughed. "Clicks. It's all about clicks, Jessie. What do you think is running across the bottom of every TV news segment broadcasting this bullshit right now? What link is being displayed on blogs and tweets and Youtube videos? Manpower's URL. Traffic's going to be through the roof." He rubbed two fingers together.

"Page views," she said. "Advertising revenue. That's what this is all about. The only reason Vaughn Truman is visiting the city at all." The thought was depressing on too many levels.

"You got it."

She watched Truman drone on. "It never bothers you, representing sleaze bags like this?"

Snyder burst out laughing. "Are you kidding? Truman's a saint compared to my typical client base."

LARRY A. WINTERS

She couldn't argue with that.

"Hey," Snyder said. He was staring intently at her. "You look like you could use a vacation." He must have seen that he'd struck a nerve, because he smiled knowingly. "This job will kill you if you don't take care of yourself."

"I don't need a vacation, Noah. I need your client to end his, and get the hell out of Philadelphia."

"I'll be sure not to pass that along."

"Of course not. Every day Truman spends in Philly is a good day for your firm's bank account."

"You know it."

As always, she parted ways with Snyder feeling slightly dirty, but any worries she had about Truman's showmanship vanished quickly as she replayed her victory in her head. Prevailing in a hearing didn't bring quite the same rush as winning a trial, but it still felt pretty damn good. Jessie spent the rest of the day buoyed by the ruling. Let Vaughn Truman make all the spectacle he could—it wouldn't change the fact that the information Manpower was now required to produce would likely be the key to her case. Even the most eloquent speeches about freedom of speech and the right to due process would fizzle in the face of evidence showing a person manipulating a teenage boy into murdering sixteen of his classmates and their coach, especially when the warrant to expose that man's identity and the content of the private messages was legally valid. That night, Jessie slept very well.

Little did she know what tomorrow had in store.

# 20.

In Graham's experience, warrants were usually handled quietly and without much fuss. Manpower, on the other hand, had scheduled a press conference in front of City Hall to publicly hand over its data in front of as many cameras and microphones as possible. Thirty minutes before this publicity stunt was scheduled to begin, Graham was at her desk at Police Headquarters, looking over her case notes and trying to distract herself from the maddening wait.

She knew she might be on the verge of a groundbreaking case if the evidence supported a murder charge against a person whose part in the shooting had taken place entirely over the internet. A victory like that would boost her reputation in the PPD. But she was just as likely to discover that all of her hard work had been for nothing, in which case she'd become the butt of jokes for months, maybe longer. It all came down to whether the private messages revealed a conspirator to murder or just another woman-hating internet troll. She supposed Jessie was under similar pressure. After all, pursuing the case had been the assistant DA's call. If, at the end of the day, she had nothing to show for it but tons of negative publicity, she'd have to answer to the District Attorney himself.

Her cell phone vibrated, jarring her out of her thoughts.

"This is Detective Graham."

At first, only hitching sobs and rapid breathing came through the phone. Graham felt a pit open in her stomach. The voice that followed was even more unnerving—high-pitched, wavering, barely in control. "It's Tanya. I ... I need your help."

From his own desk, Novak looked up with a questioning expression. She gestured for him to come over.

"What's the matter, Tanya?" she said, keeping her voice calm. "Tell me."

"I think ... I think Wesley's about to do something. Something terrible."

"Okay, Tanya. I need you to take a deep breath. Calm down. Start at the beginning."

A long intake of breath whooshed against the phone's speaker. It collapsed into a series of hitching sobs.

"Did Wesley hurt you?" Graham said in a careful voice

"No. No, of course not. He would never."

"Tell me why you're upset."

"Wesley took the day off work today, to help get the house ready to show. We were ... watching TV.

The news came on. All about that website, Manpower, and how a court was requiring them to turn over information. The reporter said that the man who runs the site ... he—" Her sobs caught up with her and she had to pause.

"Vaughn Truman?" Graham said.

"The reporter said he's going to turn over the data to the DA personally, as part of a ... part of a press conference."

"Yes, that's right." Graham glanced at the clock on her computer screen. The press conference would start in about ten minutes, assuming Truman didn't arrive late to add drama to his big moment, which sounded exactly like something the guy would do. According to Jessie, Manpower's whole opposition to the warrant had been a ploy to get free publicity. It had worked, obviously. Now Truman planned to hand over the data on live TV, probably along with a rousing speech about life, liberty, and the pursuit of happiness. She assumed he'd work the full URL of his site into this speech at least six, maybe seven times.

Tanya half-spoke, half-sobbed. Graham strained to make sense of her words, but over their cellular connection, they were unintelligible. Something about being safe?

"Slow down," Graham said. "I'm having trouble understanding what you're saying."

"The gun safe," Tanya said. "It's open. He took the rifle."

Graham felt her body go cold. "What?"

She remembered Lanford telling her that Russell had left one rifle behind when he'd looted the gun safe. A Browning X-Bolt SSA Predator, bolt action, he'd said. Good for hunting.

Or sniping.

"I think...." Tanya said. "I think he's going to do something bad."

"Is there somewhere you can go? Somewhere safe? A friend's house, or family?"

"My sister...."

"Go there. Stay there until I call you back."

Graham ended the call. Her heart was racing. Cold sweat broke out across her face.

"What is it?" Novak said.

"I think we need to get to City Hall."

Graham jumped out of the car before Novak fully stopped. She could see the crowd of people in front of City Hall, waiting for the press conference. She turned, slowly scanning the surrounding buildings. Windows and roofs. Looking for Wesley Lanford and his rifle. *Where are you?*

Novak jogged over to her. He'd double-parked the car at the curb. Now he pointed up. "Emily!"

She followed the direction of his finger and spotted the dark outline of a figure standing on a roof across the street. *Son of a bitch. The old detective hadn't completely lost his touch after all.*

They ran.

* * *

Jessie gritted her teeth. Vaughn Truman had turned City Hall, a historic landmark of the city, into the backdrop for his latest circus act. And what was worse, he'd drawn her into it. And by extension, the DA's office. There was already a crowd—a mix of reporters, curious civilians, and a few angry-looking cops—and the crowd was getting bigger by the second as curious passersby stopped to see what was going on.

Watching Truman take his place in front of his audience, her stomach sank.

*Who cares? Let the blowhard squeeze a little more attention out of this tragedy, in service to his website and political agenda. The people will see him for the slime ball he is. The data is what matters. The private messages and the identity of True_Man.*

Truman held a thumb drive in one hand. He raised it and faced the cameras.

"My name is Vaughn Truman. I'm an activist." He spoke loudly and surely, and his voice carried through the crowd. "My cause is men's rights. I know that most of you probably weren't aware that men's rights were a cause, or were in need of protecting. Part of the reason you don't know that is because, at every opportunity, your government silences this movement."

Jessie tried to be inconspicuous at the periphery of the crowd, but Truman spotted her and pointed a finger at her.

"There they are now," he said. "The state, as

represented by assistant district attorney Jessica Black."

A hundred gazes turned to look at her.

She supposed she could have derailed his stunt by insisting that Manpower deliver the data without any grandstanding public show, but that would have meant a delay. It would have meant having to wait longer for Manpower to comply with the warrant. A dangerous predator was out there, prowling the internet, and she needed to find him and stop him before he caused more mayhem and death. That concern had to come before saving face, before politics.

Didn't it?

She wasn't so sure. The last person she'd known who put his job ahead of politics had been Leary, right before he'd been pushed out of the Philadelphia Police Department.

*Too late now for second thoughts.*

She stepped forward. Cameras flashed. A reporter called out, "Do you have a response, Ms. Black?"

She made eye-contact with the reporter. "This is not the appropriate forum to discuss an ongoing criminal investigation into a possible co-conspirator in the Stevens Academy killings. I'm here to collect the data per the court's order."

*There.* Best she could do. Hopefully she'd still have a job tomorrow.

She reached for the thumb drive, but of course Truman held it just out of her reach. He wasn't done. He was just getting started.

He wore a dour expression, but she sensed he was all smiles on the inside.

"I am in your city today to face the latest attempt by our government to silence the men's rights movement. You see, as part of the movement, I operate a website message board called Manpower, where people can come together to discuss their views on the issues facing men in our modern world. Manpower users have the option to post their opinions anonymously or under nicknames, so that they can speak freely without fear of being punished or persecuted for their beliefs. Because of this, our forum has grown into a large community with lively, healthy debate and discussion."

One of the cops in the crowd gave Jessie a questioning look. *Should we break this up?* She responded with a barely perceptible shake of her head. She wasn't sure yet what the right move was, but she knew it wasn't that.

Graham looked up. The building was shorter than City Hall—maybe four flights—and on the other side of the street from the government building. The ground floor was an Indian restaurant Graham had never noticed before, called House of Spice.

"Call for backup," she said as she and Novak ran toward the door.

"On it."

She rushed inside, Novak right behind her. The hostess, a tall, matronly Indian woman, looked up from her counter. Going by the woman's wide-eyed expression, Graham figured she understood immediately that they weren't here for lunch. Patrons glanced up from their tables, curious.

Graham said, "How do I get to the roof?"

The hostess shook her head. "The roof's off-limits."

She held up her badge. "Not today it isn't."

The woman looked uncertain. "The landlord, he gets angry...."

"This is an emergency. How do we access the roof?"

The woman seemed to come to a decision. She sighed and said, "Follow me."

A door in the back of the restaurant, near the restrooms, led to a small office. The office connected to an internal hallway. "Elevator and stairs are that way," the woman said. "Can you tell me what's going on?"

"No time," Graham said. Already striding away from the woman.

"Is there danger?" the woman called after her.

Graham hesitated. She believed there was danger—a man on a rooftop with a rifle was pretty much the definition of danger—but she didn't want to cause a panic. "Stay inside and you should be okay," she said.

That's when they heard the first gunshot.

* * *

"The District Attorney," Truman lectured, "seizing on the recent tragedy at Stevens Academy, has convinced the court to issue a warrant forcing us to divulge the identity and private messages of one of our users. We fought the warrant in court, and we lost, and now we must provide the state with this confidential information—a terrible outcome for us, for you, and for democracy."

Jessie tried to gauge the reaction of the crowd. Some seemed to be buying into Truman's rhetoric, turning accusatory stares in her direction. But others looked skeptical, and some were even laughing.

"We could have just sent the data to the DA's office, or even emailed it," Truman went on. "But that would be a cowardly manner of accepting defeat. Instead, I am here personally, as the owner of Manpower, to make sure that everyone knows what's happening today. I hope that all of you who share my disappointment with the erosion of our constitutional rights and our expectations of privacy will loudly condemn this unlawful search and seizure, which, as the founders of this country anticipated when they drafted the Bill of Rights, can only lead to the chilling of free political speech in this country.

"Make no mistake. Manpower will appeal this miscarriage of justice all the way to the Supreme Court, if that's what it takes to protect the right of all of us to free political discourse."

And with that, he handed the thumb drive to Jessie. Aware of the multitude of eyes and cameras eager to read her expression, she tried to keep her face neutral. She took the thumb drive, offered Truman a curt nod, and turned to make her escape.

It wasn't going to be easy. Sensing that this was the right moment, the reporters in the crowd surged forward, thrusting microphones toward her and Truman. The noise level rose to an ear-battering din as they shouted questions.

Then there was a loud, sharp *crack* and the crowd went silent. In the stretch of seconds that followed, Jessie's eyes met Truman's. She wasn't sure if he recognized the sound, but she did. *A gunshot.*

It was followed by another one. *Crack!* She felt something zip past her face. The bullet struck the building right behind her and sent chunks of the wall flying like shrapnel. Something caught Jessie's neck. Sharp pain. Blood.

The crowd burst apart and people fled in all directions. Someone dropped a camera and it was trampled instantly, broken into a thousand pieces and scattered under hundreds of shoes. Jessie stared, holding her neck, thinking, *I'm shot.*

*No, just a cut. You'll be fine. Just get the hell out of here.*

She grabbed Truman's arm. "Come on! We need to move!"

He gawked at her. His eyes were wild with panic. All his cockiness seemed to have abandoned him. She tugged his arm again, but he didn't move. Petrified, frozen in place by fear. *Where the hell were his bodyguards?* She spotted them, running away.

"Mr. Truman! Vaughn! Snap out of it. *Vaughn!*"

Hearing his name seemed to bring him around. His gaze focused on her. He opened his mouth, about to say something, when a perfect circle appeared to the left of his nose. A hole. It filled with blood even before she heard the *CRACK!* He fell.

Then there was a different sound—also recognizable as gunfire, but from a different weapon. Four shots, in rapid succession.

And then the wail of sirens.

Graham and Novak raced down the hallway. The sound of the gunshot still echoed in Graham's ears. "Take the elevator!" she said. "I'll take the stairs."

She didn't wait for his confirmation. There was a door with a picture of a stick figure mounting a staircase. She threw her body against the crash bar and burst into the dimly lit stairwell. Up she went, pounding the stairs, wishing she were wearing her sneakers instead of her work shoes. But her morning running ritual paid off. She practically flew up the stairs, rushing past the second-floor door, the third-floor door.

Finally she hit the end of the stairwell and a door marked *Roof Access*. It was more solid-looking than the inner doors, and had an ancient but complicated-looking combination lock built into it.

*Please don't be locked.* There was no time to drill.

Novak entered the stairwell below her, coming from the third floor elevator. "Jesus," he said. "You're

169

not even out of breath?"

She gestured at the door to the roof. "Ready?"

He drew his Glock and nodded.

Graham pulled her own gun and gripped the cold, steel doorknob with her other hand. She turned the knob. The door didn't budge at first, and she thought it really was locked. But it was only stiff. She added pressure and the rusty hinges squealed and the door opened. Sunlight flooded the stairwell.

Novak bounded past her through the doorway, gun raised. She followed him outside, coming in lower and sweeping left to right with her own gun. Adrenaline flooded her system. Her heart jumped into her throat, pumping like crazy.

Noises from the streets below reached her ears. Screams, cries, shouts, running feet—the unmistakable sounds of panic.

She spotted Wesley Lanford just as the second gunshot went off. A blunt, brutal sound that seemed to bounce off the sky above them.

Lanford's back was to them. He knelt at the edge of the roof, his bald head glistening with sweat, the rifle braced against his shoulder. He didn't look panicked. He looked calm. Totally at ease. Like a zen Buddhist in meditation. Except for the Browning X-Bolt SSA Predator bolt action rifle. Nothing zen about that. He slotted in another round.

"Stop!" Graham yelled. "Drop your weapon!"

She aimed her gun at his back. Her heartbeat seemed to slow down—just a notch—as she lined up her shot. She realized this was the second time she'd confronted a shooter in a matter of days. And that the shooters were father and son. She'd managed to take the son alive. The father? She hoped so. God, she hoped so. As much as she disliked the man, she didn't want to shoot him.

"I said drop it, Lanford! Now!"

"Don't be stupid," Novak said. "Drop the rifle."

Lanford pivoted and turned a cold stare toward them. Instead of dropping the rifle, he aimed it at her. Graham didn't hesitate. Her finger squeezed the trigger. Four times. The shots rang out. Lanford's body jerked as all four bullets hit him center mass. He slumped to the roof. The rifle fell out of his hands.

She darted to his side, kicked the rifle away. It skidded across the surface of the roof until Novak brought his foot down on it, stopping it.

Lanford was bleeding, which meant he was alive. Graham half-knelt, half-collapsed beside him. She felt his pulse. Already slowing. "He's bleeding out." Backup would be arriving soon, and with it, an ambulance, but by that time, it would be too late. "Damn it." She rocked back on her heels. A ragged breath tore out of her. She was suddenly exhausted. Spent. She didn't even have the energy to look past the edge of the roof to watch the chaos below.

It was a good shooting. A justified shooting. She knew that. But it didn't change the fact. She'd put a man down. Killed him.

First time.

"You alright, Emily?" Novak said. He squatted beside her and placed a tentative hand on her arm.

"Not really."

"It's okay. You will be." She didn't realize she was still gripping her pistol, finger inside the trigger guard, until Novak gently took the gun from her. "All part of the job," he said.

"I was right about Lanford," she said.

"You sure were."

"I sensed something."

"Remember this," Novak said. He looked in her eyes. "If you ever start to doubt your instincts, remember this."

She nodded, already starting to feel better, to feel stronger. She'd stopped a bad guy.

But she had to wonder, as the sounds of frightened civilians continued to fill the streets below, if she'd stopped the danger.

# 21.

An emergency room doctor at Thomas Jefferson University Hospital treated the wound in Jessie's neck and sealed it with surgical glue. "Shouldn't leave much of a scar," he said. "Whenever you're ready, you can go home."

"Thanks."

Leary paced beside her. The whole event had obviously disturbed him. He'd rushed straight here from his office, and was still dressed in the business casual attire that she knew he was still getting used to after years of wearing a suit as a homicide detective. The doc watched his restless prowling and glanced at Jessie with a concerned look. "I think he's taking this harder than you."

"He'll get over it."

The doctor smiled and left them alone.

"Leary, relax. I'm fine."

"You're lucky," he said. His face looked strained. "Lucky that Wesley Lanford was a relatively good marksman. If he'd had slightly worse aim, it might be you in the morgue right now instead of Truman."

She winced. Somehow, Vaughn Truman's death hadn't fully sunk in yet. Counting Wesley Lanford, whom Graham had taken out one second too late to save Truman, the death count was now up to nineteen. And True_Man, whoever he was, was still at large.

But not for long, hopefully. The police had the thumb drive and were perusing its contents right now. With luck, they'd have True_Man identified and under arrest by the end of the day, and then Jessie could bring the full weight of the DA's office down on his head.

"How are you feeling?" said a familiar voice. Jessie looked up to see Emily Graham walking toward her.

"I'm fine. What about you? I know it's never easy, having to shoot someone."

The detective shrugged. "I'll be okay."

"You might not really believe that right now," Leary said, "but it's true. You'll be alright."

Graham gave him a half-smile. "Thanks. That's what Novak keeps telling me. How're you doing, Leary? Private sector getting any more tolerable?"

Now it was Leary's turn to shrug. "I don't get shot at anymore, so I guess that's a plus."

"What's the latest on True_Man?" Jessie said.

Graham's face seemed to darken. "Actually, that's why I'm here. I wanted to deliver the news in person. We looked at the flash drive Manpower provided. It contains logs of the private messages—and they're illuminating, believe me—but we don't have True_Man's identity."

Anger coursed through Jessie. "But Judge Katz ordered them to give us that information!"

"They gave us what they had. But True_Man never gave any identifying information to Manpower. Even his IP address was hidden. He visited the website using a VPN, a proxy service. He could be anywhere and anyone."

Jessie shook her head, momentarily forgetting her injury. The motion brought a stabbing pain to her neck, which only made her angrier.

"I want to see everything Manpower gave us," she said.

"I assumed you would," Graham said. She handed Jessie a folder and a thumb drive. "I printed everything out for you. Here's a hard copy, and a copy of the digital files."

"Thanks."

"Don't thank me yet. You've got some unpleasant reading ahead of you."


Later, Jessie was officially discharged and she and Leary left the hospital. Outside, the sun was beginning to set behind the Philly skyline, a red glow between the buildings.

"Wait here," Leary said. "I'll bring my car around."

"My neck is hurt, not my legs. I can walk with you to the car."

He gave her a look. "Just humor me, will you? Let me take care of you a little."

She sighed. Even though her only wound was to her neck, the truth was the experience had fatigued her. "Okay. Thanks."

She watched him walk away. Her phone vibrated and Warren Williams's name appeared on the screen. Not a surprise. She'd been expecting his call. Still, with her neck hurting and her frame of mind shaken, he wasn't a person she wanted to deal with right now. She considered sending the call to voice mail, then reconsidered. He was her boss, after all.

"Hello?"

"What the hell is going on?" he said.

"I'm okay. Thanks for your concern. It's touching."

"Sorry," he said, and his voice actually sounded abashed. "Of course I want you to be okay," Warren said. "But I just spent ten minutes getting chewed out by Rivera and his political advisers, so my social skills are a little off. I'm sorry."

"Who are you kidding, Warren? Your social skills are never on."

She watched traffic pass the hospital. No sign of Leary's car. She was starting to wish she'd walked with him.

"Two deaths today," Warren said, "and we pretty much martyred this guy Truman. Doesn't put the district attorney's office in a great light. In fact, quite the opposite. We look like fascists trying to suppress political speech. I hope you found something that justifies this warrant, Jessie."

She gripped the folder Graham had given her. "The warrant's already been justified. By a court of law."

"You know that's not what I mean. I'm talking about the court of public opinion. Just as important, as you know. More important, as far as Rivera is concerned."

She made an effort not to sigh into the phone. The higher she rose in the prosecutor's office, the more politics seemed to enter into her job. She didn't like politics. "Tell him not to worry. I'm on top of it."

"That's what you keep saying, but it's not what I'm seeing. First your warrant is challenged as unconstitutional. Then a press conference puts you in front of the cameras looking like a deer in the headlights. The shooter's father goes on a vigilante attack and murders an innocent man right in front of City Hall, while you're standing next to the victim on live TV. And then that same father, who was probably out of his mind, crazy with grief about his son, and needing help, gets gunned down by the police. So you tell me, Ms. I'm-On-Top-Of-It, do you think the media is praising the city's response to the Stevens Academy shootings right now?"

"I'm guessing that's a rhetorical question. I know you're fond of those."

"The mayor is blaming Rivera. Rivera is blaming me. And now I'm telling you—*fix this.*"

Jessie touched the bandage on her neck. As far as she was concerned, there was nothing to fix. Truman's and Lanford's deaths had been unfortunate, but they hadn't been her fault or the fault of the DA's office. There was nothing fascist or unconstitutional about the warrant. She was doing her job, and doing it well.

"The police are already reviewing the new evidence Manpower produced," she said. "And I'll personally read every page tonight. It's going to lead to the arrest of a very bad guy. By the time this is over, Rivera, the mayor, and everyone else will be fighting to take credit."

After a pause, Warren said, "That's a nice story."

"It's the truth. Just trust me on this."

"I do. I will. But not for much longer. You need to wrap this mess up, and quickly. Do you hear me?"

She did. Loud and clear.

## 22.

Jessie didn't look at the Manpower file until she was back in her apartment. Then she sat on the couch with the hard copy printouts, a legal pad, and a pen, curled her legs under her, and prepared to dive in. Leary pulled his button-down shirt out of his pants and took it off. He was wearing a plain white tee shirt underneath that hugged his toned torso. Her gaze tracked him and she suddenly found it impossible to focus on the documents.

"I need to do some work, okay?" she said. "You can watch TV in the bedroom if you want, or surf the web."

She wondered if this was how other people in the crime fighting profession acted—*honey, why don't you keep yourself busy while I look at this grisly evidence*—of if she was just hopelessly bad at this.

"Shouldn't we eat first?" Leary said. He had watched her set up her working space on the couch with a wry smile, but now he looked serious. "You might lose your appetite if the messages are as unpleasant as Graham implied. I could order Chinese."

Jessie was starting to wish he hadn't come home with her. It was an ungenerous thought, and brought an immediate rush of guilt, but it was the truth. She was used to being alone, working when she wanted to work and eating when she wanted to eat, without having another person distracting her. She looked up, trying to think of a polite way to ask him to leave, and was caught off guard by the feeling of affection elicited by the sight of his eyes, his stare—tender, protective, and intense all at the same time. All of a sudden she didn't want him to leave at all.

*Clearly, this whole relationship thing is going to take some getting used to.*

"Good idea," she said. "I could go for some General Tso. An egg roll, too." She thought for a second. "And wonton soup."

He laughed softly. "Getting shot at makes you hungry, right? I've experienced it. Something about coming close to death, facing it. It can awaken ... uh ... other appetites, too." His gaze dropped to her body.

She smiled back. "Maybe later. Let's just stick with food for now."

"Got it."

He took his cell phone into the kitchenette and called in their order. Jessie took advantage of the moment to flip through the pages in the file, not reading anything yet, but trying to see the big picture. The messages varied in length, from a couple of words to walls of text that went on for pages. She didn't do a count, but figured there had to be twenty, maybe twenty-five individual messages to and from True_Man and Russell Lanford (alias Betaloser). All of them sent within a span of a few days just prior to the Stevens Academy shooting. The last line of the last message, sent from True_Man to Russell on the morning of the shooting, caught her eye: *Make sure you kill them all.*

Nice. She closed the file. Leary was right. If she read the messages now, she might lose her appetite. She didn't want that to happen. She was really looking forward to that eggroll in particular. Her stomach rumbled at the thought of it.

Leary came back into the room. "Food should be here in twenty minutes. You sure you don't want to ... do that other thing?" He flashed a mischievous smile.

Jessie looked at his eyes again, deep and blue, and the way his toned arms extended from the sleeves of his tee shirt. The tattoo on his left bicep was on full display.

*What the hell?* she thought. *Why not?*

In bed, she realized he'd been right about the "other appetites," too. She attacked him with a vigor that surprised both of them. Wrapping her legs around his hard body. Thrusting her hips. Gripping his hair as she kissed him deeply. By the time they were done, they were both totally spent and totally satisfied. Her toes actually curled as a final wave of pleasure rolled through her.

"Wow," she said. Her voice was breathy. "Maybe I should put myself in danger more often."

He propped his chin on his hand and studied her. His expression turned serious again. "Don't say that. You could have been killed today. It's not a joke."

"I know." She reached out and touched the firm muscles of his arm. "Thanks for suggesting this. It was wonderful. Sometimes I forget to be a person as well as a prosecutor."

His smile returned. "Anytime."

The doorbell chimed. A few minutes later the apartment filled with the aroma of fresh Chinese food. The True_Man file waited on the couch, untouched.

But not for long. No matter how enjoyable sex and food might be, she was still an assistant district attorney, and her work could only wait for so long before she itched to do it.

"You want to watch a show in the bedroom while I read through the file?" She put their leftovers in the fridge, stuffed the garbage into the trashcan under the sink. "Should only take me an hour or so."

"Actually," Leary said, "I was thinking we could review the file together. I can help you."

She felt some of the glow of a great evening fade. "Leary, we talked about this."

"I know," he said. "I'm not a PPD homicide detective anymore. I promise you I'm not trying to insert myself into the investigation. I'm just saying, I'm here, right? And I have the experience, the expertise. Why not look at the messages together? It won't go farther than that."

She watched his face warily. There was a note of

pleading in his tone—not quite desperation, but a close cousin of it—that she didn't like at all. She wished he found his new career more fulfilling. She didn't want their relationship to become a substitute for the job he'd given up. She couldn't allow that to happen. "I don't know...."

"I just want to help," he said.

She sighed. She supposed it wouldn't hurt to get his thoughts on the messages, as long as that was as far as it went. She was a lawyer, not a detective. Leary might well catch something she missed.

"You can help me tonight, offer some thoughts on these private messages. But that's where it ends."

"Deal," he said.

They sat on the couch together and began going through the pages, each of them reading quietly. It was actually kind of nice, except for the hateful, murderous content of the messages themselves.

"Jesus," Leary said at one point. She didn't ask him which part of the message he was responding to. It was all bad.

For example, True_Man wrote: *I get that it won't be easy finding out the code to your dad's gun safe, but you can do it. Call the safe company. Pretend to be your dad and you forgot your combination. Give them the safe's serial number, any other info they ask for. They'll give you the code and bingo. Guns. Think of the bullets hitting those bitches. Imagine their screams.*

Russell's response: *You really think that will work? The company will give me the code to the safe, just like that?*

And True_Man: *Happens all the time. Don't wait. Do it today. The sooner you call, the sooner you can walk through the gate of your school, onto the field where the sluts are practicing their teasing little slut moves, and put them down like the vermin they are.*

That explained how Russell gained access to the gun safe. One mystery solved. It also showed the critical role True_Man had played in the shooting, safely hidden behind his screen.

"There really is a conspiracy case here," Leary said. "They're planning the crime together, step by step."

"Unfortunately, without True_Man's identity, there's no one to file charges against."

"Don't give up yet." He tapped the stack of print-outs. "There's a lot of paper here. A lot of words. Maybe his identity is right here in front of us."

Jessie shook her head. "I think this guy's way too smart to identify himself to Russell, even in a private message."

"Too smart to do it on purpose," Leary said. "But sometimes people slip up. Look here." He pointed to the message she'd just read. "Look what he wrote. 'Walk through the gate of your school.' How does True_Man know Stevens Academy has a gate? Maybe he's local. Maybe he's here in Philly."

Jessie was skeptical. "You're deducing that from one detail he could have gotten from a Google street view?"

"I'm not saying I'd put True_Man in Philly based solely on one detail. My point is there may be other details in here, words or phrases pointing toward the same conclusion. One local detail might have come from a Google search. Ten and it's looking a lot more likely the guy lives in or close to Philadelphia. So, reading through these messages, one thing we should be asking is whether there are more details pointing toward a likelihood of local knowledge."

She smiled at him, still not fully convinced, but appreciative of his help. "You're sexy when you go into detective mode."

"Oh yeah?" He arched a brow.

"Like a man on a mission."

The lighter mood was a nice break from the grim reading, but it didn't last long. Soon enough, their heads were filled with True_Man's voice again—one of the most hateful, most evil she'd ever encountered.

"Look at this," he said, pointing at another message. "Betaloser says, 'How will I get away after?' and True_Man says, 'There will be more of an impact, more of a legacy, if you don't. Have you heard of suicide by cop?'"

"Sick bastard," Jessie said.

"Right, but look what comes next. Russell says he might not be ready to die, but doesn't want to go to prison either. And True_Man says, 'Isn't there a SEPTA station right by the school? Maybe you could disappear into the tunnels, get some distance, and then pop out in a random part of the city and make your escape.'"

"He knew about the subway entrance," Jessie said.

"And he referred to it as a 'SEPTA station,' like a local would. Convinced yet?"

"Getting there."

They flipped more pages.

True_Man: *You need to make sure all the girls are there. You'll only have one chance at these sluts, so you need to wipe them all out in one go, the whole squad. If you get there and not every bitch is at practice—if someone's sick or whatever—just turn around and go home. Don't take SEPTA. Not with a bag full of guns. Just catch a taxi.*

Betaloser: *Makes sense.*

"Another reference to SEPTA," Jessie said.

"I'm telling you, True_Man knows Philly."

The thought made Jessie shiver. "Okay, let's go with that assumption, for the time being. It still doesn't tell us who he is. There are a lot of people in this city."

"True," Leary said. "But there may be other clues in these messages." He started flipping pages again.

"You're enjoying this, aren't you?"

He looked at her, and appeared genuinely surprised. "You're not?"

"Well," she hedged, "I don't know if I'd use the word 'enjoy.'"

He cracked a smile. "Come on, Jessie. Sex, Chinese takeout, and crime-solving? This is our best date yet."

She had to laugh. "This is why we desperately need that Caribbean vacation."

His expression turned pensive as he turned back to the documents—his analytical mind taking over, she thought. "Why is this guy doing this?" he mused aloud. "What's his end game? Just to kill a bunch of random cheerleaders? Can someone's hatred be that strong?"

Jessie thought of something. "What if he's interested in these cheerleaders in particular? These girls. What if they're not random?" She tapped the stack of paper. "More than once, True_Man emphasizes that Russell needs to kill *all* of the girls on the squad. He wants *these* girls dead, specifically."

"Or maybe," Leary said, "*one* of those girls, specifically. He can't name her, because that would be suspicious and it wouldn't fit the story he's selling Russell about making some kind of men's rights statement. But what if that's what all of this really is— just an elaborate cover for the murder of one girl?"

Jessie nodded. The theory had a kind of logic. "This crime wasn't about two misogynistic men making a point with violence," she said, testing the theory by speaking it aloud. "There was another agenda here. A hidden one."

"Hidden even from Russell Lanford," Leary said.

Jessie could feel the familiar rush of the hunt. The truth was within their grasp. And so was justice. "Russell was a puppet, an unwitting tool, used by True_Man and then thrown away."

Leary said, "Did anyone have reason to want any

of these cheerleaders dead? Maybe someone at the school? Another student, a parent, a teacher? If we find the person with the motive, maybe we find True_Man."

"Let me call Emily." Jessie picked up her phone. "She oversaw the initial interviews at Stevens Academy. Maybe there's something in the police reports that seemed irrelevant at the time but means something now, in light of our new theory."

"I love when that happens," Leary said.

Jessie called Graham and caught her up on their analysis of the evidence and their thoughts. She walked the detective through her reasoning. When she'd laid it all out, she braced herself for skepticism as a response.

Instead, Graham said, "I like it."

"You do?"

"I'll go through the reports again. Officers canvassed the school, interviewing students and teachers. Maybe something will pop."

"That's what we're hoping."

## 23.

Jessie settled into her office the next morning, and, after chugging sixteen ounces of coffee, braced herself to tackle the mountain of backlogged emails that she'd let pile up during the last few busy days. Before she could read the first one, her phone buzzed.

Turning away from Outlook, she grabbed her phone like a lifeline. Emily Graham.

"We may have caught another break," the detective said over the phone.

"I'm listening." Jessie felt her heart rate kick up, and it wasn't because of the massive hit of caffeine she'd just ingested. Well, it wasn't *only* because of that.

"A student at Stevens Academy—a junior named Arabella Minsky—might have information that could be helpful in finding True_Man."

Jessie leaned forward in her chair. The DA's office was quiet at this hour, the hallway outside her open doorway silent. "The police didn't interview her before?"

"They did. Uniformed officers, as part of a general canvas. The statement Minsky provided was kind of

189

dismissed as useless at the time, because frankly she came off as a gossip, a teenager looking to add some drama to her life. But now, suspecting True_Man might be local, some of what she said seems more relevant. So I called her back in to talk."

"And what did she say?"

"She's still saying it. She's here right now, at the Roundhouse, sitting in an interview room with Novak. I thought you'd appreciate a heads-up and a chance to come by and watch."

"I do appreciate it." Jessie was already shutting down her computer. The long queue of emails would have to wait another day.

Jessie arrived at the Roundhouse ten minutes later and found Graham. The detective let her into an observation room, through which she could observe the interview through one-way glass. The girl, Arabella Minsky, was pretty in a wholesome, girl-next-door kind of way. Blonde, smiley, petite. And young. God, these kids all looked so young, so naively innocent. It only underscored the tragedy.

Arabella Minsky was cradling a cardboard mug in her hands. Starbucks—probably one of their sticky, sweet concoctions that bore only the slightest connection, if any, to coffee. Jessie could practically smell the syrup through the wall. Novak sat across from her. His phone was on the table. He wasn't looking at it, but every so often his fingers inched toward it as if he were dying to grab it off the table and check Facebook. Jessie shook her head and couldn't help smiling. The veteran detective was more addicted to social media than the teenage girl. She supposed there was a first time for everything.

The door opened and Graham walked into the interview room. She pulled up a chair and said, "Sorry about the wait. I had to make some calls. I hope my partner here kept you entertained."

Arabella Minsky offered a half-hearted smile. "Yeah, it's fine."

"So," Graham went on, "you were telling us about some of the girls on the cheerleading squad. The victims."

The girl's face seemed to light up, and she leaned forward with a conspiratorial expression. She didn't make any effort to try to look sad or mask her glee in spilling super secret school gossip to her new detective friends. Jessie felt a flash of distaste, but forced herself to dismiss it. Teenagers weren't fully developed human beings, even though they thought they were. In time, Arabella Minsky would probably mature into a fine, empathetic young woman. In the meantime, if her gossipy nature could help the police find the man who'd helped end the lives of seventeen people, Jessie could cut her some slack.

"I told the police lots of important stuff before," the girl said. She pouted. "They didn't seem very interested."

"They were," Graham said with an assuring voice. "They sent your statement straight to me. I'm the lead detective. We're all extremely interested in what you have to say."

From the look on Arabella's face, you'd think she'd just won the Mega Millions jackpot. Maybe, in her teenage world where social currency was at least as important as the kind printed on paper, she had.

"I heard you're looking for someone now," Arabella said. "Some guy on the internet who helped Russell." She shuddered. "So creepy."

"It's an ongoing investigation and we're exploring numerous leads," Graham said vaguely. "In your statement, you told the officers that you knew a lot about the victims. That you were close and that we should talk to you if we wanted to know about them."

"People have secrets, you know? And I respect that—everyone would tell you that you can trust me to keep a secret, normally. But I just think when there's been a crime and people are dead, you can't keep secrets anymore."

"I agree," Graham said. "I don't think anyone would argue with that. Right, Detective Novak?"

Novak nodded. "Better to get everything out in the open."

Arabella beamed. Jessie sensed that the detectives' permission was all the excuse she needed to blurt out the juicy info she'd been bursting at the seams to reveal.

"For example, Jordan Dunn. She had a big secret."

Graham glanced at her notes. "Jordan Dunn, junior, age 16. One of the victims."

"Right. She was, like, super pretty. If you asked anyone on the street to describe what a cheerleader should look like, they'd describe Jordan. She could have any guy at Stevens Academy for a boyfriend. She could have college guys."

"But she didn't?" Graham said. There was a little bit of discomfort visible in her expression, and Jessie thought she probably found the girl's gossipy tone distasteful, too.

Arabella leaned forward and lowered her voice to the point that the room's microphones barely picked it up. "Jordan was hooking up with a teacher."

"Really?" Graham said. "What was this teacher's name?"

"Jordan wouldn't tell me." Arabella rolled her eyes theatrically. "I know, right? *Total* drama queen."

The irony of this girl labeling anyone else a drama queen was too rich to ignore, and Graham shot a covert smirk toward Jessie through the one-way glass.

"But she told you she was having an affair with a teacher? A member of the Stevens Academy faculty?"

"Well, she didn't call it an 'affair,' but yeah. They were hooking up."

"Was this person one of Jordan's teachers, or just a teacher at the school?"

"I'm not sure." Arabella frowned. She looked a little disappointed in her own lack of details. "It was a man, though, a male teacher. She definitely called him a him. So it wasn't, you know, a lesbo thing."

"Okay," Graham said. "So one of the victims, Jordan Dunn, was involved in an affair—or, let's call it an inappropriate relationship—with a male teacher at the school."

"Crazy, right?" Arabella said. Some of her enthusiasm was returning. "You think that only happens on TV, but it happens in real life, too. Probably all the time."

"Did Jordan give you any other details about the teacher? What class he taught, how old he was, whether he was single or married?"

Arabella suddenly blushed, her cheeks reddening so much that Jessie could see the change through the one-way glass. "She said he was great, you know, at *doing it*. Is that helpful?"

Graham, in a tone of grave seriousness, said, "It's extremely helpful, Arabella."

The girl smiled ear-to-ear. "I have more information. Do you know about Kaelee Teal?"

Graham looked confused. She flipped through her notes, then shook her head. "Her name hasn't come up in the investigation. She wasn't one of the victims."

"That's because she was cut from the cheerleading squad two weeks before the shooting."

Graham shot another quick glance toward Jessie through the one-way glass. "How did Kaelee feel about that? Do you think she held a grudge against the rest of the team?"

"Oh, she definitely did. She said they were a bunch of stupid whores who didn't know anything about cheerleading. She said they didn't know a cupie from a basket toss. She said Ms. K. didn't care about the sport and that's why she let Kaelee get cut."

Jessie noted the use of the word "whore," and was sure Graham did, too. Echoes of True_Man and the Manpower forum.

"And by Ms. K., you mean Ms. Kerensa, the coach," Graham said.

"Uh-huh. Kaelee said she was as stupid as the rest of them and wasn't qualified to coach a pre-school dance class."

"Sounds like Kaelee was very angry."

"Yup. She said they'd regret it. She said she was going to get back at them."

Graham arched an eyebrow. "Did she say how?"

"No."

"Why was Kaelee cut from the squad?"

Arabella shrugged. "Grades. You need at least a B average to participate in varsity. There's a rule about it. But Kaelee said that's bullshit because the school breaks the rules for the football and basketball teams all the time. She said she's just as much an athlete as those guys, and more of an athlete than any of the other girls on the squad."

"The 'stupid whores,'" Graham said, reading from her notes.

"Her words, not mine. I like the other girls. I mean, *liked*. It's still hard to believe they're gone."

"Is Kaelee good with computers?"

Arabella looked surprised by the question. "I don't know. It's not like she's making her own apps or anything."

"Does she have any family members who work with computers? A boyfriend, maybe?"

Arabella laughed. "She doesn't have a boyfriend. I don't know her family."

Graham paused. Jessie could see her processing all of the new information, thinking of follow-up questions. Jessie didn't need to be a mind reader to know what the detective was thinking. Both the salacious rumor about Jordan Dunn and the existence of an angry, former member of the cheerleading squad both had the potential to be important leads.

## 24.

After a brief conference, Jessie Black left the Roundhouse to catch up on her work at the DA's office, and Graham and Novak went to Jordan Dunn's house to follow up on the lead Arabella Minsky had provided.

Novak drove. In the passenger seat, Graham silently cautioned herself not to get too excited. This case seemed perpetually on the verge of breaking, yet they never managed to make real progress. The dead bodies were piling up, but were they any closer to making a solid conspiracy case against True_Man, a person they still hadn't even identified?

Novak parked and they got out of the car. The house was a two-story colonial, light blue, sitting on a quiet street in the suburbs. The mailbox at the foot of the driveway was in the shape of a sailboat.

Graham led the way to the front door. A small army of wind chimes tinkled in the breeze. She and Novak exchanged a look.

Then they heard screams through the front door.

Not the type that gave rise to probable cause,

thankfully. These were happy screams, high-pitched and full of gleeful energy. Kids.

Graham rang the bell. A few seconds later, a woman opened the door. It seemed to take her a moment to focus on Graham and Novak. Her eyes were red-rimmed and the bags under them were puffy.

"Ms. Dunn?" Graham said.

"Yes?"

"We're from the Philadelphia Police Department. My name is Detective Graham. This is Detective Novak. We'd like to ask you some questions about your daughter. May we come in?"

"Questions about Jordan?" the woman said. Her voice cracked on the last syllable.

"Yes. It could be important."

"But she's ... already gone. All those poor girls are. What could be important about asking questions now?"

A squeal of laughter issued from inside the house.

"Please, Ms. Dunn," Novak said. "We only need a few moments of your time."

Dunn cast a look behind her into the house. "I have guests. My younger daughter is having a play date."

"We won't be long," Graham said.

The woman hesitated for another second, then gestured for them to enter. She led them through a cheerful-looking entryway, but her bearing was anything but cheerful. Her walk seemed slow, dragging. Her grief was almost palpable. "We're sorry for your loss," Graham said, wishing she'd said it earlier.

"Thanks."

There was a carpeted staircase leading upstairs, with a few stuffed animals scattered on the steps. Dunn led them past the stairs and into a brightly lit kitchen. Two children streaked past them, barely as tall as Graham's knees.

"That's my daughter Ellie," Dunn said. "And her friend from down the street."

A woman entered the kitchen from another room. "Everything okay?"

Dunn nodded. "These are detectives. They want to talk about ... you know. Do you mind watching the girls?"

"Of course not. Take your time." The woman smiled awkwardly, then disappeared as quickly as she'd appeared. Dunn looked like she wanted to disappear, too.

"Is there a place we can sit down?" Graham said.

"I'd rather not." Dunn crossed her arms over her chest and leaned her back against the refrigerator. It was a white fridge, not the fancy stainless steel kind, and it was covered with drawings and notes and magnets. Dunn's shoulder brushed against a magnet shaped like a watermelon, and it dropped from the fridge and clattered on the tile floor. Dunn didn't seem to notice until Novak bent to pick it up. "Thanks," she mumbled.

"I don't know if you've been following the news," Graham said. "We're investigating the possible involvement of a second person in the shooting, someone who may have been helping Russell Lanford. We think this person may live in the area and may have had a personal motive for wanting to hurt these young women."

Dunn nodded. "I saw on TV. You got a subpoena for that website."

"A warrant, yes." An unwanted image flashed through her mind. Wesley Lanford turning toward her with his rifle. Her mouth went dry. She swallowed. "Did Jordan have any enemies?"

Dunn's face twisted, and Graham thought she might laugh out loud. She wouldn't be the first person to laugh at that question. The word "enemies" was so overly dramatic, and the context of a murder investigation so stressful, that a lot of people burst into giggles just from sheer nerves. Dunn didn't, though. She wiped her eyes and shook her head. "No enemies."

Graham glanced at Novak. He looked as uncomfortable as she felt. They both knew what was coming next wouldn't be easy for anyone in the room. "I know this is difficult," Graham said, "but we only have a few more questions. Was Jordan seeing anyone?"

"Like ... a boyfriend?" Dunn said. She wiped her eyes again. "No. She went to parties, stuff like that. We gave her freedom as long as she came home by eleven. But no boyfriend."

"Are you sure? One of the other students at Stevens Academy seems to be under the impression that Jordan was seeing someone."

Dunn shrugged. "I don't know why she would keep it a secret. She was very open with me."

"Well," Graham said, "what if the person she was seeing was older? Do you think she might keep that a secret?"

"Older?" Dunn's shoulder knocked another magnet off the fridge. "What do you mean? How much older?"

"A teacher," Graham said.

Dunn shook her head so vigorously that her hair fanned around her head. "Not possible. Jordan would never. She ... no. Whoever told you that is a liar."

"I know this is difficult to hear—"

"It's not true."

"Would it be okay if we had a look at Jordan's bedroom?"

Dunn stared at her as if Graham had requested to deface her daughter's grave. "No. Absolutely not. I want you to leave my house right now. This is ridiculous!"

"We can get a warrant," Novak said, "if we have to."

She wheeled on him. "Are you threatening me?"

"We're just looking for answers," Graham said. "Don't you want the people responsible for Jordan's death to be brought to justice?"

"I'm calling my husband." She moved to the kitchen counter and detached a cell phone from its charging cable, then started tapping the screen.

Graham chewed her lip. "Okay. I think that's a good idea. We should talk to your husband, too. While you get him on the phone, would it be alright if we went upstairs?"

"No! It would not be alright!"

Graham gave Novak a look. He turned his back on the kitchen and pulled out his own phone. Started the process of getting a warrant based on Arabella Minsky's statement. Meanwhile, Dunn was talking into her phone, her voice edging closer to hysteria. Graham could just barely hear a male voice on the other end of the line, loud and angry.

Dunn ended the call and glared at Graham defiantly. "My husband is on his way."

"Warrant's in progress," Novak said, putting away his phone.

"It's going to take longer this way," Graham said, trying one more time. "We were hoping to have a quick look around, then get out of your hair."

Dunn glared at her. "And he's calling our lawyer, too. I heard all about how you bullied that website into releasing the private information of its users, and you got that guy Truman killed trying to protect his users' privacy. All for some witch hunt when everyone knows the only person to blame here is Russell Lanford, and he's dead! Now you come here and accuse my daughter of.... Enough is enough!"

The other woman poked her head into the kitchen again. "Are you okay?"

"Just watch the girls!" Dunn snapped. The woman hurriedly backed out of sight. Dunn shook her head. Tears streamed down her face. "What do you think you're going to find, anyway?" she said to Graham.

"I don't know. Maybe Jordan kept a diary. Maybe there are love letters, or—"

"You people are shameless!"

The husband arrived before the warrant. He had thick silver hair and wore a dark gray power suit. He didn't really look anything like Wesley Lanford, but that didn't stop a chill from dancing up Graham's spine. He was an angry father, and his entrance triggered something in her—post traumatic stress?—left over from her rooftop shooting. Novak, seeming to sense this, touched her arm and stepped forward to take the lead.

"Mr. Dunn, my name is Detective Novak. This is—"

"I want you out of my house right now."

"Mr. Dunn," Novak said, "we're here because your daughter may have been involved in a romantic relationship with one of the teachers at Stevens Academy. If that's the case, that teacher may have had something to do with the shooting in which she died."

"I don't see how that makes any sense—"

The two little girls burst into the kitchen. The one in the lead yelled "Daddy!" and crashed into her father's legs, hugging him. The woman followed the girls, an apologetic look on her face.

"They heard his voice," she said. "Sorry."

"It's okay," Ms. Dunn said. She crouched beside her daughter and peeled the girl away from her father's legs. "Ellie, Mommy and Daddy need to do grown-up things now, okay? Why don't you show Susie the new doll Grandma gave you?"

Ellie looked at her mother, and for a second, Graham was taken aback by the expression on the little girl's face—old beyond her years, tired and skeptical and even cynical. Then she was beaming, and excitedly telling her friend about her new toy, and the two girls took off like rockets out of the kitchen.

"Jordan wasn't having a relationship with a teacher," Mr. Dunn said. His voice was thick with anger.

His wife's gaze was still on the spot where Ellie had recently stood hugging her father's legs. "You know what she asks me every morning?" she said, looking at Graham as if daring her to ask.

"What?"

"She asks me if Jordan is still dead. Every morning, it's her first thought. Her first question. Is my sister still dead?" The woman's voice broke. "I can't stand this anymore."

"Go lie down," her husband said. "I'll handle this."

Ms. Dunn seemed to hesitate. Her husband nodded reassuringly. She cast a final scowl at Graham and Novak, then left the kitchen to join her friend and the kids.

Mr. Dunn regarded them with barely concealed rage. "I'm going to file a complaint with the police department. Harassment. How dare you come into our house and upset my wife? Our daughter was just killed, for God's sake. We're grieving."

"And we respect that," Novak said.

Graham said, "We're not here to upset anyone. We're trying to find the other person responsible for Jordan's death."

"Don't say her name," he snapped. Then, with an angry laugh, "Other person? What a joke. As if there's a shadowy conspiracy to kill cheerleaders."

"In this case, we believe there was," Graham said.

Something about her tone must have affected him, because his harsh laughter cut off as sharply as if someone had flipped a switch. "This is ludicrous," he said.

"Why don't you show us your daughter's bedroom?" Graham said. "If it's ludicrous, then we'll find nothing and that will be the end of it."

"Fine." His teeth flashed. "This way."

They followed him upstairs. There were four bedrooms. The master, one for each daughter, and a guest room, Graham supposed. The doors all stood open, but Mr. Dunn stopped at the threshold of Jordan's room as if stopped by an invisible wall. Graham heard him suck in a long, shaky breath, and then he stepped inside. She and Novak followed.

"This is Jordan's room?" Graham said.

Dunn nodded. He wiped a finger under one eye, looked away from them.

"It's very ... neat," Novak said. "I have a daughter. She's an adult now—a mother—but when she was a teenager, her room was always a mess."

Graham took another step into the room. The double size bed was made. There were no clothes on the floor or draped over the furniture. The closet doors were closed, as were the drawers of the dresser. Graham didn't have a teenage girl, but she'd been one herself not long ago. Compared to this, she'd lived like a hobo.

"Did you clean up in here?" she asked.

Dunn wiped his eye again. "A little bit. Not much. Jordan was very neat."

Not just neat, Graham thought. *Mature.* Framed prints from the Philadelphia Museum of Art adorned the walls where she would expect to find posters of bands or movie stars. There were no stuffed animals on the bed, no magazines on the nightstand. On a small desk under a window, there was a stack of SAT prep books, an Asus laptop, and a Kindle. Graham picked up the ereader, turned it on, and looked over a library of literary works. *Not your typical teenage reading material.* She put the Kindle down. Through the window, she could see the backyard, where a swing set had been erected.

Dunn came up beside her. "The girls usually don't—I mean *didn't*—play together. Because of the age difference. But sometimes they would swing together out there. Now I look at those swings and I want to ... I don't know. Tear it all down."

Graham gazed down at the swings and imagined the teenager and her little sister swinging side-by-side, laughing, talking. She felt a pang in her chest and knew it could only be the faintest echo of the pain the Dunns were experiencing.

"Do you mind?" She opened the desk drawers, one at a time, forcing herself to work slowly and meticulously. And sensitively, to the extent that was possible.

"Would it make a difference if I said I did?" Dunn said. On the other side of the room, Novak crouched and looked under the bed. "What are you looking for, anyway?"

"Even when people want to keep an affair secret, they often can't resist keeping mementos. A ticket stub, a small gift, that sort of thing."

Dunn made a sound of exasperation. "Look, even if it were true, even if Jordan was having some kind of affair with a teacher, what's the point of proving it? Haven't we been through enough? Jordan is dead, a victim of a random act of senseless violence. Why tarnish her memory by making her out to be some kind of...."

His voice trailed off, but the unspoken word hung in the air. *Slut.* Graham felt a spike of anger. "If she was involved with a teacher, it wasn't her fault. It would mean she was taken advantage of. And it's possible that this teacher orchestrated her death just to cover up his inappropriate behavior. If that's what happened, don't you want to bring it to light? Doesn't Jordan deserve that?"

Dunn seemed to struggle with these questions. At last, he said, "I don't know."

Novak had moved on from the bed to the dresser. Graham finished searching the desk and opened the closet. Dunn hovered by her shoulder but did not interfere. Every so often, they heard the children laughing downstairs. That was the only sound.

After forty-five minutes, it became clear they weren't going to find anything.

"Can I see her phone?" Graham said.

Dunn stared at her blankly. "We don't have it. We assumed the police recovered it from the crime scene."

Graham shook her head. They hadn't found any phones at the crime scene, but then, they hadn't really been looking for phones. The shooting had seemed so cut-and-dried at the time—senseless, random killing by a disturbed adolescent—Graham had not even thought to look for the victims' phones.

"We'll need to take the laptop with us," Graham said.

"Go ahead. You won't find anything. I told you. It's not true. It's a filthy lie."

Given the total lack of evidence, Graham was beginning to doubt the story herself. After all, how likely was it that the young woman who'd lived in this room—mature beyond her years, intellectual, responsible—would be friends with a gossipy airhead like Arabella Minsky, much less confide secrets to her? The thought prompted Graham to ask the question aloud.

"Was Jordan friendly with a girl named Arabella Minsky?"

"Arabella? Of course. John Minksy is my business partner. The girls have been friends since they were toddlers. Why? What does Arabella have to do with this?" His face shifted as understanding dawned on him. "Arabella is your source?"

"I didn't say that," Graham said, silently cursing herself for asking the question in the first place.

But now that it was out in the open, the information had an unexpected effect. Knowing that the rumor had come from Arabella Minsky seemed to force Dunn to consider it more seriously. He sat down hard on the bed. "A teacher. Oh, Jordan." Tears leaked from his eyes, and this time he didn't bother to wipe them away. "Oh, why didn't you say something to us?"

Graham waited patiently for Dunn to regain his composure. Novak, meanwhile, collected the laptop.

# 25.

Jessie met Graham and Novak at the Roundhouse. The detectives were returning from a visit to the house of Jordan Dunn's family, but judging by what Graham had told her on the phone, they hadn't found much. Their hope was that Kaelee Teal, their other new lead, would be more promising. They had asked her to come in for an interview.

Jessie arrived ahead of them and was waiting in the Homicide Division when Graham and Novak walked in. Graham had a frustrated frown on her face. Novak was holding a laptop under one arm. Jessie caught their attention and they headed toward her.

"Jordan Dunn's computer?" Jessie said.

Graham nodded. "Maybe there's something useful on it. If the girl was really sleeping with a teacher, there's got to be some evidence somewhere. A photo, an email. *Something.*"

"What about her phone?" Jessie said.

She thought she saw a look of embarrassment flash across Graham's face, but it vanished as quickly as it had appeared. "We don't have it."

"Are you looking for it?" In the modern world, phones had practically become extensions of people's personalities, and the contact lists, notes, web browser history, GPS data, and other information stored on the small devices could be invaluable. Novak, who seemed excessively attached to his, should have known that better than anyone.

"How's it going, Toby?" said a deep voice.

Jessie turned, then looked up. They had been joined by a giant—a man who had to be close to seven feet tall, and who sported a thick, black beard that would have fit in better at a lumberjack convention than a metropolitan police station. He had hands that were bigger than some people's faces, and he used them to take Jordan Dunn's laptop out of Novak's grip.

"I've had better days," Novak said to the man. "Emily Graham, Jessie Black, meet Eldon Greenfield, one of the department's best computer geeks."

Graham stared at him with an openly skeptical expression. "You don't look like a computer geek."

Jessie had to agree.

Eldon sighed. "Sorry, I left my pocket protector at home today. So, what's the story? Perp delete the hard drive? Use some kind of fancy encryption?"

"It's not the perp's computer," Novak said. "It belonged to one of the victims. And I don't know if it's encrypted. We never turned it on."

Eldon stared at him. "And you called me because...."

"You're a computer guy. We're hoping, I don't

know, that you could run some kind of search for us. We're looking for information about a boyfriend, or a teacher."

Eldon scratched his beard. "You don't need 'one of the department's best computer geeks' to run a search like that, Toby. This is beneath me."

"Did I mention she may have been having sex with the teacher?" Novak said.

Eldon perked up, apparently developing a sudden interest in his assignment. "I'll see what I can find."

Fifteen minutes after Eldon Greenfield left with Jordan Dunn's laptop, Kaelee Teal arrived. Once again, Jessie retreated to the observation room to watch through one-way glass. Graham and Novak escorted the former cheerleader into the same interview room they'd used for Arabella Minsky. But the teenager that entered the room was nothing like Arabella.

Kaelee walked with the confidence of a runway model—all hips and long legs—and had an outfit to match. She slid out of her jacket, flashing the tell-tale plaid lining of Burberry, and handed it to Graham as if the detective were a coat check attendant. Jessie wasn't exactly a fashionista, but she knew enough about designer labels to surmise that Kaelee's blouse, pencil skirt, and heels probably cost more than Jessie's, Graham's, and Novak's wardrobes combined. Not to mention the Fendi bag she placed on the battered metal table, or the meticulous makeup, salon-perfect blonde hair, or professionally pristine maroon fingernails. Not bad for a teenager.

The question was, why dress up for a meeting with the police? Was this a case of a wealthy but oblivious teenager not knowing any better, or was there intent behind her choices? A message sent to her interrogators that she was not intimidated by them, that she was above the law? Watching her, Jessie wondered.

Kaelee took a seat in one of the metal chairs. She leaned back and draped one long, bare leg over the other, appearing totally at ease in the grim police interview room. Graham sat down across from her. Novak remained on his feet, leaning against a wall and trying to be unobtrusive in a corner. Jessie smirked. Apparently, the plan was for Graham to try to make a connection with Kaelee and initiate some "girl talk." That strategy had worked with Arabella Minsky, but Jessie had her doubts it would be effective here.

"Thanks for coming, Kaelee."

"Did I have a choice?" There was no anger or even irritation in the girl's calm voice, just a simple question. But the girl's blue eyes seemed to watch Graham with the sharp attentiveness of an opponent.

Graham put on a surprised expression. "Of course. We asked you to stop by as a favor, not an order."

"I didn't realize that. You should be more careful not to give the wrong impression." Again, no overtly adversarial tone, but the girl's eyes seemed to glint with subdued anger.

*I don't like her.*

"I didn't mean to give you the wrong impression," Graham said. Of course this was a bald-faced lie—half of the police department playbook involved giving people the wrong impression, whether to get them to waive their right to counsel, consent to a warrantless search, or voluntarily come to the Roundhouse to be interrogated—but Graham managed to sound sincere.

"No worries," Kaelee said. She glanced at her watch. Diamonds reflected the overhead fluorescent lights as she turned her wrist. She said, "I have lunch plans in an hour. Do you think this will take a long time?"

"It shouldn't take long at all. We're just wrapping up our investigation of the shooting, and we're hoping you can help us fill in some of the blanks in our investigation."

"Wrapping up?" Kaelee said. "What about that warrant that was on the news? It didn't lead anywhere?"

Jessie leaned forward and tried to read the girl's face. Was that a hint of a smirk? A mischievous twinkle in her eyes? Jessie couldn't be sure. Kaelee was frustratingly calm, her features as smooth as polished stone.

"I can't discuss that part of the investigation at this time," Graham said.

"I see." Kaelee shrugged. "So what do you want to know?"

"You used to be on the Stevens Academy cheerleading squad, right?"

"I was the best one on it. The only one with a private coach outside of school. Not that anyone cared, obviously."

"You were pretty angry when they cut you from the squad because of your grades?" Graham said. Her voice was all sympathy, as if she were describing an outrageous injustice.

"I don't know if I'd use the word 'angry.' Say I was disappointed. I thought the school's administrators had better judgment." She shrugged. "Life goes on."

*For you, it does*, Jessie thought.

"Just disappointed?" Graham said. "Are you sure? I mean, there's nothing wrong with being angry when something like this happens. It's an appropriate reaction."

Kaelee shrugged again. Her poise didn't slip even a notch. "I wasn't angry. This is only high school. It's nothing, in the scheme of things. I was disappointed. But I moved on."

"Okay," Graham said. Then she paused, as if thinking. "I only ask because we heard that you told some people you were going to do something to get back at the squad."

Kaelee's lips turned down in a frown of distaste. "You talked to Arabella. I thought I smelled that idiot's prescription dandruff shampoo." She wrinkled her nose. "If you believe anything that girl says, you must really be grasping for straws."

"Well, like I said, we heard that you said you were going to do something to the squad."

"That's called hearsay, right? When someone tells you what another person told them?"

Jessie stiffened at the girl's use of the legal term. She was right. And presumably she raised the issue because she knew that, generally, hearsay wasn't permitted as evidence in court because it wasn't a witness's first-hand knowledge, and denied a defendant the right to question his or her accuser.

*The girl's done some legal research. Why?*

Was Kaelee Teal actually True_Man? It didn't seem out of the question. Even from this brief interview, she came across as smooth, calculating, a game-player. All traits of a sociopath. With her long legs and cold blue eyes, she might make a hell of a femme fatale one day—assuming she didn't spend the rest of her life in prison.

"It won't be hearsay if you tell me yourself," Graham said.

"I don't remember ever saying I was going to get anyone back."

*Not quite a denial,* Jessie noted.

"Did you refer to the other girls on the squad as 'stupid whores'?"

"I don't remember saying that either."

"But you were disappointed," Graham said, her tone rich with sarcasm. "Were you disappointed in yourself for not studying harder, or did you just blame everyone else?"

"Studying harder? Please. Do you think the

troglodytes on the football team study hard? Some of them can barely tie their shoes."

"A double standard," Graham said. "But what about the other cheerleaders? Could they tie their shoes, and keep their grades up, too?"

"Grades aren't always about studying."

"What do you mean?"

"Oh, I don't know. Maybe I should have spread my legs for a few of my teachers," she said with a sarcastic grin. "That seemed to work for at least one of my squad mates. Maybe that's the only way for a woman to succeed, right? The lessons we learn at the august Stevens Academy school for gender equality."

As she spoke the last two words, she seemed to challenge Graham with her gaze. *That's right*, her eyes seemed to say, *I know all about Manpower.*

Graham didn't take the bait. "Are you talking about Jordan Dunn?"

"I'm just repeating some vague gossip I might have heard."

"Do you know the name of the teacher?"

"Like I said, vague gossip. Unlike some girls, I don't really take an active interest in that kind of drama. I'm too busy living my own life. What business is it of mine if a girl wants to whore herself out to turn a C into a B?"

"For someone who's only disappointed, and not angry, you sure sound angry."

Jessie agreed. And she had to wonder, how could

someone so young and so obviously privileged be so bitter? At her age, Jessie would have given anything for what Kaelee had—flawless beauty, fancy clothes, two parents.

When Kaelee didn't respond, Graham said, "Okay. So you're cut from the squad, while other girls less deserving than you—girls without private coaches, girls who trade sex for grades—get to stay on the squad. And you're disappointed. What did you do about it? Did you complain to the administration? Or did you decide to handle things in your own way?"

Kaelee was silent for a stretch of seconds as she studied the detective. "Am I some sort of a suspect?"

"We're just gathering information," Graham said.

"Because I don't recall you reading me my rights. Or asking my parents' permission to question me without them being present."

"You're not under arrest." Graham did an admirable job of sounding confident, but Jessie suspected she knew she was on shaky ground. Very shaky ground. This teen was too well-informed.

"So I'm free to leave?"

Graham hesitated. "I'd prefer if you stayed. You've been incredibly helpful, and we have a lot of other questions about the cheerleading squad."

Kaelee rose from her chair. "I'm done with your questions. May I have my jacket, please?"

Graham rose from her chair as well, but she didn't reach for the jacket. "Can you spare another ten minutes? We can move on to another subject."

"I'll tell you what, Detective Graham," she said. She reached past Graham and grabbed the jacket herself, then swung it over her shoulders and thrust her arms through the sleeves. "If you have other questions, you can ask my lawyer."

Enough was enough. They'd pushed the boundaries of the *Miranda* law as far as they could go. Jessie leaned forward, found the right button on the console in front of her, and spoke into a microphone linked to a receiver in Graham's ear.

"Let her go."

# 26.

That night, Graham and Novak sat in a parked car. Across the street, the Teal house stood on a spacious suburban plot. Graham had ended the Kaelee Teal interview earlier than she'd wanted, rather than risk a *Miranda* violation. She'd had to let the girl go just when she'd begun to disturb her icy veneer. Graham hoped Kaelee might still be rattled enough to do something rash. Something stupid. Hence, this good old fashioned stakeout.

Sitting in a car for hours with Novak was no picnic, though.

She'd forgotten how irritating her partner could be. She tried not to glare at him as he noisily sucked a Frappacino from a Starbucks cup and thumbed through the latest Facebook updates on his phone. Her fingers tightened painfully around the steering wheel.

"Would you put that thing away?" Her voice came out harsher than she'd intended. "The screen's glow is going to give us away. You may as well bust out a spotlight and shine it on our car."

Novak gazed doubtfully at the Teals' house across

the street. Several of the rooms in the mini-mansion were lit up. Graham knew what he was thinking. The family was awake and busy, probably not paying much attention to the quiet residential street beyond their windows. But he stuffed his phone in his pocket anyway.

"Thanks," she said.

Novak slurped his frozen drink. By the time he'd sucked the final dregs from the cup, she was grinding her teeth. After that, they sat in blissful silence, punctuated only by an occasional breeze buffeting the car. They watched the house.

"If we can't use our phones, how are we supposed to not die of boredom?" Novak said.

"You were a cop before cell phones existed. You tell me."

"You say that like I'm a hundred years old."

"How about talking?" Graham said. "You want to talk?"

"Now you sound like my wife." His voice was dour, but he cracked a smile. "What do you want to talk about?"

Graham exhaled. She was feeling fidgety, just as bored as Novak. She needed to focus her mind on something while her eyes continued the dull task of staring at the house.

"How about our other lead?" she said. "You make any progress finding Jordan Dunn's teacher-with-benefits?"

"Not really. I checked in with Eldon. He scoured Jordan's laptop and came up empty."

Graham took a swig from a bottled water. "And we still don't have her phone."

"Nope. Wasn't in her house. Wasn't at the crime scene."

She looked at him with more interest. "Do you think that's meaningful?"

Novak shrugged. "Hard to say."

"Well, we should look harder for it. Add that to the To Do List."

"Agreed." Novak yawned. "There are seven male teachers employed by Stevens Academy, and an eighth who was employed but retired last year. None of them was Jordan Dunn's teacher at the time of her death. I suppose we'll have to interview all of them. More items on the To Do List."

"The nonstop thrills of a homicide cop," Graham said.

Even while talking to Novak, Graham focused part of her attention on the house. Now something caught her eye—movement near the side of the building. She leaned forward and peered into the darkness. It was Kaelee Teal, walking from the house to a Mercedes Benz parked in the driveway. There was no attempt at stealth. She strode with purpose, opened the door, and slid behind the wheel. A second later the engine thrummed to life and the headlights went on.

"She's on the move," Graham said, starting their own vehicle.

"In Daddy's Benz," Novak said. "At least I hope it's her parents' car. If it's her car, then I was really deprived as a child."

The Mercedes drove past them and down the quiet street. Graham waited until it made a right turn onto a side street, then put their unmarked car in drive and followed.

"Where do you think she's going?" Novak said.

Graham didn't know, but she was going to find out. They tailed the Mercedes from the suburbs to downtown Philly, keeping two cars between them when possible. Pretty quickly, Kaelee's destination became apparent. "She's heading for Stevens Academy."

"At 10 PM? Is the school even open at this hour?"

"I guess we'll find out."

Kaelee parallel parked along the street in front of the school. Graham and Novak circled the block once, then parked a block away and followed on foot, arriving at the school just in time to see her climb the fancy wrought-iron fence and leap gracefully over it.

"Guess all those private lessons paid off," Graham whispered.

Novak smirked. "Cheerleader skills in action."

Kaelee had swapped her skirt, blouse, and heels for sneakers, black yoga pants, and a sweater—an ensemble that probably cost just as much, but was eminently preferable for skulduggery. Graham supposed if you're going to sneak around at night and break into your school, you may as well do it in style.

"How are your climbing skills?" Graham said.

Novak stared doubtfully at the fence. "I'll go around, try to find another way in."

"Okay. Call for backup, too." She faced the fence, then turned back to Novak and added, "and Jessie Black. Let her know."

Novak let out a quiet laugh. "You two are tight now, huh?"

"We girls gotta stick together."

"Even though she's a lawyer?"

"Nobody's perfect."

She spent a few seconds studying the fence, then took a running jump, hit it about four feet off the ground and clung like a monkey. The wrought iron was thankfully rust-free, but the metal was cold and bit into her bare hands. She grimaced. Her legs swung beneath her and the pull of gravity was more intense than she'd anticipated, but she managed to haul herself up to the top of the fence, swing over, and drop. Her shoes hit the grass on the other side with a silent but ankle-jarring impact. She looked back through the bars to give Novak a reassuring nod, but he was already gone.

*Okay*, she thought. *Time to find the cheerleader and see what the hell she's up to.* The school grounds were lit sporadically with in-ground spotlights and a few blue safety lights mounted on the side of the school building, but it was still hard to see. She peered into the darkness. Then a sound reached her, quiet but instantly recognizable. The sound of a metal key clicking and scraping against a lock plate as it searched for a keyhole. Graham jogged in the direction of the sound.

There she was, blonde hair tucked into a neat ponytail, dressed all in black except for the stray designer label catching the ambient light. The world's most glamorous burglar.

Apparently, she had a key to the school. Graham pondered that. Maybe a leftover from her days on the cheerleading squad? Her theory was somewhat confirmed when Kaelee pulled the door open and Graham saw that it led to the school's gymnasium.

Kaelee slipped inside. Graham debated waiting for backup, then dismissed the idea. Even if this girl turned out to be True_Man, she wasn't a physical threat. Graham waited a beat, then followed her inside.

The gym was even darker than the nighttime grounds outside. Graham entered quickly and moved to the side so she wouldn't be silhouetted by the light. The smell of the gym's waxy hardwood floor brought a rush of memories, most of them unpleasant. She saw Kaelee head for a door to what she assumed were the locker rooms. She almost laughed. She'd spent a good chunk of her high school years trying to avoid the gym locker room. Kaelee was breaking into one.

She pursued the girl into the locker room. At first all she saw was darkness. She took a tentative step forward, touching a hand to the cold metal lockers lining one wall in an attempt to keep her bearings.

The lights went on in a blinding flash. Graham

raised a hand to shield her eyes, then realized her mistake as Kaelee charged past her, almost knocking her over. *Shit!* Graham turned and gave chase. Kaelee pounded halfway across the gym before the lights in the gym came on as well. This time, it wasn't Kaelee who'd turned them on, but Novak. He stood with two uniformed officers. Kaelee looked at them and stopped running.

"Do you want to call your lawyer now?" Graham said. "Because this time, you are under arrest."

# 27.

"The locker room?" Jessie held her phone to her face as the taxi sped through the mostly-empty streets, rushing toward the school. "Why?"

"We don't know yet." Graham's voice sounded tense through the connection. "She must have spotted me or sensed I was there. I don't know. I never had a chance to see what she sneaked into the locker room to do. She blinded me with the lights and bolted. We'll have to see what information we can get out of her once her lawyer shows up." The detective did not sound optimistic.

"The locker room," Jessie said again.

"What are you thinking?"

"Not sure yet. Let me go. I'll see you in a few minutes." She ended the call and made another—this time to the mobile number of Clark Harrison, the principal.

"Hello?" She heard a TV in the background.

"This is Jessica Black, the assistant DA—"

"I remember." The sound of the TV cut off. "Is something wrong?"

"I'm on my way to the school. There's been a break-in. One of the students tried to access the girls' locker room, and we believe it may have something to do with the shooting."

"What student?"

Jessie watched the street signs pass her window as the taxi drew closer to the school. "We can talk about that later. Right now, I need you to tell me who has the ability and the legal right to open the lockers."

"Oh. Well, I guess I do. I have a master key in my office. It opens all of the lockers in the school."

Jessie nodded. "That's what I was hoping. Can you meet me at the school now?"

"Whatever you need."

"Thanks."

Jessie arrived at Stevens Academy a few minutes later. The taxi dropped her off behind two police cruisers. The gate was open. A uniformed cop stood beside it, drinking a Red Bull. Jessie showed him her ID and he let her through.

Harrison arrived soon after her, looking disheveled in jeans and a sweatshirt. They walked to his office first and she waited patiently while he collected a keyring from his desk drawer. Then they walked together through the darkened hallways toward the gym.

"Can you tell me who broke into the school?" he said as they walked.

"Kaelee Teal."

"Hmm. Kaelee is, well, I guess you could call her headstrong."

"We understand she was recently cut from the cheerleading squad."

He shot her an anxious look. "That was based purely on grades. The policy's been vetted by our legal counsel."

Jessie gave him a sideways glance. Did this guy have any mode other than ass-covering? She tried to imagine him in a teaching role and couldn't quite manage it. "Let's take it one step at a time," she said.

They found a strange assemblage of people in the women's locker room. There were three uniformed cops, all of them men and one of them, who was sitting on a bench, looked almost young enough to be on a high school sports team himself. Kaelee Teal stood with her back to a row of metal lockers that had been painted a garishly bright green. Graham stood beside her but didn't speak. Jessie knew they were waiting for the girl's parents and lawyer to arrive. Novak was checking something on his phone.

When Jessie entered the room, Kaelee's back straightened. At first, she wondered if the girl knew who she was—Jessie had watched her meeting with the detectives through one-way glass, but they'd never met—then realized she was probably responding to Harrison's entrance, not hers. Apparently a roomful of cops didn't rattle this girl, but the school principal did. The thought was almost comical.

"What are you doing here, Mr. Harrison?" Kaelee

said.

"Cooperating with the police. I'd recommend you do the same."

She shook her head. "I know my rights."

Jessie said, "My name is Jessica Black. I'm an assistant district attorney. I understand you've invoked your right to counsel. No one will ask you any questions about the shooting until your lawyer arrives."

She was hoping this statement would draw a reaction, and it did. "The shooting? What are you talking about? All I did was sneak into the school."

"I'm sorry I can't say more," Jessie said. "It's a legal restriction. If you're willing to waive your right to counsel, then we can talk and hopefully sort all of this out."

Kaelee opened her mouth, and for a second, Jessie thought she might do it. But then she closed her mouth and shook her head. The girl was too smart to fall for the usual tactics.

"Okay," Jessie said. "That's fine. We'll wait for your lawyer." She turned to Graham. "You searched the room?"

Graham nodded. "We didn't find anything."

Jessie turned to Harrison. "Which locker is Kaelee's?"

Harrison checked a document he'd brought from his office. "214."

"Open it."

"You can't do that!" Kaelee said. She positioned herself in front of the locker to block Harrison. Harrison glanced at Jessie, unsure what to do. Jessie looked to Graham. Graham gently took the girl's arm and forced her to step aside. Kaelee glared at Jessie.

"In my experience," Jessie said, "when a suspect sneaks away right after a police interview, it's usually not for a lawful reason. It's usually to hide something, to cover something up."

"I have rights! You can't just open my locker!"

"I'm not going to engage in a legal debate," Jessie said. She was confident that the law was on her side, and wanted to minimize her exchanges with Kaelee before her lawyer and parents arrived.

Harrison opened the locker. "What the hell?"

There was a stuffed teddy bear attached to the inside of the locker door with strips of duct tape, its furry face pressed to the door as if it were looking out through the gaps in the metal slats. Jessie didn't know what she'd expected to find, but it hadn't been that. Everyone else seemed equally surprised. For a moment, no one spoke or moved.

Then Graham put on a pair of latex gloves and stepped forward. She pried the bear loose and studied it under the locker room's fluorescent lights. "There's a pinhole camera in the left eye," she said. "Wireless nanny cam would be my guess." One of the uniforms held out an evidence bag, and she dropped the bear into it.

Jessie pivoted on her heel, following what would

have been the bear's line of sight when the locker door was closed. The shower, of course. Jessie shook her head. *Seriously?*

"It was just a prank," Kaelee said. "A little revenge on those bitches for not sticking up for me when I got cut."

"Revenge?" Graham seemed to think that over. "What were you going to do? Record nude video of them and upload it to the internet?"

A small, cruel smile appeared on Kaelee's lips for a second before she could hide it. "You know what they say. High school is temporary, but the internet is forever. I wanted to teach them a lesson."

The natural follow-up question was whether she'd taught her former squad mates the same lesson through Russell Lanford, but no one asked it. They had to wait for her lawyer, or any response she made would be considered tainted, inadmissible evidence.

"Does that key open all of the lockers?" Jessie asked Harrison. When he nodded, she said, "Please open the other cheerleaders' lockers. Maybe we'll find something else."

The uniformed officers, detectives, and Kaelee stood in silence as Harrison opened each of the sixteen cheerleaders' lockers, one by one, with his master key. The process took on a strange rhythm— the click of his key in the lock, the squeak of the hinges, the *clang* of a metal door flung open. Harrison picked up speed as he went. Within a few minutes, all of the murdered cheerleaders' lockers were open.

Jessie walked the length of the locker room and peered inside the open compartments. The girls had died in their cheerleading uniforms, during practice, and their street clothes were still in their lockers, waiting for owners who would never return. Jeans. Skirts. Sweaters. Blouses. Some were neatly folded, others carelessly shoved in. Shoes, too. Looking at these articles of clothing made Jessie's heart ache. The sight of shirts, pants, boots—it was so *mundane*. How many of the girls had doubted for a second that they'd be changing back into their clothes right after another routine practice?

"You didn't check the lockers as part of the initial investigation?" she asked Graham.

Graham looked sick. "We were focused on the primary scene. The field. I.... It was a mistake."

Jessie let it go. In addition to clothing, she saw phones, some jewelry, purses and bags, other personal items. Each narrow rectangular space was like a snapshot of a life cut short.

She turned to Harrison. "Which one was Jordan Dunn's?"

The principal looked surprised by the question. "Who?"

"Jordan Dunn," Jessie said more slowly. "She was one of the cheerleaders."

Harrison nodded. "Oh, right. Jordan. I know who she is. A good kid. Model student, really." He checked his list and told her the number.

Jessie and Graham approached the locker. It

didn't look much different than its neighbors. A pile of clothing—Jordan, not surprisingly, was one of the folders rather than stuffers—and a nice pair of shoes. A coat and a book bag.

Graham, still wearing her latex gloves, reached for the bag. It was a dark red Jansport backpack. Graham unzipped it and began removing its contents. Textbooks, two spiral notebooks, a tin of Altoids mints. Pens and pencils and one of those bulky Texas Instruments graphing calculators.

"What are you looking for?" Harrison said. "Why are you interested in Jordan?"

Jessie debated telling him, but decided not to.

Kaelee Teal wasn't as tactful. "She was banging a teacher."

Harrison's eyes widened. "What?"

"Yeah," Kaelee said. Her voice had an ugly, gloating tone. "How's your model student now?"

"You had no idea?" Novak asked Harrison.

"No." The principal fumbled with his keyring, looking extremely uncomfortable with the subject matter. "I don't really hear rumors like that. The students tend to go silent when I walk down the hall."

"Any idea who the teacher might be?" Graham said. "Someone with a history of inappropriate behavior, maybe?"

Harrison's face flushed red. "No teacher here has a history of inappropriate behavior. That kind of ... relationship with a student wouldn't be tolerated even

234

once. We have very strict rules at Stevens Academy. The safety of the students always comes first!"

"Gather up everyone's things," Jessie said. "Maybe we'll find something useful."

"What about her?" Graham said, indicating Kaelee.

The girl glared at Jessie. Jessie glared right back. Her parents and lawyer were apparently taking their time getting here. Once they did, full questioning would be in order.

# 28.

It was close to midnight when she returned, exhausted, to her apartment. She was bone-tired, and the only thing she wanted to do was stumble into her bedroom and drop onto her bed. It wasn't until she saw Leary sitting on her couch with a bottle of wine on the coffee table in front of him that she remembered they'd made plans to watch a movie and share a bottle of Cabernet.

"Oh no. I totally forgot. You must be so pissed."

"Nope," he said. His smile looked genuine. "Just really, really thirsty."

"It was work."

"I assumed." He produced a corkscrew and went to work on the wine bottle. She watched the muscles of his arms bulge as he pulled the cork, and a tremor of excitement ran through her. She suddenly felt less fatigued. He patted the couch cushion beside him. "It's pretty late, so I'm guessing a two-hour movie is off the table. How about we have a few glasses of wine?"

"Thanks for being flexible."

"After the wine, I can show you just how flexible I

am."

She smiled and walked across the room, then dropped onto the couch next to him. They kissed.

He handed her a glass and lifted his. "To flexibility."

"Yes." Their glasses clinked. She sipped her wine. It was good.

One of his arms circled her waist and she leaned against him. The feeling of his body against hers felt both comfortable and exciting at the same time. She almost sighed with contentment. And yet, despite these feelings, she knew she wasn't fully there. Part of her was still in the Stevens Academy girls' locker room. She wanted to focus on Leary. God knows he wasn't a hard man to focus on. She pushed thoughts of the case from her mind and lifted her wine glass to take another sip.

"Why don't you tell me about it?" Leary said.

"About what?"

He gave her a knowing look. "Come on, Jess."

"Am I that transparent?"

"I just know you really well. That's a good thing."

She knew he meant it, but she felt a twinge of concern anyway. They'd had to cancel their tropical vacation because of the shooting at Stevens Academy, and she'd been working nonstop ever since. Tonight had been her idea. It was supposed to be a chance for the two of them to enjoy a romantic evening together—no computer or legal pads in sight. So what did it say about her—*about their relationship*—that she'd completely forgotten about it and even now couldn't get her mind off of the case?

"Okay," Leary said, as if reading her mind. "Let's talk about something else. You called your dad the other day, right? How's he doing?"

She felt a small sense of relief. "He's doing well. You know, he seemed a little bored, I guess, but overall, I think he's good."

"Good," he said. "That's really good to hear. Any news about your brother and his family?"

"Not really. Just the usual." Her voice fell away. They sipped wine. Finally, after what seemed like the longest awkward silence in history, she said, "You really don't mind talking about my case?"

He hugged her more tightly against him. "Jessie, I'm *dying* to talk about your case."

"But this is supposed to be, you know, romantic."

"It is. It's absolutely infused with romance. Now, tell me."

She sat up straighter. "You're not going to believe it." She told him about the stakeout of the Teal house, about how Graham and Novak had tailed Kaelee to the school, about the hidden camera they'd found set up in the girls' locker room.

"That's like something out of a movie," he said.

"I know. That's what Emily said. It's an insane thing to do, right? Unfortunately, it doesn't look like it has anything to do with the shooting."

He paused, then said, "But?" Leary seemed to be studying her. Seemed to be reading her mind again.

"But I can't stop thinking about the locker room." She shook her head. She was having trouble expressing her thoughts, and the wine wasn't helping. "I don't know. It's like, I feel like there was something there. Something important. But I can't put my finger on it."

Leary winced. "I know that feeling. Drives you crazy."

"No kidding."

"The best thing to do is talk. Go over it, every detail."

She smiled. "And you're not just suggesting this because you want to hear all about it?"

He shrugged. "That's true, too, but it doesn't change the fact that talking works. Trust me. I've been there many times. It's one of the most frustrating parts of trying to solve a crime. You sift through all the evidence, and then—if you're good at the job—your brain makes connections. It's not something you consciously control. Not something you can force. It just has to happen on its own. And sometimes it takes its damn time."

"And talking helps make it faster?" she said.

"Talking helps. If you're up for it."

"I am," she said. "Some romantic evening, huh? We're going to snuggle while dwelling over the worst aspects of human nature."

"Sounds like my kind of date. So Graham and

Novak watched the Teal house after they brought her in for an interview, and the surveillance paid off."

Jessie nodded. "Emily's got good instincts."

"Good for her." She saw something sour in his expression. "It takes more than instincts, though, to get ahead in Homicide. I hope she learns that more quickly than I did."

"Maybe you should tell her."

Leary waved away the suggestion. "She's better off without me." He drank more wine. She watched his throat move as he swallowed. "I'm no wise man. Nobody's mentor."

"I don't think you give yourself enough credit."

He arched an eyebrow. "Are we talking about me or the case?"

"Fine. So, Graham and Novak tailed the girl to the school, watched her sneak in, and cornered her in the girls' locker room. When Harrison opened up her locker, there was the camera. A wireless nanny cam disguised as a teddy bear."

"Cute."

"Adorable."

"Who's Harrison?"

She realized she'd left some gaps in the story. Must be her exhaustion and the wine diminishing her narrative skills. "Clark Harrison. He's the principal. We called him there as a representative of the school to open Kaelee's locker."

"You mean *you* called him there. Let me guess. He

hasn't been principal for very long. Not very experienced with dealing with the police."

"He was a science teacher until he got promoted last year."

Leary grinned. "So you told him you needed him to hurry over to the school right away and open Kaelee Teal's locker for you," Leary said, "and he did it. Without ever thinking to demand a warrant."

"Actually, I asked him to open all of the cheerleaders' lockers, which would have been beyond the scope of a warrant." She shrugged. "So, as the kids say, *go me*." She blushed a little. Yes, the wine was definitely affecting her narrative skills.

"Find anything interesting in the other lockers?"

"Nothing you wouldn't expect. The clothes they'd changed out of for practice. Jewelry. Bags. Phones, of course—" She stopped mid-sentence, put her wine glass down on the coffee table.

"What?" Leary said.

"I think my brain just made one of those connections."

He leaned forward. "Tell me."

"I'd have to double-check, but Jordan Dunn's locker ... I don't think there was a phone in hers."

"And Jordan Dunn is...?"

"One of the cheerleaders. She's rumored to have been having an affair with a teacher."

"A teacher who might have wanted to get rid of her phone, just in case it contained photos, texts, who knows what," Leary said. "A teacher trying to cover up their relationship."

"Or cover up her murder," Jessie said.

"Or both." Leary nodded, clearly liking the idea. "Anyone besides this Clark Harrison guy have a key to the lockers?"

"Probably."

"Yeah, probably. But how many of them are men? And how many of them used to teach?"

Jessie leaned back in her chair. Clark Harrison? Was it possible? "He doesn't seem like the murderer type."

"No?" Leary said. "Let me guess. Harrison's been super helpful. More than happy to assist the police with their investigation. And all the while, subtly steering you away from the school. Away from himself."

*Son of a bitch.* She started to stand up.

"Woah. Don't tell me you're going to leave," he said.

She rose to her feet, grabbed her bag, and slung it over her shoulder. "I think I have to."

He looked up at her, smiling. In that moment, she knew they had something special, something true, even if their relationship didn't fit the classic mold. He didn't just accept and understand her devotion to her work—he loved her for it. She leaned down and kissed him. The flavor of the wine mixed with the strong, sturdy flavor of him, and she didn't want to stop.

When she finally pulled away, she said, "I'm really sorry."

"Don't be," he said. "Go be you."

# 29.

There were no questions, no sarcastic comments, no having to explain herself. One phone call, less than a minute long, and Emily Graham agreed to meet Jessie at the Roundhouse at 1:15 AM. Jessie reflected on that as she took a taxi to Police Headquarters. She and Graham had come a long way since their first meeting, when Jessie had had to fight the detective just to spare ten minutes to walk her through the crime scene.

Graham was waiting for her in front of the building. Novak was there, too. "So what's this about?" Graham said. "You've got something about our investigation that couldn't wait until the morning?"

"I think I do."

Novak arched an eyebrow. "This I gotta hear."

A cool night breeze fluttered Jessie's hair. The streets around the police station were quiet. She laid out her theory for Graham and Novak, step by step, the same way she'd talked it through with Leary. The locker without a phone. The cheerleader with the illicit affair. The teacher with the motive to cover it up and the key to access the lockers.

"I don't know," Graham said. "That sounds pretty shaky. How many glasses of wine did you say you had?"

"Bring him in," Jessie said. "Tonight. Question him here at the Roundhouse." She tilted her chin at the huge building behind them, looming in the darkness. "I really think he may be our man. True_Man."

Graham and Novak exchanged a glance. Novak shrugged. "Let's go get him."

"I have his home phone number," Jessie said. "I guess we should call first, given the time."

Graham shook her head. "You want a confession, right? Then we don't call first."

"It's almost 1:30 in the morning," Jessie said.

"Exactly. We show up at his house unannounced while he's sleeping peacefully next to his wife, dreaming about violating minors."

"A lot more intimidating that way," Novak said.

Jessie felt a tremor of doubt. "What if it turns out he's not the right guy? I don't want to be so aggressive we give him grounds for a civil case against the city."

"You called us here in the middle of the night," Graham said. "I know you're a workaholic, but I don't think even you would have done that unless you had a really strong feeling about this."

Jessie nodded. "I do."

"Go inside," Graham said, indicating Police HQ. "You must have a favorite chair in front of the one-way glass by now. Make yourself comfortable."

Jessie turned to do just that, then thought of something else and turned around again. "Make sure you get his computer," she said. "We'll need Eldon to search it for evidence linking Harrison to the True_Man identity."

Without evidence conclusively linking Harrison to True_Man, their whole case would be circumstantial. There would be no trial. She'd never get past the preliminary hearing.

"If there's a computer in his house, we'll get it," Graham said.

Jessie watched them leave, then went inside the Roundhouse. She walked through the mostly-deserted workspace of the Homicide Division and returned to the same observation room in which she'd watched the interviews of Arabella Minsky and Kaelee Teal through one-way glass. She leaned back in a swivel chair—Graham was right, she did have a favorite—and looked through the window. In shadowy silence, the interrogation room looked like a theater stage before the curtain goes up.

She hoped Graham and Novak returned with Harrison soon. She was looking forward to show time.

# 30.

Novak parked their unmarked car. He and Graham took a moment to watch the street. The Harrisons lived in the Germantown section of Philadelphia, in a suburban, middle-class neighborhood. Their house, a white colonial, was not exactly a shack, but not particularly nice, either—that was obvious even with the building shrouded in darkness at close to two in the morning. Compared to the houses of the Stevens Academy students she'd seen—Lanford, Minsky, Dunn—the principal's house looked shabby, even a little sad. Graham wondered if that pissed Harrison off, coming home to his modest little house after a long day serving the educational needs of the city's elite? Did it make him feel better to screw the daughter of one of those high and mighty moneyed families? No, she decided. Probably not. Probably, she was giving him too much credit. He'd just been horny.

It was a sequence she'd seen before, and one any homicide cop would recognize: Horny. Then ashamed. Then afraid. Then desperate. And eventually, after fear had eaten away any moral restraints he might have possessed, desperate enough to kill to cover it up. In this case, to stage a massacre.

"You ready?" Novak said. He pulled his Glock, checked the magazine, and holstered it again.

"Ready." She climbed out of the car. The street was quiet, almost silent, save for the faint buzzing of insects in the grass. The sound of Novak closing his door was like a gunshot, and she winced.

There were lights on in the downstairs of the house. She watched the windows for signs of movement, didn't see any.

Novak joined her at the front door. "You know, I think I'm going to enjoy making this arrest," he said. "I still remember my high school principal. A real sanctimonious prick."

"Spent a lot of time in detention, did you?"

"When I was lucky. Most of the time, they just suspended me."

She looked at him. "Guess you were a rebel back then."

"Nah. I just thought it was funny to stick cherry bombs in toilets."

"And now you're a police detective."

He cracked a half-smile, his teeth white in the darkness. "Yup. My principal never saw that coming."

And, if they were lucky, Principal Clark Harrison wouldn't see *them* coming. Not at 2:00 AM on a quiet night.

Graham rang the bell. They waited as minutes

passed. The door swung open and a disheveled woman in pajamas and a bathrobe looked at them through narrowed, suspicious eyes. Her brown hair was pulled back in a severe knot, and her face was lined and tired-looking. Even so, Graham could see that she had been pretty, maybe even beautiful, before life and a scumbag husband had ground away her youth.

"Mrs. Harrison? My name is Detective Emily Graham. This is Detective Tobias Novak. Is your husband at home?"

"Of course he is." The woman didn't open the door wider or invite them inside. The creases in her face seemed to deepen. "It's the middle of the night. Is this about the ... incident at the school? Hasn't Clark helped you enough already?"

"I apologize for the late hour," Graham said, "but it's really important that we speak with your husband now."

She tried to peer past the woman, but all she saw was a dark and dreary entryway. After a moment, Mrs. Harrison sighed and took a step backward with one slippered foot. "Come in, I guess." Then, half-turning, she called over her shoulder, "Clark!"

He appeared a second later, also wearing a robe, his feet covered in dirty-looking white socks. His first reaction upon seeing the two homicide detectives standing in his entryway was unmistakable—*fear*—but he recovered quickly with a smile that looked way too big to be genuine.

"Detectives Graham and Novak. I wish you'd

called...." He looked down at his robe and cinched the fluffy belt at his waist. "I would have gotten ready."

*I bet*, Graham thought.

"Well, come inside," he continued. "How can I help you?"

Harrison was already walking deeper into the house. Novak followed him, and so did Graham, but with an uneasy feeling. Harrison didn't feel dangerous to her—not in a hands-on kind of way—but all the same, she didn't like being here on his home turf. Better to get him into the back of their car and drive him to the Roundhouse, ASAP.

The inside of the house was as unimpressive as the exterior. Everything looked outdated—wallpaper that looked vintage 1980's, shaggy carpeting straight out of the 70's. No fancy appliances in the kitchen. She wondered again how the disparity between his life and that of his students made him feel. Maybe Graham would ask him later—on *her* home turf.

"Actually, Mr. Harrison, we'd like you to accompany us to the police station."

Harrison's wife let out a little gasp. Harrison turned to look at Graham. "Right now?"

"Yes."

"What is this about?" Mrs. Harrison said. Her voice became shrill, laced with fear. "Why can't it wait until morning?"

Harrison shot her an irritated look. "It's fine, Barbara. The school comes first."

Barbara shook her head. "It's not right."

Graham kept her focus on Harrison. For the space of a few seconds—seconds in which Graham stopped breathing—he looked like he might do something stupid. Guilty people often did, at the moment the police arrived to take them in. She didn't know what was going through Harrison's mind right now. Grab a knife from the butcher block on the counter? Throw the glass coffee carafe at her head? But something in his eyes had changed. She felt the reassuring bulk of her holster and willed him not to act on whatever panic impulse was rushing through his system. She was still suffering sleepless nights from shooting Wesley Lanford. She didn't want another firefight.

Then Harrison shrugged and the tension in the room evaporated. Graham breathed.

"May I at least put on some clothes?" he said.

"Be quick," Graham said.

Harrison stepped past her and Novak. They heard boards creak as he ascended a staircase, then more creaking as he walked around upstairs.

His wife stared at them with a look that was equal parts fear and anger. At last, she said, "You're not really here for his help, are you? What did he do?" She looked pained, and more tired than ever.

More sounds reached them from upstairs. Suddenly, something seemed to occur to Novak. He said, "Shit!" and pounded after Harrison. Graham, confused but trusting his instincts, followed her partner up a narrow staircase to the second floor.

"Stop!" Novak yelled. He burst into a room off the upstairs hallway, and Graham, still following him, saw it was a bathroom.

Harrison was in there, still wearing his robe and white socks, standing over the toilet with a laptop in his hands. The toilet seat was up. He looked at Novak, bared his teeth in a snarl that reminded Graham of a raccoon her father had cornered in their driveway when she'd been a kid. He dropped the computer.

Novak lunged forward and swung an arm. The flat of his hand connected with the laptop just before it could hit the water, and sent the computer flying. The laptop hit the tile wall above the bathtub and shattered in an explosion of bathroom tile, plastic, and circuitry. Then he grabbed Harrison, wrenched the man's arms behind his back, and handcuffed him.

Graham squeezed past the two men. The laptop was in pieces in the bathtub. She pulled on latex gloves from one pocket, grabbed an evidence bag from another, and began gathering the smaller pieces.

"Good reflexes, Toby," she said. A second later, and the laptop would have been submerged in toilet water, its innards probably fried beyond recovery.

Novak was frowning. "I meant to grab the thing. Not bash it against the wall."

"At least it's dry. Hopefully Eldon will be able to recover something."

Novak looked doubtfully at the mess in the tub. "Yeah. Hopefully."

"We don't need the laptop, anyway," she said as

she straightened up. She made eye-contact with Harrison. "We have more than enough evidence against this creep."

Judging by the victorious grin on his face, Harrison thought he knew better.

"You have the right to remain silent," Novak said, beginning the *Miranda* warnings.

"So now I'm under arrest?"

"Anything you say or do can be used against you in a court of law."

"I want my lawyer," Harrison said. He craned his neck toward the open bathroom door. "Barbara, call Hyram Brand!"

"Let's go," Novak said, and hauled him out of the bathroom.

"You're going to regret this," Harrison said. They pushed him toward the stairs. "I know people. I have a lot of friends."

"In my experience, friends tend to disappear when you're arrested for murder," she said.

Harrison turned on her with a grin that chilled her blood. "Not friends like mine."

# 31.

Jessie crossed her arms and stared at the closed door of the police conference room in which Clark Harrison was conferring with his lawyer, Hyram Brand. As an attorney-client communication, the meeting entitled Harrison and Brand to privacy. Jessie and the police couldn't listen in. All she could do was chew her lip.

Someone walked up to her. She turned and saw Emily Graham. "Eldon took the hard drive and RAM chips to the computer lab," Graham said. "What was left of them anyway."

"And?"

"He'll do his best. He didn't sound particularly optimistic, though."

"Damn it." Without the laptop, they had no physical evidence tying Clark Harrison to the True_Man identity. And if they couldn't prove that Harrison was True_Man, then they had no case. "How did this happen?"

"We shouldn't have let him go upstairs alone to get dressed," Graham said. "It was a lapse in judgment."

Jessie didn't contradict her. It *had* been a lapse in judgment, and it might just result in Harrison walking out of here. But there was no sense dwelling on it.

"Do you think if we work together we can get him to confess?" Graham said. She stared at the conference room door as if trying to see through it.

"With Hyram Brand at his side? Doubtful."

"He's good?"

"You could say that." Good didn't begin to describe Hyram Brand. He was one of the most respected criminal defense attorneys in the city. Harrison must have anticipated that he might need a lawyer one day, and had done his research ahead of time to find the best. Now his preparation was paying off. Jessie wondered what other preparations he might have made.

"Still worth a try," Graham said. "Maybe we can rattle Harrison, get him to say something incriminating before his lawyer can shut him up. I've seen that happen plenty of times. Even the best lawyer can have trouble protecting a client from himself. Especially a client with a guilty conscience."

"I'm not sure Harrison has a conscience," Jessie said. "But I agree," she added, seeing the look of anxiety on Graham's face. "It's worth a try."

A familiar voice grumbled from behind them. "You want to tell me what the hell is going on here?"

Jessie swung around and saw Warren Williams striding toward them. He was breathing hard and his face was red, as if he'd run here from the DA's office. Maybe he had.

"Who's this man you arrested in the Stevens Academy case? Clark Harrison. Why wasn't I given a heads-up?"

How the hell had he found out about the arrest so quickly? Jessie didn't bother thinking too hard about it. The man really did have eyes and ears everywhere. Very little happened in the DA's office or the police department without Warren receiving an alert. Whoever his sources were, they were reliable.

"He's the principal at Stevens Academy," Graham said. Even though she stood a head taller than Warren, her voice faltered and she looked intimidated.

Warren glared at her, then turned his attention to Jessie. "And?"

"He's True_Man," she said.

"Ah, the internet mystery man who supposedly orchestrated the massacre. You do know who's in there with him, right? That's Hyram Brand, in case you didn't notice."

"I noticed."

"You know I was skeptical about this whole conspiracy angle from the beginning," Warren said, "but now it looks like you've compounded the problem by making an arrest prematurely. Do you have any tangible evidence that Harrison is True_Man? I mean, other than your stellar instincts?"

Jessie forced herself to breathe. "We're working on it. It's a long story. Harrison's computer—"

"I already know the long story."

Of course he did.

"Your case is shit," Warren said.

"We're going to try to rattle him," Graham said. "See if we can trip him up."

Warren stared at the detective, incredulous, then turned back to Jessie. "Is she serious? I'm starting to miss Leary."

"It's a long shot," Jessie said, "but worth a try."

Warren barked out a laugh. "That's not Noah Snyder sitting in there. That's *Hyram Brand*. You're not going to get anywhere with Harrison. Release him now, with an apology, before this gets any more embarrassing."

"What?" Graham looked outraged. "What's there to be embarrassed about? He caused the deaths of seventeen people—nineteen, if you count Wesley Lanford and Vaughn Truman—and we arrested him for it."

Jessie raised a hand to quiet her. "Warren, just give us fifteen minutes to talk to him, okay? If we don't get anywhere in fifteen minutes, we'll let him go and cut our losses."

She could sense Graham fuming beside her, but didn't dare turn to look. She needed to maintain eye-contact with Warren.

Seconds passed before her boss let out a little snort of disdain. "Fine. Fifteen minutes. But that's it. If you don't get results, we pull the plug. And not just on this arrest, Jessie. On this whole investigation. It'll be over. Agreed?"

He'd raised the stakes on her, the way only he could. And there was nothing she could do about it. She clenched her teeth and nodded. "Agreed."

Warren glared at Graham. "Move them to an interrogation room. One of the comfortable ones—we don't want to give his lawyer any ideas about a civil claim. Let's get this over with."

# 32.

This time, Jessie joined Graham in the interview room. Per Warren's request, this space was one of the bigger, less dungeon-like rooms, with a nice wooden table large enough to accommodate four. On the other side of the table from Jessie and Graham, Harrison sat with Brand. The principal still wore his terrycloth bathrobe. Brand wore a five-thousand-dollar suit.

Novak and Warren were out of sight in the observation room behind the one-way glass. That glass looked like a mirror on Jessie's side of the wall, but even though she couldn't see them, she could feel Warren's stare boring into her.

"Hello, Hyram," she said.

"First of all," Brand said, indicating Harrison's robe, "this is outrageous." So much for starting things out on a pleasant note.

Jessie wasn't surprised by the bluster. It was Brand's style. The man was barely five feet tall, and had the kind of Napoleon complex common to short men. He always seemed to be on the attack. In the courtroom, he'd been known to browbeat witnesses and lawyers—and even judges, on occasion—into submission. She was determined not to let this tactic work on her.

"Your client resisted arrest," she said as she calmly took a seat.

"Not true. Your police overreacted when Mr. Harrison accidentally dropped his laptop computer."

"Over a toilet bowl," Jessie said.

Brand shrugged. "I fail to see how that warrants the demeaning treatment of being taken to the police station without his clothing. The behavior of the police tonight was beyond inappropriate." He leveled an icy stare at Graham, who stared right back at him.

"After his attempt to destroy the laptop," Jessie said, "Detectives Graham and Novak did not want to give your client any additional opportunities to tamper with evidence. That's why they took him into custody in his robe."

"Well, Mrs. Harrison is on her way here now with a change of clothes. If she hurries, she should reach the building in"—he looked at his Rolex—"just enough time to let Mr. Harrison put on some trousers before he walks right out of here."

Brand's face was dead serious. Harrison's bore a smirk. Jessie glanced at her own watch and saw her fifteen minutes slipping away. She could feel the weight of Warren's unseen stare.

"No one's walking anywhere," Graham said. "We arrested your client for murder." She focused her gaze on Harrison, and Jessie was pleased to see the principal's smirk falter, if only slightly. "You're looking at the death penalty, Mr. Harrison. The best thing you can do now is tell us everything. If you save the state the cost of a trial, Ms. Black has the authority to take death off the table. You'll serve a life sentence, seventeen of them, but—"

At this speech, Hyram actually let out a snort. "Is this Philadelphia Police Headquarters, or are we on the set of a bad TV cop show?" He looked past them at the mirrored wall. "Warren, are you there? Are you watching this farce?"

But Graham kept her eyes locked on Harrison, and he was starting to squirm in his seat. Jessie decided to help Graham keep the pressure on. "Mr. Harrison, it's easy for your lawyer to joke around. But this is no joke for you. Do you really think a jury exists that wouldn't look at your list of victims and give you the death penalty?"

Harrison's Adam's apple bobbed as he swallowed hard. Brand put a steadying hand on the man's arm. "Those were Russell Lanford's victims. My client is a principal, a teacher, a model citizen. And because you're out for blood, you want to make him a scapegoat. *That's* what the jury will see."

"He was having sex with a sixteen-year-old girl," Graham said.

"You have no evidence of that."

"Only because he killed her," Jessie said.

Brand looked from Graham to Jessie. "You guys tag-teaming us now? As I said, the only person who killed any students was Russell Lanford."

"Your client conspired with Russell Lanford," Jessie said.

Brand laughed. "That's a novel and interesting legal argument. Unfortunately, we won't have the opportunity to test it, because you have no evidence."

There was a knock at the door. Jessie glanced at her watch. Only ten minutes had passed since they'd entered the interview room, but apparently Warren had seen enough.

"Excuse us for a minute," Jessie said. She and Graham rose from their chairs.

Brand smiled knowingly. "It's Warren, isn't it?" His eyes seemed to twinkle with glee. "I knew he was there."

Jessie didn't respond. She and Graham stepped out of the interview room. Warren was waiting for them. He did not look happy.

"It's over."

"You agreed to give us fifteen minutes," Jessie said.

Warren gave her a beleaguered look. "Oh, I'm sorry. I didn't realize you were five minutes away from a full confession. Come on, Jessie. Brand is right. We don't have the evidence to support the charges."

"Actually," a deep voice said, "we do."

They all turned to see Eldon's seven-foot-frame leaning against one of the homicide desks, a thumb drive gripped in one hand and a sheaf of printed pages in the other.

"You were able to recover data from Harrison's laptop?" Graham said.

"It was busted up pretty bad—a real challenge, unlike rifling through Jordan Dunn's laptop. Novak must have a hell of a throwing arm. But I salvaged most of its memory. Including more than enough data to prove that the user of this laptop was the internet user calling himself True_Man."

Jessie felt an urge to hug the bearded giant. Instead, she turned a triumphant smile on Warren. "Well?" she said. "What do you think now"

To her surprise, Warren smiled back. "I think we're going to have a chance to test that novel and interesting legal argument after all."

# 33.

Two months later, the trial of *Commonwealth v. Clark Harrison* began.

In Courtoom 303 of the Juanita Kidd Stout Center for Criminal Justice, Judge Letty Sokol waited for the crowd to quiet before she invited Jessie to present the prosecution's opening statement.

"Are you ready, Ms. Black?"

Sokol was one of the newer judges, having practiced law as a civil litigator until ascending to the bench two years ago. She lacked the crusty wrinkles and jaded cynicism of some of the old-timers, and was also less of a known quantity. Both the DA's office and the defense bar were still trying to figure her out. In the three cases Jessie had tried in her courtroom, she'd found the judge to be knowledgeable and fair, but not particularly open to new legal ideas. That could pose a problem in her current trial. One of many.

"Ms. Black?" the judge prompted again.

Was she ready? The question sent a flutter of nervousness through her belly. But she expected the sensation and was able to mentally shake it off. She never felt ready to begin a trial, no matter how much she prepared.

"Yes, Your Honor."

She rose from her chair at the prosecution table. She didn't take any notes with her, and she didn't bother with the podium. She walked to the railing of the jury box. Years of experience had taught her that delivering her opening statement from memory, and looking straight into the eyes of the jurors—talking directly to them as if they were her colleagues—was the most effective way to open a trial.

She had two goals with her opening statement. The first was to come across as a genuine and likable person, and the second was to give the jury a short, easy-to-understand version of her case. She was confident in her ability to achieve the first goal— already, some of the jurors were returning her smile. It was the second goal that worried her this time. Her case against Harrison wasn't simple and easy to summarize like most murder cases. She couldn't just tell her audience of twelve jurors and two alternates that defendant X used weapon Y to kill victim Z, and that the state was going to prove it. Harrison's crime was more complicated. More subtle. His weapons had been words and the power of the internet.

"Good morning," she said. "Thank you for being here today to help us with this very important matter. My name is Jessica Black. I'm an assistant district attorney."

They waited for her to continue. Their faces

looked patient, receptive.

She remembered the advice of a favorite law professor, guiding her during mock trials back at Penn Law: *Just start at the beginning, and lay it out in chronological order until you reach the end. Jurors want to hear a story they can understand. Get that right, and you'll be more effective than half the trial lawyers out there.*

"This case," she said, "is about the murder of seventeen people—sixteen of whom were kids, teenage girls. Each of those people had family, friends, hopes and dreams, a favorite ice cream flavor. They had lives. One of them had a story of particular importance to us today. Her name was Jordan Dunn. She was sixteen when she died from a bullet wound that punctured her left lung. Jordan's story is that she was having sex with one of the teachers at her school. That teacher, now the principal, is the defendant sitting here today, Clark Harrison."

She turned sideways to give the jurors an unobstructed view of Harrison. She would have liked to look at him, too, to see how he held up under their scrutiny, but it was more critical that she study the jurors' faces. She watched them, tried to determine which ones were already leaning towards a guilty verdict and which ones would need more convincing.

She noted with a sense of dismay that several of the jurors looked skeptical, and a few looked confused. She could practically hear their thoughts: *What's she talking about? I thought that kid Russell Lanford—the crazy one who hanged himself—shot those people.*

She resisted the impulse to glance into the gallery, where she knew Warren was sitting amongst the throng of spectators. Leary was there, too, but she didn't look at him, either. She was on her own, for better or worse.

*Come on, Jessie. You've got this.*

She'd written and rewritten at least ten drafts of the opening statement. Looking at her jurors now, she wished she'd had a few more nights to fine-tune it further, to make it clearer. For some reason, the time between an arrest and a trial always felt shorter than it was. Two months ago, when Eldon declared that he'd managed to recover vital evidence from Harrison's laptop, she'd felt like she had an eternity to prepare for trial. But here she was, as if time had compressed itself and pushed her from one moment to the next with barely a second to breathe.

That wasn't true, obviously. It only felt that way. In reality, she'd had time. Time to prepare her arguments, her witnesses, and herself. Time to prepare this statement. She was nervous, but she was ready.

She resumed her position in front of the jury box. The jurors focused on her again. "What does Jordan Dunn's affair with a teacher have to do with the murder of seventeen people? The evidence is going to show you that there was a direct connection. That the defendant, Clark Harrison, planned and assisted in— *choreographed*—the murders for the purpose of covering up his affair with Jordan Dunn."

Usually, at this point in an opening statement,

after presenting the theme of her case, she'd have some of the jurors nodding along with her. Not this time. But several of them looked interested, even intrigued, and that was better than nothing. She'd take it.

The spectators in the gallery also seemed interested. The media had used the months after Harrison's arrest to turn the upcoming trial from a government proceeding into a full-blown event, and the payoff was a packed house. Those in seats squeezed in shoulder-to-shoulder, while those unable to find seats lined the back wall. She knew that this audience—the court of public opinion—was only slightly less important to win over than the jury. Warren and Rivera would probably consider them *more* important.

There was a lot riding on this trial, and therefore a lot riding on her.

Finally, she allowed herself a quick glance at the defense table. Brand and Harrison sat side-by-side, both of them dressed in nice suits. Brand was taking notes—or maybe just pretending to—on a legal pad in front of him. Harrison was watching her. Now he caught her eye, and even though his mouth remained a neutral straight line, she thought she saw a smile in his eyes. The bastard was confident that he'd outsmarted the authorities, that he'd covered his tracks, that he was going to win and walk out of here. Jessie took a deep breath and turned to face the jury again.

"You may be wondering how Clark Harrison could be responsible for a mass shooting committed by another person. The defense will certainly raise this question, and tell you that the answer is he can't be. But under our laws, that's not the case. After both sides have presented their evidence, Judge Sokol will give you instructions about the law. Her Honor will explain that under Pennsylvania's criminal code, an individual can be guilty of murder even if that individual doesn't personally pull the trigger. Think of a person who hires a hit man. If the hitman commits a killing for hire, then both the hitman and the person paying him are both guilty of the murder. The evidence will show that Russell Lanford was like a hitman—only, unlike a hitman, Russell Lanford didn't get paid. *He* paid, with his life, while Clark Harrison derived all of the benefit."

She watched the jurors' reactions. Leary had actually been the one who came up with the hitman analogy, during one long night spent working on her statement. She'd thought it was pretty good. Still thought that. But the jurors didn't look convinced. She continued to face expressions of skepticism and confusion.

Her old professor's advice played in her head again: *Just start at the beginning, and lay it out in chronological order until you reach the end.*

"Like I said, Jordan Dunn was sixteen. You're going to meet her parents and her little sister Ellie, who will tell you all about her. They will tell you that she was bright and helpful and loving. Ellie will tell you that even though they fought sometimes, as sisters will, Jordan was always there for her. Her father will tell you about visiting potential colleges, and the excitement in Jordan's voice as they spent the long drive home from Amherst talking about her future. Her mother will tell you about the time they spent an afternoon volunteering together at a soup kitchen. And then you will hear from another witness, Jordan's friend Arabella Minsky, who will tell you that Jordan had a secret. She was involved with a teacher."

Jessie watched the jurors closely. She knew that some of them would blame Jordan Dunn for that affair, consider her a seductress and home-wrecker. Based on the questions the jurors had answered during jury selection, she could even guess which ones. She'd removed as many as she could during the *voir dire* process, but a few remained on the jury—Elizabeth Armstrong, a widow who looked and spoke like a zealot who'd stepped out of the days of the Puritans, and Jane Grange, a forty-something, recently-single mom whose husband had left her for his eighteen-year-old secretary. Both women looked angry at the thought of an affair between Clark Harrison and Jordan Dunn, but angry at whom, she didn't know. Either or both might well see Harrison as the victim, seduced by a manipulative woman.

This was one of the challenges of the American legal system—juries were people, who brought their own histories, prejudices, and other baggage with them into their deliberations. Being persuasive on the facts and the law wasn't always enough to overcome that hurdle. You had to read the mood of the jurors as you engaged them in a strange, one-way dialogue, in which you communicated with words and they communicated in less obvious ways—a quiet intake of breath, a widening of the eyes, the impatient jittering of a leg. You had to shift gears mid-argument— sometimes mid-sentence—to respond to these signals.

Jessie was lucky in that she seemed to have an innate talent for "feeling" the mood of a jury. She thought she had maybe a third of these jurors shifting toward her side now, with another third undecided and a final third against her for reasons that might be logical or illogical.

To convict, she'd need all of them.

"Mr. Brand, the defense attorney, will tell you we don't really know what happened between Jordan Dunn and Clark Harrison. He's right. Jordan was secretive about the affair. She didn't talk about it, except with her oldest childhood friend, or keep a diary. We suspect there may have been photographs or other materials on her phone, but we'll never know, because that phone disappeared on the day of her murder. We will present evidence to you indicating that Mr. Harrison was one of the few people with access to the locker where we believe she stored the phone during the cheerleading practice at which she was killed, and a motive to hide it and any evidence it may have contained."

Some of the jurors peered accusingly at the defense table.

"At any rate," Jessie said, "we can surmise that a married man, who has recently been promoted to principal, would have a lot to lose if a secret, sexual relationship with a student came to light."

"Objection!" Brand said, half-standing.

Judge Sokol nodded. She said, "Stick to the facts, please, Ms. Black."

"Sorry, Your Honor. I'll move on."

She was supposed to limit her opening statement to the facts, and refrain from making arguments or drawing conclusions for the jury. But sometimes you had to break the rules a little bit. The idea that Harrison had a motive for murder was critical to her case. She'd gotten the idea into the jurors' minds, and that was what mattered. She could see Jane Grange, one of her problem jurors, thinking it over.

"The facts," Jessie said to the jurors, "lead us next to another student at Stevens Academy. That student's name was Russell Lanford."

She watched the jurors' reaction to the name, and saw looks of distaste, disgust, anger, and sadness. The jury wasn't supposed to come to a trial with knowledge of the case, but that was impossible here, and everyone knew it. The shooting had been national news.

"The evidence will show that Russell Lanford was a troubled and unhappy young man. He blamed a lot of his unhappiness on women. He believed that they rejected him unfairly. On the internet, he found a message board called Manpower, a forum supposedly about men's rights, but in reality about hatred of women. The posts he found there stoked his hatred and his anger. During the trial, you will have to read some of these posts, which may be unpleasant but will be necessary for your understanding of the facts."

Unpleasant? Several jurors were leaning forward as if they couldn't wait to see the message board posts. Jessie felt a grim satisfaction. It was an old trial lawyer trick. Give the jurors a preview, like a movie trailer, to increase their interest.

"One of Russell's teachers, Christiana Weaver, will tell you that she was so disturbed by an essay Russell wrote in her English class—an essay about the men's rights movement as he understood it from the Manpower website—that she brought it to the attention of the principal, Clark Harrison. Mr. Harrison did not take action. Not in his capacity as school principal, anyway."

She gave the jurors a few seconds to ponder that.

"It was on the Manpower message board that Russell Lanford connected with a user going by the online handle of True_Man. True_Man seemed to share Russell's anger and frustration toward women. Moreover, he seemed sympathetic to Russell's experiences. For example, you will see an interchange between Russell and True_Man in which they commiserate about Russell failing to get a date to a dance. As the two became closer, they took their conversation off of the public forum and used the website's private messaging functionality instead."

Many of the jurors were looking at Harrison now. Some seemed to be wondering what this story had to do with him. Others had clearly already figured it out. Jane Grange had her arms crossed over her chest and was staring at Harrison with narrowed eyes. *I've won her over*, Jessie thought.

"The evidence will show that True_Man was in fact Clark Harrison," she said. "When you see the private messages that passed between them, you will see that Mr. Harrison, posing as the sympathetic True_Man, persuaded Russell to take violent action against female classmates. True_Man was careful to suggest a specific group of female classmates, too—the cheerleading squad, which included Jordan Dunn. Finally, Mr. Harrison helped Russell plan the attack, every detail from how to obtain the combination to his father's gun safe, the time and place, and the escape route. Several times, Russell expressed doubt and fear and tried to back out of the plan, and each time, Mr. Harrison convinced him to proceed."

She had more of the jurors on her side now. Instead of a third, she had half of them, maybe more. The spectators, too. She could feel it, a sea-change in the courtroom, a swell of outrage. She looked at the defense table and saw Harrison staring at his hands, Brand scribbling on his legal pad. Could they feel it, too?

"On a seemingly typical day, a day that will now haunt the families of the victims for the rest of their lives, Russell Lanford returned to school at around four in the afternoon carrying a large gray duffel bag filled with guns and ammunition. He walked through the gate of Stevens Academy, then circled around the building to the athletic field where the cheerleaders were practicing their routines. He took a seat in the bleachers, watched them for a moment, and then started shooting them."

Even though every juror had known this was coming, several of them gasped anyway.

"Russell shot and killed every person on the squad, as well as the coach. Even when he must have heard the sound of approaching police sirens, he kept shooting. Those had been the instructions he'd received from True_Man, the online friend he had no way of knowing was actually his principal, Clark Harrison. True_Man had emphasized the importance of killing every girl. There was nothing more critical, he'd said. Russell Lanford followed that instruction. He killed everyone, including Harrison's real target, Jordan Dunn. Some of the women died instantly. Others died later, after hours of suffering."

Six of the fourteen people in the jury box had tears in their eyes. One was audibly sobbing. Those with dry eyes still looked uncomfortable, exhausted, disgusted, or all three. How many were on her side now? Two-thirds? More? All of them?

"This story started with Jordan Dunn, and it ends with Jordan Dunn, because it is and always has been *about* Jordan Dunn. Clark Harrison, after engaging in a risky sexual affair with her, decided he would be better off if she was dead. So he used Russell Lanford to kill her. The coach and the other fifteen young women were collateral damage, their lives callously sacrificed so that the killing would look like a random school shooting and not the targeted murder that it really was. But the truth will come out now, here, in this courtroom. And I will ask you, at the close of evidence, to find Clark Harrison guilty of murder in the first degree."

She paused, thanked the jurors, and returned to her seat. The courtroom was silent. The spectators in the gallery seemed frozen. Brand and Harrison sat stiffly in their chairs. Judge Sokol took a moment before she cleared her throat and suggested a short recess.

Opening statements were critical—part skill, part art, part luck. Jessie knew that many cases were actually won or lost in opening statements.

She sensed that this might be one of them.

# 34.

Graham was on another blind date when she received the phone call from Novak. At first, she thought it was a prank. Just Novak, bored at home, having some fun with her. "Funny," she said. She gestured to the man sitting across the table from her—a nice enough guy, definitely better than the last one her mother had dug up. *One second.* "Listen, I'm kind of on a date," she said into the phone. "I'll call you later—" Then, abruptly, she realized Novak wasn't joking.

To her date, she said, "I'm sorry. I have to go."

"Police emergency?" He said it with a sardonic smile, as if the thought were amusing. It wasn't amusing to her. Her blood felt as if it had gone ice-cold in her veins, and the pleasant buzz she'd attained from her cocktail was gone. All she could think was, *I need to call Jessie.*

She rose from her chair. Dropped her napkin onto her bare place setting. Their salads had not even arrived yet, but she'd have to forego dinner and the man who was buying it.

"Another time, okay?" she said.

"Wait. You're really just going to leave?"

She turned before he finished the sentence and headed for the door, dodging around waiters and other diners until she emerged into the chilly darkness of night.

Her hand still gripped her phone. She brought it up now and called Jessie. The phone rang, but the prosecutor didn't pick up. Probably busy preparing for the next day of the trial.

She clicked off without leaving a voice mail, and texted her instead: *Harrison escaped. Call me asap.* She stared at her own message for a moment.

Remembering her reaction to Novak's call, she added: *Not a joke.*

She put her phone away. She stood on a sidewalk on Walnut, in Center City. Jessie's apartment building wasn't far. She could probably get there in five minutes, even in heels. But there was no guarantee Jessie was home. She might be at her office, which was in the other direction. She might be at Leary's place, wherever that was. She might be anywhere.

A group of young guys, loud and reeking of beer, surged past her. One of them bumped her shoulder as he stumbled past and almost knocking her over. Indecision gripped her. She looked at her phone again. Jessie had not responded to her texts.

Just because Clark Harrison had escaped from his cell didn't mean Jessie was in danger, of course. But the circumstances bothered her. Someone had helped

Harrison escape. A guard, presumably. According to Novak's terse update, the working theory was that Harrison had made friends with another woman-hater on the Manpower message board, possibly using a different alias than True_Man. And if that theory turned out to be correct, then she had to wonder how many aliases Harrison had. And how many people he'd influenced.

*"I know people," he'd said. "I have a lot of friends."*

He'd used Russell Lanford to murder seventeen people. If he had other willing online buddies, what was to stop him from using them as well? She could think of several women Harrison might want dead, but she and Jessie probably topped the list.

*I'll try her apartment*, Graham decided. *Better than just standing here.*

She started heading west. After four strides, as she was passing the mouth of an alleyway between two restaurants, someone shoved her. She wasn't expecting the collision and it almost knocked her off her feet. She staggered into the dark alley, catching herself by grabbing the side of a Dumpster. Turning, she saw a man stalking into the alley after her. The light from the street silhouetted him. He was a dark figure. She couldn't see his face.

Whoever he was, he'd messed with the wrong person.

"I'm a cop, moron." She reached for her gun, thankful that she'd made the decision to carry concealed tonight, even though doing so had a tendency to spook some of her dates.

She knew something was wrong when her fingers brushed the top of her holster and felt the strap there open. Her gun was gone.

"Looking for something?" the man said. "You might want to check the garbage can a few blocks east."

*The man who'd bumped into her,* she realized. *Oh, shit.*

"Don't they teach you anything at the police academy?" he said. He stepped forward, cracking his knuckles. "Or do bitches like you get a free pass so the police department can show what an equal opportunity employer it is?"

"Let me guess," she said, straining to keep the panic from sounding in her voice. "You've got some unresolved issues about women."

He didn't answer. He came at her.

Close up, the man's face became visible in the faint light of the alley. Middle-aged, with deep grooves and pockmarks hinting at a difficult life. Graham figured the crew of young men he'd appeared to be walking with earlier had actually been strangers. He'd used them as cover, to get close enough to bump into her and steal her gun.

He was a big man, easily twice her weight. His body seemed to fill the alleyway. She considered trying to run past him—if she could get to the street, she'd be safe—but she wasn't sure she'd make it. She didn't want to risk running straight into his grasp. She considered reaching for her phone, but ultimately rejected that idea, too. She wanted to have her hands free when he closed the distance between them.

She didn't have any other weapons on her. No backup gun, no knife. If she lived through this, she'd have to be more paranoid in the future.

The man lumbered forward. His face was screwed up with malevolent determination. Whether his intent was to pummel her, strangle her, stab her, rape her, or all of the above, she had no idea. But she could tell he wasn't here to give her a back rub. She shifted her weight, balancing on the balls of her feet and tensing to meet his attack. She'd trained in close quarters combat, although she'd rarely had occasion to use her skills. Now she felt the muscles in her arms and legs tense, felt her hands curl into fists.

"You think Harrison's your friend," she said. Part of her was still hoping a fight could be avoided with words, even though instinct told her it could not. "He doesn't give a shit about you, or about the men's rights movement, or about anything. He's just a coward who talks other men into fighting his battles for him."

The man didn't stop. His expression didn't change. She couldn't even tell if he'd heard her. He swung a punch and she just barely ducked under it. She heard the whistle of air above her as his fist missed her head by inches.

She backpedaled until her spine pressed against the brick wall of the building behind her.

He threw another punch. She tried to dodge it, but

this time he anticipated her direction. His fist connected with her right breast. Pain exploded in her chest. The air went out of her lungs.

"That's right," he said. He breathed heavily through his open mouth, watching her. "Not so arrogant now, are you? I'm going to beat you to death and leave your body here. Your face won't even be recognizable."

She might have asked him why, if she weren't struggling with all her strength just to catch her breath. His fist shot forward. She realized two seconds late that it was a ruse, distracting her from his leg. His boot, hard and huge, slammed into her left knee and she crumpled to the pavement. There was a puddle of water that smelled like the Dumpster. He stomped his foot in it and splashed her face.

She tried to crawl away. Broken pavement raked her palms and tore up the knees of her pants. Her fingernails snapped and splintered.

He kicked her hard in the gut and she flipped over. She curled into a fetal position.

*This is where I'm going to die*, she thought. Right off Walnut Street, ten feet from a million oblivious people.

"You've got this coming to you," he said. She didn't know if he was trying to justify his actions to her, or to himself. She didn't care.

He lifted one heavy boot over her head.

Before he could stomp her skull into the street, she reached out and grabbed his other foot with both of her hands. She wrapped her fingers around his ankle and pulled with all her strength. His foot came up and he lost his balance, falling backward. There was a loud, metallic *clang* as the back of his head connected with the Dumpster behind him. Then he was sitting on the pavement, gawking at her.

"You're gonna regret that, bitch."

"Oh yeah?" She scrambled to her feet. He was bigger, but she was faster. She made a run for the mouth of the alleyway and the busy street beyond.

Before she made it, he tackled her. Two-hundred or more pounds drove her to the ground. She screamed, but her voice was driven out of her, along with her oxygen, when he landed on top of her. She struggled to crawl forward, to free herself from him. One of her hands swept past something hard and rough. She looked. A brick.

She grabbed it but he grabbed her hand. His hand seemed to envelope hers. He squeezed, crushing her fingers painfully against the brick. Intense pain flared in her hand. In another moment the bones of her fingers would snap.

Desperate, she clawed at him with her free hand. But she only touched air. He grunted and squeezed her other hand harder against the brick. She felt the skin of her palm tear open.

"Get ... off ... you crazy ... bastard!"

"My wife called me crazy. That's how she took my kids away from me. My little boys. But I'm not crazy. I'm not—"

Her hand continued to claw at the air. It brushed his mouth. The softness of his lips and his wet tongue repulsed her. But only for a second. Then she thrust her hand into his face, past his teeth, and stabbed her jagged, broken nails into the soft bed of his tongue.

He reared back. He released her throbbing hand and grabbed her other wrist with both of his hands, pulling her fingers out of his mouth. Her hand was numb and throbbing, but she managed to maintain her grip on the brick. Twisting around, she swung it with all her strength against the side of his head.

He went down. She rolled clear of him. She didn't want to look at the damage. But at the same time, she *did* want to. Half his skull was misshapen, concave, like a dented fender. The ear on that side of his head was a bloody, torn mess. One of his eyeballs bulged, and blood leaked from the tear duct. His tongue lolled from his mouth, bloody and raw-looking. A piece of fingernail jutted from it. She was pretty sure he was dead. If he wasn't, he was going to wake up wishing he was.

# 35.

Jessie and Leary were relaxing at a coffee shop near her apartment, drinking decaf cappuccinos and reliving the excitement of the trial's first day. They both felt it had gone really well. If she could maintain her momentum through the rest of the trial and closing arguments, she was confident the jury would follow through with a guilty verdict that would put Harrison away for the rest of his life.

"He can talk to his fellow inmates about men's rights till he's blue in the face," Leary said.

She reached across their little table and wiped a dot of whipped cream off his nose. "Just as long as they don't give him internet access," she said.

"I think Clark Harrison's online days are over."

Her cell phone vibrated. She'd placed it on the table, just in case someone needed to reach her about the trial. Now, it inched toward the edge of the table as it buzzed. She picked it up. "Jessica Black."

As she listened to the voice on the other end of the line, the taste of coffee in her mouth turned sour. Leary must have read her expression, because when she thanked the caller and put down her phone, he said, "What happened?"

"Clark Harrison escaped from his cell."

"*What?*"

"Apparently one of the deputy sheriffs helped him." She remembered something Graham had told her on the day of Harrison's arrest. "He boasted to Emily that he had friends."

"Jesus," Leary said. "You think this deputy sheriff was someone he met on the Manpower forums? Didn't you read all of Harrison's online messages?"

"The warrant covered records for the True_Man account. Harrison could have had other accounts, though. Other names. Who knows how many angry men he connected with on the Manpower forums using various identities?"

"Are there that many angry men? I'm starting to feel like I should apologize for my gender."

Jessie shrugged. "Your gender's fine overall. The bad ones are a small percentage of the population. But the internet makes it easy for someone like Harrison to find them."

Leary pushed aside his cappuccino. "I think I've had enough."

"Me, too. Let's go back to my place."

It wasn't that late, but knowing Harrison was loose made the streets feel darker and quieter than usual. Jessie caught herself peering into shadows and throwing quick glances over her shoulder.

There was another couple on the sidewalk a few steps behind them, twenty-somethings holding hands. There was a man behind the couple, walking casually, hands in his pockets. Across the street, there were a few other people. A homeless man. A middle-aged woman wearing headphones. Every so often headlights lit the night and a car glided past them on the street.

They passed the entrance to a SEPTA subway station. The black stairwell yawned like a cave. Jessie felt herself stiffen as they walked by, as if she were bracing herself for an attack.

"Relax," Leary said. "This is a safe part of the city."

"Are you carrying?"

He tapped his hip reassuringly. "Always."

"Good."

Leary shook his head. "You think Harrison cares about you? He's focused on one thing right now, and that's getting out of the country. He'll never make it. His face has been all over the news. He'll be back in a jail cell so fast there will hardly be a pause in the trial."

"You think so?" His confidence was infectious, and she found herself agreeing with him. With the state of modern surveillance, fugitives rarely made it far.

"I know—" Leary's voice choked off. His body jerked and spasmed. He dropped to one knee and stared up at her with a stare of wide-eyed surprise.

That's when she saw the cords extending from his back like tentacles. She turned around. The twenty-something couple was gone. So were the homeless man and the middle-aged woman who'd been on the other side of the street. But the man who'd been walking with his hands in his pockets was still there. He'd chosen a moment when the street was abandoned. His hands were no longer in his pockets. One held a device from which the cords extended. A Taser.

Leary rolled on the ground, incapacitated. He opened his mouth, tried to speak. No sound came out, but his mouth seemed to form the word *Run!*

The man tossed aside the Taser and came at her. Jessie resisted the impulse to run. Leary's jacket had opened when he fell, and she could see the holster at his hip, with his Glock tucked snugly inside. She crouched beside him and unbuttoned the strap on the holster.

The man grabbed a handful of her hair. Pain raced across her skull. She saw Leary's arms twitch as he struggled to regain control of his body. He managed to wrap one arm around the assailant's leg, hooking his elbow against the man's ankle. The man lost his balance and let go of Jessie's hair as he fell on top of Leary.

Jessie got the holster opened and yanked the gun free. She aimed it at the man's chest just as he rose to his full height.

"Don't move. I'm a good shot."

"Fuck you, bitch." The man was average-looking—about five-ten, normal weight, plain face, maybe mid-thirties. He didn't look like a criminal. He was dressed in a nice pair of khakis and a button-down shirt. She thought there was something strange about the shirt, but it was hard to tell because he was wearing a jacket over it.

Leary twitched on the ground, staring up at her with a helpless expression.

Jessie took one hand off of the Glock and pulled out her cell phone. "I'm going to call the police. You haven't done anything terrible yet. We can still sort this out."

"That's what the cops told me last year when they pretended to be on my side. All I wanted to do was show a woman how much I liked her, but she called me a stalker and a woman judge agreed. Now I have a restraining order and I lost my job."

"I don't know anything about that." Jessie struggled to use her phone's touchscreen one-handed. She managed to hit 9, then 1.

The man charged forward. She dropped her phone as the hand holding it instinctively joined the other around the grip of the gun. She fired two bullets into the man's chest, stopping him no more than a foot away from her. She smelled his bad breath as he collapsed onto the street.

She bent down to pick up her phone. As she did, her eyes met Leary's. His mouth moved again as he tried to tell her something.

"I can't hear you."

He tried again, and a thin voice came from his lips.

"Vest. He's wearing a vest."

She looked up just as the man was getting to his feet again. That was why his shirt had looked strange. He was wearing a Kevlar vest underneath it. The vest had stopped her bullets.

He charged at her again, and this time she wasn't able to bring the gun to bear in time to stop him. His body slammed into hers and she staggered backward. She had just enough time to realize he was shoving her toward the subway entrance, but not enough time to do anything about it. The back of her left shoe came down on empty air and she fell backward down the staircase.

Her body hit the concrete steps with a series of bone-jarring impacts. She let go of the gun and the phone and used her arms to protect her head. She spilled to a stop at the bottom of the stairs. Her whole body was in pain. She wasn't sure she could get up.

From the corner of her eye, she saw the man descending after her. There was no one else on the subway platform.

"You bitches are all the same, but you're about to get what's coming to you. There's going to be a revolution. Men like Harrison are leading the way, but there will be more. A lot more. We're taking back our lives."

"You're crazy." She got onto her knees. Pain flared in her knee caps and raced up and down her body. She crawled away from the stairs, but there was nowhere to go. A wall on one side, and the edge of the platform on the other, with the tracks beneath it.

"I used to think that," the man said. "But now I think I'm one of the only sane people on Earth."

The station rumbled. A subway train was approaching the station. Hopefully that meant people. She crawled toward the platform's edge.

The man loomed over her. He seemed oblivious to the sound of the oncoming train. He reached down and grabbed her throat.

"I'm going to make an example of you," he said. "I'm going to send a message."

The sound of the train grew louder. She met his insane stare and knew there was nothing she could say that would stop him from his crazy mission. She knew what she needed to do if she wanted to live.

She grabbed his arms. He looked surprised, but not concerned. He was bigger than her. Stronger. He increased the pressure around her throat. She struggled to breathe. Her lungs burned. Black spots floated in her vision. Using the last of her strength, she twisted sideways, toward the edge of the platform, and pushed. He rolled over the precipice, but for several seconds, his hands continued to clutch her throat. The skin of her neck stretched painfully. She slid sideways. The weight of him almost pulled her over the edge. She gritted her teeth and wrenched her body in the opposite direction. His fingers slipped off her neck and he fell. She heard the *thump* as his body hit the ground.

The train blared its horn. The tunnel filled with

the sound of squealing brakes, but the train rushed into the station, unable to stop. Jessie squeezed her eyes closed as the engine roared in her ears and the warm wind of the speeding train blasted her face. From below, she might have heard the punch of steel plowing into a body, or she might have just imagined it.

After what felt like an eternity, the train ground to a halt. She heard the buzz of an alarm. There was yelling. People surrounded her.

Then she heard Leary's voice in the crowd and knew she was going to be alright.

# 36.

Jessie tried not to limp as she walked into the courtroom. She had suffered some injuries during her fight with her attacker—mostly bruises on her neck from his attempt to strangle her, and on her arms and legs from her fall down the subway station steps—but they weren't debilitating. Graham, sitting in the front row of the gallery, looked to be equally worse for wear. She offered Jessie a sympathetic nod, and Jessie returned it.

Passing through the gate, she looked at the defense table and said, "Good morning, Hyram."

Brand sputtered a response that was incoherent. His usual bluster seemed to have abandoned him. Apparently, the escape of his client and the attacks that had followed were events beyond his experience, and he looked like he had no idea how to deal with them. Jessie almost felt bad for him. She was grateful to be on her side of the aisle and not his. One of the benefits of representing the state was that your client generally didn't surprise you with jail breaks and attempted murders.

Her attacker, identified as Michael Walter, turned out to be a troubled software engineer with depression and alcohol problems who had been in and out of institutions for years. Graham's attacker was an out-of-work, former US postal service employee who'd been terminated after several inappropriate outbursts at work. A search of their computers and phones revealed that they were both frequent posters to the Manpower forums. Ditto for Rick Tyler, the deputy sheriff who'd been missing since the night of Harrison's escape. All of them blamed their troubles on the women in their lives.

If the courtroom had been crowded before, it was an absolute mob scene now, as every reporter and curious bystander in the city tried to cram into the room. Not surprisingly, Clark Harrison's mysterious escape from custody and the attacks on the lead detective and prosecutor on his case had led to a storm of national news coverage. A massive manhunt involving state and federal law enforcement was underway, but so far had failed to find the fugitive. With each passing hour, she knew, the chances of catching Harrison lessened.

Judge Sokol pounded her gavel until the room subsided into silence.

"Ms. Black, I assume, given the circumstances, that you are here to request a continuance." A continuance would postpone the trial, in this case until Harrison could be retrieved, assuming he ever was.

"Yes, Your Honor."

Brand jumped up. He puffed out his chest. The lawyer had apparently recovered some of his bluster. He said, "Your Honor, the defense objects to a continuance."

Judge Sokol arched an eyebrow. "You want to proceed in the absence of your client?"

"Not at all, Your Honor. The defense moves for a mistrial. Recent events have tainted these proceedings beyond any possibility of my client receiving a fair trial."

"'Recent events' that your client caused!" Jessie snapped.

Brand cringed. Desperation showed on his face. "That's beside the point. It is still the responsibility of this Court to ensure a fair and impartial—"

"Oh, come on, Mr. Brand," the judge chided. "You can't think I'm going to reward Mr. Harrison for his alleged criminal activities which have brought us to this point."

"I'm not asking you to reward him, Your Honor. The prosecution can charge him again at such time as—"

"Denied," Judge Sokol said. "Ms. Black, I am granting a continuance. This trial shall resume as soon as Mr. Harrison is back in custody, and"—a concerned expression crossed her face—"when you have recovered from your injuries."

"Thank you, Your Honor."

Brand shook his head, looking more bewildered than angry, and hurried out of the room. With a smile,

Jessie noted his attempts to dodge the reporters. *Good luck with that.* As she gathered her things, Graham came up next to her.

"How are you feeling?"

"Terrific," Jessie said dryly, "except for the whole wrestling a man on a subway platform and throwing him in front of a train experience."

"You were pretty bad ass, though," Graham said, "for a lawyer, I mean."

"Thanks. From what I heard, you were pretty bad ass yourself."

"Do you think he'll get away? Spend the rest of his life sipping tequila in some pueblo in Mexico?"

Jessie shook her head. "I don't know. I hope not."

There was a commotion at the courtroom door. Jessie looked up and saw Noah Snyder push his way through the crowd. He was heading in her direction. "Great. What now?"

Graham crossed her arms over her chest. "Want me to get rid of him?" Jessie noticed a protective tone in her voice.

"It's alright."

"Jessie, I need to talk to you," Snyder said.

Jessie turned to face him. At this point, the silver haired lawyer was about the last person she wanted to see. "What is it, Noah?"

"Not here," he said. He glanced at Graham, then backed up a step from her threatening stare. "Let's go to your office."

\* \* \*

They sat around a conference table in the DA's office—Snyder, Jessie, and Graham. Warren Williams and Jesus Rivera participated through the speaker phone at the center of the table, and although unannounced, Jessie didn't doubt that Rivera's advisors were listening, too.

Snyder had just dropped a bombshell.

"You're sure about this?" Jessie said.

"My client is."

"Manpower, LLC."

"Yes." He tapped the stack of papers he'd placed on the table.

"They're still your client?"

Snyder shrugged. "For now. The remaining owners are planning to dissolve the company and shut down the website. They tell me it's because it's become clear to them that Manpower no longer stands for what they originally intended it to—real issues around men's place in society. But who knows? Probably they just don't know what to do with the company, now that Vaughn Truman is gone."

"And before they shut everything down, they did this?" Jessie said, indicating the stack of papers. "Out of the goodness of their hearts?"

"They do have good hearts, believe it or not. It's a small company, but the whole staff worked on this. Scouring all that data, looking for patterns around when messages were posted, which VPNs were used, similarities in user names. Piecing together the private messages, finding the conversations setting up Harrison's escape and the attacks."

"They worked hard," Warren said through the speaker phone. "We get it."

"They did all this to try to make it right," Snyder finished.

Jessie picked up one of the sheets of paper and skimmed the private messages printed there. On its surface, the series of messages looked like a conversation between two forum members arranging to meet IRL (in real life) for a few days while one was visiting Philadelphia. But the staff at Manpower believed that one of the users was Clark Harrison, and that the other was someone agreeing to harbor him after he escaped custody.

"If this is true," Graham said, "if Harrison is really at this location, then he never left the city."

"That's why no one can find him," Snyder said. "He isn't running. He's hiding. Right here, in someone's house."

Jessie nodded, gripping the sheet of paper more tightly. "And we have the address."

Once Manpower's intel was forwarded up the ranks, the authorities moved quickly. A force was mobilized, including a SWAT team and a hostage negotiation unit. They converged on a house in the Fox Chase neighborhood of Philadelphia. Located in Northeast Philadelphia, Fox Chase was a suburban neighborhood of green lawns and single family houses, the kind of place where kids rode their bikes in the street. For Jessie, entering the peaceful neighborhood in the passenger seat of Graham's car, part of a winding law enforcement caravan navigating the quiet streets, felt surreal. Of all the places where Harrison might be hiding, she never would have imagined finding him in the heart of middle class suburbia.

Graham parked and they climbed out of her car. Putting on a Kevlar vest and a helmet, Graham joined the group that would breach the front of the house. Jessie hung back to watch the scene from the street. She'd had enough recent life-threatening encounters to last her for the foreseeable future.

There was a moment of eerie stillness—the proverbial calm before the storm—when Jessie could actually hear birds chirping in the trees. Then the team at the front of the house burst the door open with a battering ram and streamed inside, announcing themselves with loud shouts of "Police! Get on the ground! Police!"

A minute later, two cops dragged a civilian out of the house. He looked like a child, a boy of twelve, maybe thirteen. Jessie felt a sense of dread squeeze her chest. Somehow she knew, even before all of the facts could be confirmed, that this little boy was the person Harrison had befriended online and convinced to let him hide in his house. How many other kids, frustrated that the girls at school didn't return their attention, had Googled their way into the poisonous waters of Manpower's website? The thought was chilling.

"Hey! That's him!"

Her gaze shifted away from the boy. A window window at ground level on the side of the house opened and a figure crawled out onto the grass. It was Harrison. He'd changed from his orange jumpsuit into clothes he'd probably stolen from the boy's parents, and he'd shaved off his hair in an attempt to alter his appearance, but she recognized him. He got to his feet and ran from the house.

Jessie ran, too. Without thinking, she judged the trajectory of his path and bolted to the point where she would intercept him. Her body slammed into his and knocked them both off their feet. Pain flashed through her already bruised body as they rolled on the ground together.

Harrison came up holding a gun. She hadn't expected that, and instantly realized how foolish she'd been to go charging after a dangerous fugitive. Kneeling in front of him, she threw her arms in front of her face as if flesh and bones could stop a bullet.

"I've been wanting to do this since the first time we met," he said.

She squeezed her eyes closed. The crack of the gunshot was deafening. She rocked backward, thinking about Leary. She thought about her father, her brother, her mother whom she'd lost so long ago. But she still felt the air on her face. She felt the damp grass soaking into her pants. She blinked, touched her face, and looked down at her chest. She was alive. How was that possible? How had he missed at point blank range?

Then Harrison toppled forward and she understood. It hadn't been Harrison's gun that had fired. It had been Graham's. The detective jogged across the grass toward them. She reached a hand down to Jessie and helped her up off the ground.

Together, they looked down at Clark Harrison. Graham's bullet had hit the back of his head and taken off half of his skull. His body was sprawled across blood-stained grass, not unlike the bodies of sixteen cheerleaders and their coach found on an athletic field of Stevens Academy.

"You okay?" Graham said.

Jessie heaved in a breath. "I am now."

# 37.

Torchlight flickered in a gentle, salt-scented breeze. Jessie leaned back with a sigh and smiled at Leary across a little table. The beachside resort in Punta Cana where they'd finally taken a vacation was luxurious, relaxing, and romantic—everything she'd hoped.

"You look happy," Leary said. "Thinking about your new status as hero of the DA's office?"

"That's the farthest thing from my mind," she said, and felt as surprised by her answer as Leary looked. She hadn't thought about the events that had led to Clark Harrison's downfall—or the praise she'd received from Jesus Rivera and Warren Williams for making the Philadelphia District Attorney's Office look good—since they'd departed from the Philly Airport. She hadn't thought about her job at all.

Leary arched an eyebrow. "Really? So what are you thinking about?"

She smiled. "I guess I'm thinking about how happy I am right now, about how much I'm enjoying being here with you. How about you? What are you thinking about?"

"Mostly about how good you looked in a bikini today."

She was wearing a summer dress now, one she'd bought especially for this trip. It was short and light and colorful—about as different from her usual wardrobe as possible. Leary was wearing a neon orange Polo shirt and blue shorts.

"You look pretty good yourself," she said.

The ocean was visible from their outdoor table. Moonlight sparkled on the waves as they rolled out of the sea. The water was calm tonight, and the sound of each wave sliding up the beach and then sliding back again was rhythmic, soothing. She wanted to walk with Leary along the smooth, wet sand, holding hands and breathing the warm air.

After dessert, of course.

In the back of her mind, she never completely stopped thinking about work. She'd be returning to the DA's office soon enough. Jesus Rivera and Warren Williams were very happy riding their nice, big wave of positive publicity, but she'd been around long enough to know the goodwill wouldn't last forever. *You're only as good as your most recent case.* She'd face a new one soon enough. But she'd be lying to herself if she pretended she wasn't looking forward to it. There were more people like Clark Harrison out there—*evil people*—and she needed to stop them, just as she'd stopped him. She imagined that Detective Emily Graham, off enjoying her own temporary victory in the never-ending battle against crime, felt much the same way. Maybe they would work together again soon.

"*Now* you're thinking about work," Leary said. "I can tell."

"You caught me."

"Stop it," he said. "This is a work-free zone."

"Make me."

He rose from his chair and came toward her with a mischievous grin. "Maybe I will."

He placed his hands on her bare arms and looked into her eyes. His palms pressed the skin of her shoulders, strong and warm, and a tremor ran through her body. Then he was kissing her, and she was kissing him, and one of his hands moved to her lower back. Her body responded instantly. It still amazed her how easily he could do that to her, stir that raw attraction.

"You want to go back to the room?" he said.

"Yes." Her voice was barely a whisper.

They could get dessert another night. They had all the time in the world.

# Thank You

Thank you for reading **Deadly Evidence**! If you liked the book, please consider posting a review online and telling your friends. Books succeed or fail by word of mouth. Your help will make a difference.

Want more? I'm writing new Jessie Black Legal Thrillers as we speak, and they are coming soon! Be the first to know by signing up for my newsletter. You can do that at the following Web page: http://larryawinters.com/newsletter/ (newsletter subscribers also learn about special promotions and are eligible for free goodies, contests, and other cool stuff). I promise to never share your information or send you spam, and you can always unsubscribe.

ALSO BY LARRY A. WINTERS
*www.larryawinters.com/books*

*The Jessie Black Legal Thriller Series*

Burnout
Informant
Deadly Evidence


*Also Featuring Jessie Black*

Web of Lies


*Other Books*

Hardcore

# About the Author

Larry A. Winters's stories feature a rogue's gallery of brilliant lawyers, avenging porn stars, determined cops, undercover FBI agents, and vicious bad guys of all sorts. When not writing, he can be found living a life of excitement. Not really, but he does know a good time when he sees one: reading a book by the fireplace on a cold evening, catching a rare movie night with his wife (when a friend or family member can be coerced into babysitting duty), smart TV dramas (and dumb TV comedies), vacations (those that involve reading on the beach, a lot of eating, and not a lot else), cardio on an elliptical trainer (generally beginning upon his return from said vacations, and quickly tapering off), video games (even though he stinks at them), and stockpiling gadgets (with a particular weakness for tablets and ereaders). He also has a healthy obsession with Star Wars.

I love to hear from readers. Here's how to reach me:

Email: *larry@larryawinters.com*

Website: *www.larryawinters.com*

Facebook:
*www.facebook.com/AuthorLarryAWinters/*

Twitter: *@larryawinters*

The best way to learn more about me, my writing process, and other fun stuff—as well as to stay current on my books, learn about special promotions, and be eligible for free goodies—is to sign up for the newsletter. You can do that by typing http://larryawinters.com/newsletter/ into your Web browser.

Thanks for reading!

Made in the USA
San Bernardino, CA
30 April 2020